The Play's the Thing

Jessica Barksdale Inclán

Relax. Read. Repeat.

To Nicole —
Thank you for reading!

Jessica Barksdale Inclán

THE PLAY'S THE THING
By Jessica Barksdale Inclán
Published by TouchPoint Press
Brookland, AR 72417
www.touchpointpress.com

Copyright © 2021 Jessica Barksdale Inclán
All rights reserved.

ISBN-13: 978-1-952816-34-5

Editor: Ashley Carlson
Cover Design: Colbie Myles
Cover image: Adobe Stock, image of elegant dramatic black venetian mask over tulle background by tomertu
Scene divider: Photo by Unknown Author is licensed under CC BY-NC

Connect with Jessica Barksdale Inclán
Author website: www.jessicabarksdaleinclan.com
@ jessica.barksdale.inclan @jessicainclan @jessicainclan

First Edition

Printed in the United States of America.

But love is blind, and lovers cannot see
The pretty follies that themselves commit.

—William Shakespeare, *The Merchant of Venice*

For Michael, Mitchell, and Julien
People I'd want to be with in any timeline

Chapter One – A Very Bad Performance

Despite myself, I couldn't stop staring.

Next to me, his dark hair gleaming in the golden stage lights, Dan Gordon leaned back in his theater seat, notepad resting on one long thigh. He and I weren't on a first date, but the brilliant conversations I'd hoped to have with him shriveled in my parched throat. I coughed, crossed my legs, and pulled at my probably too-short skirt. Thank God I was wearing tights. Sad, weird nerves zinged through my chest. Instead of helping the Drama department with their upcoming play, I hoped to talk with my handsome colleague. *Where did you grow up?* I wanted to ask. *What are your hobbies? What do you do when you aren't grading English papers?*

My cheeks burned from the embarrassment I hadn't even earned yet. Maybe Dan was feeling as awkward as I was because he coughed lightly a couple of times, finally saying, "Why stage *The Merchant of Venice?*"

"What do you mean?" I grabbed on to the question and turned in my seat to face him.

"Isn't Sherry asking for trouble? Anti-Semitism and all that."

"This is nothing. Once she tried a clothing-optional *Midsummer's Night Dream.*"

Dan burst out with a low laugh, the sound a warm rumble. "Jessica! For audience or cast?"

"Cast," I said. "As you might imagine, the dean squelched the idea."

"Is that why she needs our help?" He pointed to the stage, and I noted his lean arm, the muscles under his neat button-down shirt. "Or are we here for insurance purposes?"

I chuckled a bit too loudly, blushing again. Thank goodness we were in the darkened theater.

"Too bad we can't swap out the hard parts of the play," he said, immediately holding up his perfect man hands (long, strong fingers and not a smidge of hair on a single digit). "Sacrilege. I know, I know."

I'd thought the same thing. There were a few key scenes to tweak, easy as pie.

"All Sherry wants is a reaction."

"Drama in the Drama department," Dan said, pushing his glasses back on his nose in a way that made me want to lean over, take off his glasses, adjust them, and before putting them back on his face, kiss him.

Dan chatted on, and I followed his voice as if he were speaking song lyrics. He had a perfect professor voice, one I certainly would have listened to in college. I probably would have signed up for all his classes.

One time, I peeked into his classroom and watched Dan guide the students through a digital show of images, Frankenstein's monster roaming the ice, alone and avenged. Heady stuff. The images flickered on the large screen as Dan talked them through with humor and useful information. His voice was handsome, if that was possible. Fact was, all of Dan was handsome. Blue eyes, dark hair, strong—but not too strong—chin and nose, cheeks with some stubble. Tall, nicely built, and lean, he had on well-worn jeans and running shoes. He even smelled handsome like peppermint and something warm. Cut wood. Caramel. Wheat bread.

Frankly, Dan Gordon, PhD looked like he was straight out of the most recent edition of *Totally Cool Professor* catalog. And he was cool enough that female and male students lined up in the hall during his office hours. Traffic was so congested, I had given up trying to drop in and tell him how much I'd liked his class. We'd never served on a committee together, and we only spoke briefly during department meetings and parties. *Hello, how are your classes?* and *Are you doing any traveling?* were our brief and uninformative conversational openers.

2

So tonight was the first time we'd really had a chance to talk.

"*Romeo and Juliet* would have been easier. Main characters meet and fall in love—" Dan began.

"And die," I finished. "Pesky poison."

"At least the ending isn't up for debate."

I laughed. "True. So cross your fingers we'll survive this." I opened my bag of snacks and reached over with the open bag.

"Goldfish?"

As the actors moved to their marks, the lights gleamed, brightening the stage to brilliance. Dan and I fell into darkness in fifth-row seats, hunkering to watch and listen. Sherry gave us both a wave and then called for her actors' attention and presented her final notes before the scene started.

Dan took a handful of crackers. Dust motes flickered like stars in the focused light. As assistant professors recently hired and needing to find our places in the department, Dan and I jumped at the chance to help the Drama department with Shakespearean interpretation. To prepare for tonight's endurance run of the full production, I brought snacks and Snapple, hoping Dan liked green tea with honey. As we crunched and sipped, Sherry started the actors at the end of Act II, scene v, the character Jessica telling her father Shylock, "Farewell, and if my fortune be not cross'd, I have a father, you a daughter, lost."

"Amber," Sherry called out. "Jessica is not off to a destination wedding in Bali. Lorenzo's a Christian. She's Jewish. She's leaving behind everything! Her faith as well as her father Shylock, her entire extended family, and all she's grown up with for—"

"A guy she barely knows," I whispered to Dan.

"An uncertain life," Sherry finished, turning to us.

Dan adjusted his glasses and called out, "Jessica is excited. But afraid. She doesn't know what she will find in her life behind the ghetto gates. It's exciting but scary."

"Also," I added. "Think about this. She's seventeen. Her father is getting on her last nerve. She wants to escape all his rules."

Sherry turned back to her cast, and Dan settled back in his seat. "Besides all the triggers in this play," I whispered, "these actors need more than our help. Poor Amber is walking around up there as if she's Ophelia." And, in fact, Amber was channeling poor mad Ophelia from *Hamlet*, staring out wide-eyed at the nonexistent audience, as if waiting to be extracted by military force or divine intervention.

"I've always thought Jessica is a bit of a dud," Dan said, "Not a developed character." He gave me a teasing look. "No offense."

"None taken," I said, but somehow, now, after many college years of teasing, I felt as though Dan were talking about me.

"Let's try it again," Sherry called out. I smiled at Dan, turned back to the stage, and mulled the Jessica comment as Amber gave her lines another go. But it seemed to be of little use. Amber wasn't getting it.

Sherry stopped the action again, consoling Amber in low tones. I patted Dan's arm. "Bear with Jessica. And maybe if you help out enough, Sherry will put on a production of *Frankenstein* next year. You can be the Mary Shelley expert."

"Don't think I can't handle it. No Jessica in that story," Dan said, reaching for another handful of crackers, his arm brushing mine. His shirt was soft, his skin warm. For a second, there was electricity between us, a frisson.

Or maybe it was static cling.

"Good riddance."

"Perhaps they can do something miraculous," Dan said. "Maybe they can make magic happen."

In the theater, new worlds spun out from strands of the finest language. One minute, there was a stage with a slapdash painted blue sky and some actors milling about wearing reduced-budget costumes in a plywood forest. The lights dimmed. The actors emerged, speaking their lines. The next thing I knew, I was in Venice, Denmark, or Rome, believing everything splayed before me, living a life on the stage and in my heart.

So Dan was right. Magic could happen.

I turned to him. "They have three weeks. Here's to hoping."

4

Dan shrugged, a pleased smile on his face. He didn't want the students to fail, and neither did I.

"Okay, people," Sherry called out, a now sterner looking Jessica at the front of the stage, Amber clearly trying to channel the seriousness of her character's actions. "From 'Enter Jessica.' Let's do it."

Amber cleared her throat, but nothing emerged. I whisked crumbs from my hand and leaned toward Dan. "Intermission," I whispered. "We haven't hit the magic yet."

Slipping out of my seat and then up the aisle, I sighed. I was in a bad patch, a slump, a lull—a couple of semesters of uninspired classes and difficult students had made me weary. Maybe more than weary. At times, I was overwhelmed by the task of trying to teach anyone Elizabethan English. And then there were the relentless meetings, most of which I barely made it to on time. Budget cuts, a stern department chair, and a nonexistent personal life dumped on top of my teaching, preparation, and grading. My Shakespeare class—usually my gem and delight—was case in point. When I got home tonight, I'd find my email inbox packed with 21 mostly ill-constructed essays, all supposedly analyzing the function of gossip in *Othello, Much Ado About Nothing*, and *Taming of the Shrew*. I just wasn't reaching them this semester, something was missing, most likely from me. A weekend of hair-pulling reading awaited. Frankly, this production of *Merchant* with the attractive and friendly Dan Gordon was the best thing to happen to me all week.

I pushed through the double doors, looking for the bathroom, but something stopped me. Maybe it was the feel of the air, the heat, smell, and weight, a strange change of its very texture. But then I jumped, startled as the doors clanked behind me. I whipped around, seeing not the swinging doors with porthole windows I'd just pushed through but a single massive oaken door. I stepped back, stumbling, my feet not on the expected carpet but on what? A dusty dirt floor scattered with? Bits of nutshell? I bent down, picked up something, and stood, holding out my palm. What the heck was this? Half a hazelnut? The very crushed nutshell used on Elizabethan theater floors? I rubbed my fingers over the dusty shell, feeling the smoothness under the grit. Sherry was really taking her authenticity too seriously. I needed to go through this big door and back into my right mind.

Just then, two students, late for rehearsal, pushed past me as I stood in... the wood-paneled hallway? This dark passage had most certainly not been here when Dan and I walked into the theater complex an hour earlier. Where was the lobby?

The students ignored me, speaking fast and unintelligibly. Their skirts were so wide, I was pressed up against the wall. For a second, I could have sworn they were men, as all performers would have been during Shakespeare's time.

"They're on scene five," I called out, in case they were as confused as I was. "Act II."

But they proceeded on, uninterrupted, as if I were invisible at worst, speaking Latin at best.

I dropped the hazelnut and wended my way down the hall, scanning the walls for the familiar and illuminated lady-in-her-little-dress sign, needing the bathroom with ever-increasing urgency. But no sign was forthcoming, only the gloom of the hall.

From inside the theater, I heard laughter and stomping, the crowd—crowd? Where had they come from?—enjoying something about scene five that hadn't been there before. Could Amber have made Jessica into a clown in five minutes?

When I got to the next door, I pushed it open, using both arms, and then I stepped onto a wooden ramp. Blinking into the unexpected daylight, I stomped forward and walked into a crowd standing in front of a wide, open-air stage, this part of the audience called the Penny Stinkers because standing was inexpensive and stinky. I staggered back, blinking, trying not to breathe. Where was I?

Not only was this not the stage I had just scurried away from, but the players were in a much earlier scene, back in Act I, scene iii. At this point in

6

the play, Bassanio was in love with Portia, and Antonio was going to stick his neck out to help him woo her. Here, Shylock is in the midst of his first big speech, the very act that starts all the *Merchant* plot wheels in motion. Antonio borrows money from Shylock, using ships filled with his merchandise headed to Venice as collateral. He does so out of his deep love for Bassanio, who needs the money to properly court stately, powerful Portia in princely style. The guy needs new shoes and clothes and a very big hat to really get her attention. She is rich, haughty, and full of herself.

I staggered a bit, my hand trying to find a place to comfort myself: throat, mouth, cheek. What was going on? I looked around the theater, seeing nothing familiar. Nothing university about this place at all. I stared at the thick beams, the wooden benches, the stage. My breath hitched under my ribs. If it weren't for the people around me, I'd have fallen upon the nutshell floor because no way was I staring at the university's shoestring production with its barely trained actors. This was a professional performance, with a rowdy crowd that was yelling and laughing as Shylock contemplated how he would make a bundle on Antonio's loan:

"But ships are but boards, sailors but men; there be land-rats and water-rats, water-thieves and land-thieves, I mean pirates," the actor said as he walked back and forth across the stage, wringing his hands in a bent-over, exaggerated style. He wore a red wig and sported a long fake nose. The crowd roared at the word *pirates*, this Shylock giving the speech some pause, glancing back at Antonio, who stood stiff and still on the stage, mortified to be doing business with this horrible guy. Shylock turned to face the audience, his dark eyes burrowing into the audience like a cleaver. This actor was exhausted, his makeup unable to hide the deep boats of fatigue under his eyes. Talk about ships!

"Then there is the peril of water, winds, and rocks. The man is notwithstanding sufficient. Three thousand ducats: I think I may take his bond."

The Penny Stinkers roared their disapproval. The entire audience called out, hissed, booed. Some kind of lumpy vegetable landed on the stage with a thud. Then another. Bassanio stepped forward, all eagerness. It is for him that Antonio would do anything. He, unlike any other, has Antonino's true heart.

"Be assur'd you may!" Bassanio cried.

Stomping and shouting, the house went wild, as did my heart, everything beating against my ribs like Congo drums. I backed away from the boisterous, sweltering crowd, tripped, steadied myself, turned, running down the ramp, out the huge door, and into… into the lobby of the university's dramatic center.

Body jittering, I spun around, startled, panting. Running toward the door, I plunged back into the theater to test my sanity. But there was no shouting, jeering. No flung vegetables on the stage. No Shylock looking at and through me with his dark eyes. Instead, there I was in Act II, scene iv, poor Amber struggling over Jessica's simple questions to Shylock, "Call you. What is your will."

"Amber!" Sherry clapped twice. "These are *actual* questions. *Call you? What is your will?* She's asking him if he called, even though she knows he did."

Sherry turned to Dan, who corroborated. "That's right," he called out. "There's a plan in motion. So she's asking a question that's not a question."

I stumbled down the walkway to my seat, Dan looking up and whispering, "That was fast. You should have taken your time. This is Amber's third attempt with the same lines."

My blood beat in my throat, my heartbeat rising and falling like a tilt-o-whirl. Trying to act natural, I picked up the cracker bag and put it on my lap, barely focusing on Amber giving the questions another go. But instead, I heard the Penny Stinkers' howls and catcalls and smelled the heat and dust of that other stage in that other place that was nowhere at all.

And then I remembered. I needed to go. Handing Dan the bag, I got up again, running up the walkway, through the double-doors, and—into the lobby. To my right, as she had been earlier that evening, blared the illuminated lady, indicating the proper bathroom. Turning once, I looked to see if the door had morphed heavy oaken, but no, it was still moving slightly from my exit.

As I walked toward the bathroom, I scanned the wide space for students dressed in Elizabethan garb, but there was nobody except the tech guy eating a sandwich on the upper stairway. I pushed into the bathroom and confronted myself in the mirror. Delusional. My eyes were wide and shocked, as if I'd just passed a horrifying accident on the highway. Clearly, the last few semesters had finally taken their toll.

Walking into a stall, I sat down, too stunned to pee. I put my head in my hands and tried to calm my nerves, breathing in and out slowly. I needed a paper bag to keep myself from hyperventilating, but I breathed into my palms, steadying myself, slowing down my lungs and my heart. From the vents on the ceiling, the sounds of the stage whispered out, Amber's voice thudding on in dull unquestioning bumps.

The inevitable had happened: I had lost it. But no wonder. For years, I'd held it together, doing this job I'd aspired to and mostly loved. Sure, I wasn't teaching where I thought I would end up when I graduated with my PhD. I'd graduated in a fantastic year for Shakespeare scholars (a lot of important retirements). Still, somehow, I wasn't quite right for Columbia, Harvard, Rutgers, and Princeton. Or then Vanderbilt, NYU, Cornell. Pass, pass, pass. I lowered the bar, and even that bar wouldn't have me. Somehow, there was always someone ahead of me, doing things with a little more vim, vigor, and smarts. Fluent in all technologies. Had lived in Stratford. Was trained in Cambridge. Oxford. Bath. Was a double PhD. A descendant of Shakespeare. Had written a best-selling novel. Had made a popular indie film based on the bard.

Average smarts, average looks, good grades, published dissertation (University of Nome Press), I was adrift. When the bar finally hit the floor, I found myself in the middle of California's central valley. In January, no sunshine. In July, no relief from the baking heat. The dating pool a tiny drop of water. Dan, the nicest and only single guy on the English faculty, seemed to have more interest in Mary Shelley and her monster than me. The good news? He liked Goldfish.

Okay, I was being a bit cataclysmic. I'd just been pushing since I started college and needed a break from all the reading, writing, thinking, and grading bad papers, which were all my fault. I needed a teaching reboot, revitalization, and rekindling. Maybe a break from Shakespeare. Maybe just good old thesis statements and topic sentences.

I flushed the toilet, washed my hands, and stared at myself one more time. I was exhausted, anxious, and maybe depressed. Either I'd hallucinated or had a trip of some kind. Maybe Dan had spiked the Snapple.

Still shaky, I walked back toward the play. I needed some sleep, a week away from papers, and maybe a few months away from Shakespeare, the great bard himself. In the morning, I'd call Susan Franklin, my department chair, and beg to get off this assignment. I'd teach four sections of freshman composition for a year. Anything to keep myself from having this particular mental breakdown again.

Chapter Two – Meeting Will

After rehearsal was over (Amber weeping on the shoulder of the actor who played Bassanio), Dan walked me to my car, accepted the leftover snacks and unopened Snapple, and said, "See you at the department meeting tomorrow. Don't be late."

He gave me a wink, squeezed my shoulder gently, and headed to his car. After admiring his walk—he looked pretty good in those old jeans—I sat in my MINI and watched him drive away in his Jeep.

I fought the urge to run after him and beg him to take me home. Not for anything but company. Swear! Maybe a hamburger. Some TV. After the warp of mind, time, and space I'd experienced, I was certain I'd end up in the Wild West. Or maybe worse, I'd be teleported to a future world where everyone lived in pods, ate squares of protein, and drank clear, sticky liquids. Dan's taillights glowed, faded, and then disappeared. There was nothing else to do but start my car and drive home, despite the possibility I might not get there. But my trip was without incident, fender bender, nervous collapse, or time travel.

Besides, the future might have been the present, based on my nighttime snack menu. I took my dog Horatio out for his nightly walk. Then we settled down with some cubed cheddar cheese, Triscuits, and a bottle of Cabernet, which was a mistake because the essays started to seem not half bad. Ridiculous hook (*Can you imagine a man killing his own wife?* Um, yes). Awkward, preposition-ridden tie in to *Othello* (In the play by William

Shakespeare about the noble Moor who murders his younger, innocent wife). Tepid summary. Conjunction. Verbal phrase. Thesis.

And worse, because deep into my second glass, Dan called.

"You make it home okay?" he asked.

"I wasn't drinking," I said. *Yet.*

"You seemed a little..."

Exactly. Through the portal of nutbar crazy. "I'm just tired," I said. "But I promise. Next performance, I'll be on top of things."

Dan laughed, and then there was a pause, a space for something. But what? How to fill it? How to say anything at all? So I said nothing.

"Okay," he said finally. "I'm counting on it."

We said goodbye, and then the space that connected us vanished, just like that.

Sighing, I turned back to my computer screen. I clicked through one and then another, slowly believing anything. Sure, I thought. Why not? It was entirely reasonable that the murderous male character Othello is an early feminist figure. After tonight, anything was possible. I poured myself another glass of wine and kept reading, trying to focus on my student's ideas and not Dan's rear end as he walked toward his car.

So—so nice.

Click, click, click. Horatio snored at my feet. The room spun on in silence, nothing but the whir of the furnace and my breath in the room. The heat hugged me tight. Shakespeare's characters filled my thoughts.

Tick tick tick went the desk clock. *Tick tick tick.*

The essay on the computer screen wavered, pixileting in grays and blues, the feminist treatise wobbling. I imagined the Shylock from earlier. Not the twenty-year-old student on the stage wearing a false beard and fumbling his lines, but the one from my lunacy. This Shylock hulked across the stage and turned, his dark eyes resting on me.

"This kindness will I show," Shylock said, bringing his hands together as if in prayer. "Go with me to a notary, seal me there your single bond."

"Craven clot-pole," someone else suddenly yelled.

"Frothy apple-john," said another.

I startled, grabbing for my mouse, assuming I'd accidentally clicked on a YouTube video link, something a student needed me to view. My hand touched nothing but fabric.

A door slammed, and I startled again, reaching out for my desk lamp, which was missing. My toes were cold. My back pressed against something hard. All sense and meaning were drowned out by the sounds I couldn't identify. I reached out a hand to touch a wall or door. Struggling up from sitting, I stood on cold wooden planks, worn and smooth.

In the muffled darkness, I breathed in the smelly aromas of wet wool, mildew, and dirt. On either side of me, coats and cloaks. Maybe uniforms, the fabrics thick and rough. Outside the closet, people were arguing, so I joined in.

"Help!" I beat at the door.

"Silence!" a man ordered, his mouth against the door. His voice English but somehow not.

"Open this door right now!" I banged harder. Somewhere near, others were yelling and banging too. On doors and, somehow, underfoot. The ceiling from below? What was going on out there?

The man yelled into the box. "Cease this wretched noise posthaste, or else there will be more to pay than you will ever earn in your lifetime."

What a load of syntactical baloney. He sounded fresh out of the Renaissance Pleasure Faire. But now it all made sense. Earlier, I must have fallen asleep during the rehearsal, Dan's comment, "Back so fast" had been only about the length of my snooze. He'd been too kind to let me know I'd been snoring during the rehearsal.

I was dreaming.

"What are you going to do? Lock me in my own dream?" I asked, but then he hissed hard enough his beer breath sizzled through the crack in the door.

"Keep your mouth to less than fury, and I will release you anon."

Anon, indeed. Anon! Ridiculous. Pressing my ear, and then my eye, to the crack in the door, I saw the flicker of candlelight. Shadows flitted in front of the closet. The structure around me creaked, groaning in its own ancient dream. I heard a woman's and then a man's voice. "You know why we are at your door. Stop feigning sleep or absence."

Then I heard a shuffling, a deep sigh, and the door opened. "Pray, Master and Mistress Gumble. Forgive my inattention. Tomorrow. Aye, tomorrow, I will deliver your rent."

"You told us thus yesternight," said the master. "And we had not but turned from your door, and there was a full session of caterwauling."

"Aye," Mistress Gumble said. "And the night before as well. No money and no rent. Your word is in the muck, Master Shakespeare."

This was rich. Perfect. Shakespeare indeed. I laughed and then put a hand to my mouth as if I could take back the sound. Master *Shakespeare*. What had I been drinking? That bottle of Cabernet. Probably the whole thing. Sulfites and a bad grape season could explain everything.

There was a pause, a shuffle. A flicker of shadow. Faux Master Shakespeare cleared his throat. "A rat in the room. As I stated earlier, a fouler chamber has never been noted."

"Explain it how you will, but pay you must. And forswear the nightly screaming."

"More than nightly," Mistress Gumble said. "On the hour! Worse than the town crier."

The supposed Shakespeare demurred. More shuffling, mumbles, and finally footsteps. The door closed, and there was a big sigh, an exhale to fill the world.

"Now could you let me out?" I called.

More silence. I banged on the wood, called out again, but nothing.

"Get me the hell out of here!" I pounded my fists against the door. I jiggled the handle. Pushing aside the stuffy clothes, I kicked the bottom of the door with my heels, tiny edges of light appearing and disappearing as I moved the door with each strike. But not enough to break it down and let me slip fully into this strange dream.

Breathing hard, I slumped against the wall, blinking into the dusty gloom. This all seemed too familiar. In another lifetime, I found safety in dark closet corners, sanctuary among my own silent clothing. When I was younger, my older sister Kate and I hid in our bedroom closet, waiting out the firestorms of our parents' fights. Sitting under the awning of our dresses, coats, and pants, we pressed together in the half-light. Sometimes, we rearranged our shoes like soldiers, a protection against unhappiness. My parents screamed and raged and sometimes threw their wedding china. But with my hand in my sister's, I'd always felt we'd make it through the fight. We did, and then, my father left.

But this dream closet with its bad smells? With the dream, rent-owing Shakespeare lurching about outside? I felt caught, trapped, and about ready to be served up to beasts.

"I'm suffocating!"

Shakespeare said nothing, likely hoping I would expire.

"Are you out there?" I called. Still not a sound. I closed my eyes, and the room outside dimmed, as the lights had in the theater with Dan. How cozy that had been, sitting with him, engaged in Sherry's play. He'd nudged me gently with his elbow, laughing in my ear at something funny. He'd leaned close, whispering, "Maybe you should jump up there to show them how it's done." But here I was stuck in an angry dream, trying to settle against rough fabrics and cold wood. If only I'd jumped out of my car and chased after Dan.

I shifted against the coats. "I won't bite!" I called out. "I promise!"

For an instant, I heard a soft sound, a mouth breathing at the door. Urging my whole body still, I clung to hope he'd release me. But nothing. William Shakespeare must have fallen back asleep. I banged once more and then gave up, clutching my arms and burying myself in the clothing.

This dream Shakespeare was a ne'er-do-well. At least the real Shakespeare left a legacy. When my parents finally divorced, I turned to the bookshelves, finding a thin volume of poetry my mother had read to me when I was much younger. The cover was delicate, worn, blue with faded forget-me-nots. *Shakespeare's Sonnets.*

"Gross," Kate said. "Boring."

I'd read the small poems with furious intent. I had no idea what they meant, but there was something beautiful about the language, a pattern and a reassuring sameness. Also, there was a longing I understood, even if the lines didn't always make sense.

In junior high school, my drama teacher presented us with the witch scenes from *Macbeth*. In Mr. Black's high school English classes, *Othello, Romeo and Juliet*, more *Macbeth*. All that drama! All that murder! And those speeches. By the time I applied to Cal, declaring myself an English major, William Shakespeare was my go-to read, my insomnia date. Tonight, this night—the night I was surely still in—my mother's ragged book of sonnets with the forget-me-not cover lay on my bedside table.

Of all the men in the world, second to my idealized, almost imaginary father, William Shakespeare was the one I loved best. He was first during my college love affair with Phillip and then after. No matter what I did, William Shakespeare never left me. He always entertained. He was there, 24/7, portable into every room of the house. He taught me. He gave me my career. He gave me hope the worst would be resolved. With every play, a wise and calm center would emerge—in *Hamlet*, Horatio—and explain everything, pulling the carnage offstage to make sense of it. He'd say it true. As Edgar told us all at the end of *Lear*, "Speak what we feel, not what we ought to say."

All my reading life, Will's words were on my lips, in my brain, in my imagination.

Shakespeare was my bible but better written and more interesting. Except now, of course, the bard having trapped me in a closet with his smelly clothes. If this confabulation were true and I was actually with Shakespeare, I needed to see him before the dream closed up forever.

"I'm going to die! Let me out of here now!"

A pause. "Are you there?" I pressed my eye against the crack.

A clumping toward the closet.

"I yet remain," he said. "You, sadly, do as well."

16

"Please open the door," I cried.

"Your lungs are doing nicely. No need for such distress," he said, his shadow lurching toward the closet. My body rippled, awash in gooseflesh. I wrapped my arms around my chest, suddenly wondering what I was wearing. A dress? I fingered the rough fabric, cloth thick and dense. This was one realistic dream.

"Please," I said. "I promise to be quiet."

"Ha!" he cried. "This would be an eerie and unexpected silence in a series of ludicrous visitations."

As with most dreams, the seams were showing. My brain was trying to right itself, putting order to something impossible. But why should I struggle? Any second, morning would come, plopping me smack-dab back into reality.

"I'll behave. I just need to get out of here."

The light in the crack grew brighter, and then one side of the closet opened a little.

"No bolting forth. No harsh words or violence with fingernails. No fists or feet or knees. No curses or wails. No fleeing through the chamber door with calls of my violence against you. No slashing with glass, books, combs, or plates. No attacking with knives or other deadly objects you pick up along the way."

"I don't have a knife," I pleaded.

"Swear!"

"I swear."

"Other objects perhaps have come with you?"

"I showed up almost naked. How could I have a what? A stun gun? Mace?"

"You have a mace?" he asked.

If I hadn't been trapped, I would have laughed. Yes, me. Jessica Randall, Warrior Princess/college professor with accompanying deadly metal war object, spikes and all. "No, I don't have *a* mace."

"Swear!"

"I swear," I said. "Cross my heart."

I heard the rest in my head, the promise Kate and I made to each other with important secrets: *Hope to die, stick a needle in my eye.*

At this point, I might actually stick a needle in my eye to get out of this closet.

And then slowly, he opened the door wide, the room soft and yellow with candlelight. Jittery, I stepped out and into the room. I turned to look at my place of confinement. A small, simple wardrobe filled with musty coats and cloaks.

My eyes now adjusted, I turned back to the man who had kept me in captivity. He was mid-thirties, maybe younger. Probably about 5'10", maybe taller. He was wiry, strong, 155 pounds, maybe less. Despite my surprise plummeting into his closet, his dark eyes weren't wide with amazement. He wasn't agape at the alarming and unprecedented spectacle of my arrival. No, he was pissed off, his sharp gaze harsh. Impatient, flinging one hand out as if urging me toward the door. And tired, too, dark circles under each eye, a weariness from the screaming the Gumbles complained of, no doubt. He had two days of stubble on his face, which was starving-artist chiseled, his cheekbones pronounced, his jaw defined. Giving me a head-shaking once-over, he ran a hand through his brown curly hair, sleep-wild and mussed.

And that's when I saw it. His eventual receding hairline. Years away. But coming. My breath clung to my ribs as he looked up at me, his eyes the steady gaze I'd stared at my entire life in books, journals, and paintings. Here is what my sad dream produced. Something—someone—his vast reading audience could have never appreciated, Shakespeare in his nightshirt. But here is what I saw. A beautiful, young, wiry and angry William Shakespeare.

Chapter Three – Waiting to Disappear

With a shrug, my conjured William Shakespeare turned toward his bed, getting in and pulling up the blanket. He mumbled, "Another one."

"Another what?" I asked.

"Should have been many minutes gone from the cupboard already."

"There are rules for this?" I asked.

"Gone with you!" he muttered, his voice muffled by bedding.

If there were rules, there were rules. So I waited to be gone. If I stayed still and remained quiet and focused, perhaps I'd wake up slumped on my desk, the place I had last left myself. Horatio would be snoring, the clock ticking, the papers hanging in cyberspace waiting to be graded, one last sip of wine in my glass.

I followed my heartbeat.

Thump, thump, thump, thump.

After a moment, Will looked up from where he feigned sleep and cried, "For the love of God, let it stop."

I pulled my gaze from him and turned to the room's yellowish gloam. An empty bottle teetered on its side by his bed, which, along with the chair, table, and (yikes!) chamber pot, was the only other object I could make out.

Then my nose caught up to my eyes. Bringing my hand to my face, I took in small sniffs. The room smelled like the dankest corner of a barn. But I was reassured. Since this was a dream, the smell would dissipate and be replaced by the usual aromas of coffee or early morning air or Horatio, his breath part kibble, part heat.

"What did you mean when you said, 'Another one'?" I asked, stepping forward. Under my feet straw rushes and dirt. "Another what?"

"Silence!" Shakespeare said.

I shuffled forward, wishing I could find a way out of this dream sequence into one much less disturbing.

"Are you still here?" From under his blankets, his voice rolled with a deep growl that made me nervous. Now was probably a good time to start screaming. No wonder the Gumbles were up in arms.

"I am," I said, heading toward the door, reaching for the latch. But what would I do out in the hall? The Gumbles might be there, ready to shake me down for all my nonexistent pence. Anyway, I had promised him I wouldn't run out the door.

"Why?"

"How should I know? I have no control over this. I don't know the rules."

Shakespeare arranged the blanket, staring at me from his bed.

"Mayhap you are from some world yet undiscovered?"

I sat down on the chair, trying to keep clear of the table that shone with something sticky and was peppered with tobacco flakes.

"Pretty much," I said. "My whole world is undiscovered."

He flung back the blankets and rubbed his jaw, the sound of his whiskers a *shush, shush*. "Zounds. So many of them. A plague of women."

"Lucky guy," I said, but he ignored me.

"Streams of them. Some decade—nay! Century—or another favoring the moniker unduly. What folly." He sounded pretty irritated. And it didn't seem to be just about me. Or the Gumbles.

"Slow down," I said. "You're barely speaking English."

"Your words are porridge."

"But you understand me?"

"And how not to?"

"If this seems familiar," I began, wondering how my dream could have happened before without my knowing. "Do you have any idea when this will end?"

"Wench! Begone!"

Underfoot, something alive scrabbled past my feet. I tucked my feet under me, searching the floor in the dwindling candlelight.

"Do you have another candle? More light?"

"Light, seeking light, doth light of light beguile—"

"Quote yourself already. Then go ahead and get us another candle."

"Illiterate, too. Alas."

Shakespeare shook off his blankets, a waft of underarm, musty man smells, and dirt drifted toward me. In that instant, Dan Gordon's soft shirt and zesty clean popped into my mind. Meanwhile, smelly Shakespeare searched for something in a drawer, objects clattering. "How far that little candle throws his beams."

Another quote. But it made perfect sense, given my activities of the evening. The candle from *The Merchant of Venice*. The earlier beguiling light quote was from *Love's Labour's Lost*.

For no good reason other than I was hearing Shakespeare quote himself, I laughed, a strangled, odd sound.

"This is no laughing matter," Shakespeare snarled as he continued to search.

Things were not going well.

This must be the same delirium I'd dropped into at the play. There must be an escape hatch here, too. All I needed to do was walk into the closet and then out again, back into my very own apartment. Or maybe if I thought about my apartment, I'd go back. I closed my eyes, conjured my desk, my computer, my dog. Oh! Horatio! I opened my eyes. Still awake in my dream. Still in the small, stinky room, Shakespeare lighting the second candle, a *rasp rasp* in the thick silence. But then the promised light. A candle. A tiny beam. And then more, the room glowing bright yellow.

We stared at each other, he sitting on the edge of his bed, elbows on knees. Though they resembled each other, this younger Shakespeare wasn't my Shakespeare, the almost-portly older man in a high-collar who stared out with solemn eyes. Whenever I picked up a text, I'd read a page or two and then turn back to the portrait. Read, flip, read, flip. Avuncular, kindly, and tongue-in-cheek, a man I could trust.

But this Shakespeare was my age, hipsterish with his two-day beard, cool despite his truly old-fashioned Elizabethan nightdress.

"You were never this young."

"Young is not what I feel." He shook his head, looked up at me. "In faith, conversation brings no clarity."

"You aren't the one who should be confused. It's my dream, and I'm here in this room, trapped—"

He waved a hand. "This is not your dream. But it does no good to explain," he said, his voice scratchy. "Wait but a trice, and you'll disappear back into your own time. I would venture the twentieth century? Or the twenty-first. Varies. Last week, a visitation from a girl from someplace called Man-Hattan. She screamed for thirty seconds before evaporating. It's taken me a great deal of time to figure out this nightly torture, but you are but a single cloud in a storm of many."

"What are you talking about exactly?"

"Why should I bother?" He pushed up to standing, kicked the bottle, tossed up rushes. Shaking his head, he stared at me, turned toward the window, hands on slim hips. Turned back.

"What?" I asked.

"You are still here!"

"Why don't you do something about it?" I asked.

"Do you not think I have tried? Prayers, incantations, beseechings of various and sundry kinds. Praying to all the gods at once. The only option left to me is murder, I would venture, you silly wench!"

"There's always self-slaughter," I offered.

He cut me a hard glance.

"Kidding," I said.

"Splendid. A humor artist."

Despite the novelty of this dream, I was done.

"Lumpish horn-beast." He walked toward me, eyes wide. I stood up, knocking back the chair, my heart thudding in my throat. "Saucy nut-hook."

I stepped back, the thing on the floor squeaking and scuttling away. "Horn-beast? Nut-hook? You're a real jerk, you know that?"

"And you are named Jessica."

Yes, my name. His creation. "Of course. My name is Jessica. This is my dream—"

"Perchance, one of us might get to sleep in some near future."

I stared at him. He was almost quoting himself, but not on purpose. This an almost line from *Hamlet*. When were we? 1596? 1598?

He waved a hand again. "Pray, continue. Go ever onward. You have things to say. Dream you say?"

I swallowed. "I'm not sure what sick part of me conjured you and this smelly man cave you call a bedroom, but so be it. Now it's time to wake up!"

I pressed my arms tight against my sides. I was corporeal. Strange, how I felt so alive for being asleep, as if I were really shivering in the room, looking at this sad, hungover man.

"You are still here." Again, his hard, dark glare.

"Be honest," I said. "Tell me who you are and where we are. I need a bit of truth to take back from this dream."

"Be silent. It will all pass in a moment."

"Come on!" I said, apparently with too much enthusiasm as someone in the room below roared out and banged on the ceiling. Soon enough, the Gumbles would be back, ready to kick us out and toss us to the curb. The dream was bad enough in the room, so I lowered my voice.

"Please."

Shakespeare looked up, a wide world of fatigue in his eyes, slack face, and sad lips. He began, by rote, the words well-practiced. "My name is William Shakespeare. Your name is Jessica," he paused, waved a hand. "Jessica Something. From some time un-had, un-realized. From some world only imagined. You have arrived in my chamber because I created your name."

In the fireplace, the embers red but slowly burning out, pieces breaking, sizzling, dying. "So you think this is because you invented the name?"

He nodded, his hand moving through his hair again.

"But you created a lot of things. Names. Words. Settings. Why this name? Why Jessica? She's not one of your best characters. Not well-drawn. Odd, really. Not like Portia. Someone said to me tonight—"

He almost reared back, exhaling with a snort. "You spoke of Jessica this very night?"

"Actually, yes. I was at a rehearsal of your play."

He stared at me, face slack. "My play?"

"*The Merchant of Venice*. In fact, I would swear I saw you in the role of Shylock. Did you really play him?"

I felt an academic paper forming.

"Never mind this role. You watched this play tonight? Saw you Jessica in action?"

I nodded. "Dan and I discussed Jessica."

"Dan?" Shakespeare asked.

I waved my hand and continued. "Her lack of substance. So if you were to be haunted, why her? Why not Juliet? Not so many with that name. Or Kate from *The Taming of the Shrew*. Or Rosaline from *Love's*? Or Portia. She's the one with all the power."

He didn't say a word, his eyes on me.

"I suppose you didn't make up those names," I guessed. "But still."

"If this is your dream, why not ask yourself?" He glared a bit and then shrugged, sinking back onto the bed. "This is a curse, truly. A spell incanted by a witch. If I could unname you, I would do so happily. But no matter. In minutes, you will disappear. I'll have hours of peace. Maybe a day. But then, I will be once more awakened by a scream. Another Jessica. I will bother not to light the candle. I'll wait, and then she will vanish. Like smoke."

For a moment, I watched Shakespeare watch me. Never for more than a minute—from the first time I read the name Jessica in the list of characters in

24

The Merchant of Venice—did I think more than, Wow! My name. Cool. But here, I had concocted an entire scenario involving Shakespeare's invention.

"Nothing ever stopped us?" I asked.

Shakespeare snorted. "As I said, my methods were varied and usually involved heavy drinking and much debauchery. But with some hope, the name will fall from grace. All the wretched parents will find favor with Esther or Alice or Martha—"

"Not likely," I said.

He ignored me, continuing. "But until then, all the Jessicas in all the world will travel time and space to meet me. Your creator, dear woman. Now, in this instant, begone!"

Chapter Four – No Better Than Captain Kirk: Breaking the Prime Directive

I closed my eyes, trying not to think of this narrative's bizarre turn. All I needed was to keep my eyes shut and wait for sleep to pull me out of this room and back to my life.

"You're still here!" Shakespeare yelled. I opened my eyes and wobbled on the chair, clutching the seat.

"I'm trying," I said. "Really."

"Endeavor with more urgency, you—"

I held up one hand, a universal sign—regardless of the century—for stop. "No more Elizabethan curses, you . . . you dizzy-eyed windbag."

He stopped, started, something like a smile at the corners of his eyes. But then he glowered. "Few have stayed this long before. By now, I've had time to curse, piss, and drink half a bottle before falling back to slumber."

"Sorry to have held you up," I said, kicking at the bottle and noting its dead kinsmen in the corners. "Rough month?"

"'Time goes on crutches till'—"

"'Love have all his rites.' Got it. *Much Ado About Nothing*. Long hard loveless month. Tell me about it." I relaxed into my rant, a giddiness taking over. "Try a long hard five years. Only then can you start quoting Shakespeare to me, *Shakespeare*."

"I say—"

"Don't *say* anything. You don't know what it's like to join Match.com and freak out when guys actually want to go out. But are they who they say they are?

Are their pictures current? They aren't. There's the guy waiting for you at Starbucks looking twelve years older than his online profile. Surprise! He's wearing a toupee."

"To pay?"

I ignored his question and plowed on.

"So you turn off your profile and hide for a little while. Get lonely and turn on Match again. Email with all the other misfit toys. Turn Match off and then on again. Bad date, hide, bad date, hide. Rinse and repeat. Over and over."

I couldn't shut up. But what did it matter? I was full of an unusual giddiness. Shakespeare looked at me in wonder, and his gaze made me feel good.

He scratched his chin. "Seems well said, though I am much confused."

Now I stared at his knees, knobby and hairy. But muscular and strong, like the rest of him. All that fighting on stage with fake swords. *En garde!* For a moment, I imagined him, swashbuckling up the theater walls, calling out his lines, hat in hand. Below him, the other actors landing blows. Clang, clang. If I stayed—wait, really? Did I think this would last?—could I go with him to the theater? Had he built The Globe yet? Would I be able to see his plays as they were meant to be produced? What a nice antidote to the play Dan and I sat through earlier.

"Jessica!" he said.

"What?" I sighed.

"Truly, how did you know the quote about time?" he asked.

I smoothed my magically appearing nightgown over my knees, a chill licking my toes. "It is so irritating talking to myself in a dream I can't wake up from."

He stared at me, his eyes less bleary now. "How did you know it?"

"I know it, you know it, the world knows it. It's known! It's Shakespeare!"

"I finished?"

"You finished what?"

"The play. Writing the play. *Much Ado About Nothing.*"

"You finished everything. But why are we arguing? You're a figment, a brain synapse—"

"Synapse—"

27

"Don't interrupt. You are nothing more than a terrible bit of symbolism intruding on much-needed rest. I have papers to grade. Meetings to attend."

Shakespeare stood, sexy in his nightie. The even better news? His feet were not as hairy as his knees.

"Symbolism I am not. I'm William Shakespeare."

This was too ridiculous. I burst out with an initial, "Ha," and then there were my insane giggles, the inability to stop. I leaned over, holding my sides, gasping into my knees, my forehead pressing on the fabric of my nightgown.

"Please," I managed. "Don't say another word."

"My dilemma with words this long year."

He said it with so much Shakespearean gravitas that I bent over in another peel. This long year. This long year! My troubling teaching year, full of students who seemed less than engaged, and a demanding department chair, tenure looking murky. Then off to my apartment to grade papers with Horatio, half a bottle of red wine, and a long sit on my couch. Chats with my slightly bossy sister who lives the town over and lectures from my mother, who thankfully lives across the country. More wine. More Netflix binges. Night after night, unless I had to work on the play with Dan. The big excitement? Taking Horatio for a walk.

My eyes started to fill, and then I was crying, wiping my eyes on my nightgown. Where had my Pink sweatpants gone? The ones my niece Shelby picked out for me? "Time to be a little cool, Aunt Jess," she'd said.

We'd been shopping at the downtown plaza, Shelby wearing a retro tie-dyed shirt and skinny jeans that made her peg legs even more pegged. She'd turned to me—a young Kate, but less troubled— her blonde hair frizzed from fog, her lips slightly purple with illegal lipstick. Her energy was visible, radiating in waves.

"You so totally need these!"

If Shelby were in my dream, she'd own the place, a raging eleven-year-old powerhouse, arms akimbo. More Portia than Jessica. She'd have Shakespeare explaining the entire dream and then buying her something to eat. The thought of her brace-filled mouth and wide green eyes made me start crying again.

"This is not supposed to be bad news," Shakespeare said. "I am no ravager of women. Unless they agree. You are safe here until your time to depart is nigh."

I snuffled, sat up.

"To weep is to make less the depth of grief," he said.

I wiped my nose and then pushed my hair away from my eyes. "As Shakespeare, you should know it's bad form to keep quoting yourself. Rude, my mother would say."

"I do it daily," he said.

"I take it you live alone." I eyeballed the disheveled room. "No one to talk back."

Of course, I lived alone, too. No checks and balances.

But he hadn't heard anything I said anyway. Shakespeare was rummaging in a cupboard, apparently for another bottle. He brought it back and put it on the table with a clack.

"We needs must swill from the same container," he said. "Though perhaps you will disappear mid-swig."

I eyed the amber liquid. "Not my thing, really."

"Is any of this?" he asked, pointing to himself and then the room.

"Good point."

I grabbed the bottle. The past school year, I'd taken to drinking wine at night, but I wasn't much for the hard stuff. But this stuff was 100% moonshine. I swallowed, hacked, clutched the bottle, coughed, my eyes watering.

"Not what you are accustomed to?" he asked.

The burn ripped a hot swath from my front teeth to my stomach.

It felt good.

At his nod, I took a smaller, slower swig, and passed him the bottle. He pulled long and hard at the bottle and then smacked his lips. He offered me more, but I shook my head, my throat still tingling. Going to bed tipsy was one thing, waking up another.

"What can I call you? William? Will?"

"No Jessica ever asked me that," he said.

"They didn't have time for chitchat," I said. "I'm still here."

"I see that."

"So, is it Will?

He rolled his eyes. "Matters not."

"So, Will, before I disappear or wake up or whatever, tell me what you meant about 'another one.' All the Jessicas."

Will leaned back on one elbow, reciting like a clinician about a medical condition. "They are often fair-haired and foolish. Very young. Appeared just after Shylock first tread the boards. Mayhap it was after one night I took the role myself. Of course, I have no true notion of how this magic happens."

"I looked up my name once." I took the bottle from him and rested it on my knee. "Baby name websites all say you invented it."

Will smiled. "Ah, I'm still remembered."

I took another, longer swig, licking my lips and leaning back against the chair.

"You're an industry. Shakespeare festivals all over the world. Conferences, websites, magazines. Updates. Tweets—"

"Tweets?" He raised an eyebrow. "Like a bird?"

"Never mind. Your plays—even the bad ones—performed every—"

"Bad ones?"

"Oh, come on. *Pericles?*"

"I've never penned—"

"You will. And to be honest, people will like it in your time. But listen. What I'm trying to tell you is you are huge! Every single American high school student reads at least one of your plays before graduating."

Will stared at me. "I'm not understanding. Huge in size? Graduating from schools of high? American?"

"America's in The New World. The land of Jessicas. You mention it in *Merchant.* Often in *The Tempest.*"

Will gave me a look. Even if this were a dream—my dream—I knew better.

"Sorry," I said. "Breaking the Temporal Prime Directive."

Another look. A sigh. "Of what do you speak?"

"Captain Kirk always said. You can't interfere in historical events."

"Captain Kirk?"

A television cult hero's name in William Shakespeare's mouth made me laugh. "James Tiberius Kirk," I added, barely able to get out the last word.

"Tiberius." Will seemed to muse. "Rome's greatest general. Made conquest of Germany. Laid foundations for the frontier."

"Really?" I thought of the final frontier, where no man had gone before.

Will nodded. "This Kirk must be a man to pay heed to."

I stopped laughing. Will might be right. Kirk, too. Anyway, in the audiobooks I listened to in my car on the way to work, time travel had new rules these days. People showed up whenever they pleased, said what they wanted, when they wanted, to whomever they wanted. Upon their return home, things had changed. But so what? In some other reality, the past was doing just fine. The old space-time continuum was so passé. So maybe breaking the Prime Directive was okay for one night and one night only.

"*The Tempest* is a 'first encounter' story," I started.

"Encountering who first?" Will passed me the bottle.

"The native populations. People they could have never imagined."

"I see such daily at the market," Will said. "Pray, what else?"

"A whole new world! Very colonial." I handed him the bottle. "I can tell you the entire history. I'm only here for minutes. Better take your chance."

"I am wishing for a muter Jessica."

The tingly feeling inside me spread. "All the land people are finding out there. Columbus, for one. You know about him, right? 1492, etcetera?"

Will waved a hand, his apparent trademark move.

"Okay, fine. What about this: "How many goodly creatures are there here! How beauteous mankind is! O brave new world."

I gave him a nod, waiting for him to spontaneously produce, "That has such people in't." But if I was here just after *Merchant*, we were about, what? I tried to count, something my brain was resisting. Five, seven years, ten—several years away from *The Tempest* and Shakespeare's farewell to the stage. He was in his early thirties if I had his bio right. If he were real, a young writer who didn't have his own theater yet, whose greatest work was yet to come, I was giving him way too much information.

But if he were this same writer who was being visited nightly by dimwitted Jessicas, maybe he didn't believe everything he heard. Maybe he took future information with a huge grain of salt.

He waited, sipping, the bottle, now only half full, the air around us thick with fumes. My head felt stuffed with burlap my fingers numb.

"Continue."

"Huh?"

"My illustrious career."

"So." I grabbed the bottle. "The brave new world turns into The United States of America. In two hundred years or so. A big war ensues. But the point is, we all read you."

"Say you not!"

"It's true," I told him.

"None of the other Jessicas has mentioned these facts."

"If they are young and silly, they likely have a grudge against you. Forced to read *Romeo and Juliet* and write 500 words on the use of opposites or something."

Will started to laugh. "You speak in jest."

"Dead serious. Famous and a legend. Oh, and you're a mystery."

I took another big sip and then curled up on the chair, tucking my feet under the nightgown.

"The only mystery in my life is penuary," Will said sourly before matching my last swig and then some. Again, he gestured to his room. "As you have full proof."

"That will end. Trust me. But the mystery will remain. People continue to make documentaries about your life. Of keen scrutiny is why you left Anne your second-best bed, which, I have to say, is nowhere in sight, at least in here."

"Know you my wife Anne?"

32

"Who doesn't know Anne? For one, you married her when you were but 18, she 26. Seems the baby came hard upon the wedding."

Will shrugged. "It's common."

I thought of my own mother, pregnant with Kate at her wedding. That pregnancy forced a marriage that didn't work out well, either. "I agree."

"So Anne?"

"I've visited her house in Stratford-upon-Avon. On tour after college. Then to London. The Globe. Performance after performance."

Now Will sat back, mouth agape. "We built The Globe?" he asked. He pounded his knee. "Zounds! What tremendous news."

"Sure," I said, feeling gracious. "They built the third one back in 1997."

His gaze took me in, something vacant in his eyes. "Pray, what hard year do you come from?"

I shot him a glance. "2018."

He jerked back a little, his mouth opening slightly before he whispered, "The year 2018."

"Humans have managed to survive," I said, lolling a little in my chair, my body seeming to spill over the hard wooden edges.

"Do tell me more."

"How about this. There have been theories Queen Elizabeth wrote your plays."

"That desiccated Gloriana?" he sputtered.

"Think that's bad? Try Ben Jonson, Christopher Marlowe, the Earl of Derby, the Earl of Rutland, the Earl of Southampton, the Earl of Essex, Sir Walter Raleigh. Can't forget Francis Bacon, either."

"God's Blood! Such calumny! All certainly suspect in a particular light. But Marlowe's dead."

"Some scholars think he's alive. Right now. In hiding. But I believe in you. I've always believed in you. You are my life's work."

"Enough of this madness," Will shouted. "I've listened well enough to you phantoms!" He took the bottle.

In the room below, the same angry person banged on the ceiling. I continued on with my sound advice.

"This mess could have been avoided. Sign and date your work. Save some copies in a safe. They have bank vaults in this time, I hope. Be a bit more careful about copyright. Get legal on your side. Do a bit more self-promotion. You don't even want to know what people did to your plays. One guy even kept Cordelia alive! Married Edgar! God. Totally ruined *King Lear*."

"Cordelia?" he mulled. "Such a name flows well upon the tongue."

"You haven't written her yet. But here's the deal."

I leaned forward, the world wavering like the ocean as I moved. "You weren't the best self-marketer. You put your characters before yourself. I've gone over every inch of your work looking for self-referential behavior, but there's so little. That has to change. Facebook would be ideal for you about now."

Will sat still, waiting for me to continue.

"And let's not talk about the critics and how we interpret you now. *The Merchant of Venice*? Ha!" I took another sip. "People won't even produce it, except for my university. But no wonder you're being haunted by Jessicas. Anti-Semitic payback."

"I know not this word."

I stared at him, this very real man in front of me. I reached out and touched his sleeve. A ruffle, the linen worn and needing some Clorox. He blinked, waiting.

"I'm sorry." I pulled my hand away. "The play in a nutshell. Venetian merchant borrows money from a Jewish lender. Promises the lender a pound of flesh should he not repay the loan. Mayhem ensues."

"'Tis brief but honest."

"So Shylock. He's very, very Jewish. You've given him the worst qualities you could have. A focus on money, especially. Money over everything."

"He's naught but a farce. A jibe. A jest. A comedy."

"People started taking him pretty seriously."

"You are saying his depiction caused alarm?" Will was getting a bit steamed. I handed him the bottle.

"And after World War Two—"

"One world war? And a second?"

For a moment, the fizz and gaiety went out of my rant. Right now, he didn't seem part of me and my dream. He was a man learning about the horrors of the twentieth century.

"A bad time is coming in three hundred plus years," I said, not wanting to mention the upcoming Puritan Revolution, but he would be dead by then.

Even less fizz now. Two years ago, we'd celebrated the four hundredth anniversary of his death at the university with readings and performances. I stared at him. Four hundred years. If he were 30-32, he had only 20 years left to live. I wished I didn't know that terrible fact.

Below us, the neighbor ceased his banging. Will rubbed his brow. "This is distressing information indeed."

Without thinking, I put a hand on his bare knee. "Look at the bright side. You are remembered for a lot of beautiful ideas, amazing characters, and incredible themes. You've kept hundreds of English departments alive and kicking. Ordinary people can recite your verses from memory. Even science majors."

"You speak truly?"

I nodded, taking a long swig.

"Then you must perform for me, oh Jessica who will not leave. A quote, lest I quote myself again and earn your mother's ire."

"I am an English professor, you know," I said.

He raised an eyebrow. "And yet, you do not recite for me?"

My head spun, but I steadied myself, hands gripping the chair. "I know a few of your sonnets. I make my students memorize them, so I have to prove it can be done. I usually scare them the first day with a recitation."

"Then perform it so. Perhaps midline, the poem will propel you homeward."

I nodded, closed my eyes. Which poem, I wondered, even as my brain tried to make sense of things. Maybe there was no making sense of it. So, here in William Shakespeare's rooms, drunk on moonshine, half crazy, stuck in the wildest dream of my life, I figured the moral dilemma of the 144th sonnet would suit, an angel on one shoulder, a devil on the other. The choice between goodness or passion. About duty and desire. About being neither here nor there, which fit my current situation to a T.

Standing slowly and with several wobbles, I took in a deep breath, opened my eyes, and recited:

"Two loves I have of comfort and despair,

Which like two spirits do suggest me still;

The better angel is a man right fair,

The worser spirit a woman colour'd ill.

To win me soon to hell, my female evil

Tempteth my better angel from my side,

And would corrupt my saint to be a devil..."

My breath hitched, my voice trembled, the room spun on its tiny axis. My stomach lurched and twisted in an unpromising way. I needed to sit down. But when I looked at Will, his eyes gleamed in the candlelight. He nodded, waiting. If my students could soldier on, so could I:

"...Wooing his purity with her foul pride.

And whether that my angel be turn'd fiend

Suspect I may, yet not directly tell;

But being both from me, both to each friend,

I guess one angel in another's hell.

Yet this shall I ne'er know, but live in doubt,

Till my bad angel fire my good one out."

Out finally out of my mouth, I exhaled, dizzy, feeling sick. I tried to locate my body in space, but everything was numb. Except for my stomach, which was prickles and nerves.

Across from me, Will was silent. I slowly opened my eyes, trying to quell my wooziness. His face was wet with tears.

"Did I do it wrong?" I asked, the sentence funny in my drunken ear. "Wong. Wrong!"

"I have only dreamt these thoughts," he was saying, but I was slipping and sliding off the chair, onto the floor. My head clunked something, but I barely felt it, hardly heard the thing on the floor scuttle past. Spinning, weightless, and filled with light, I prayed I was being lifted up by time and space and sleep, going, going, gone.

Chapter Five – The Goddamn Rats and No Toothpaste
or
Plague, Syphilis, Typhus, Tuberculosis, Smallpox, Malaria, Dysentery

I had to call in sick. Under the covers, I clutched my head with one hand, my stomach with another. The craziness from the night before was a virus, a rampaging, violent bug that had left me insane due to a rocketing temperature. I needed to call my sister, let her bring over her famous soup. So I turned over and slipped out one hand, searching for my bed stand and phone. I could text Kate, and in an hour, full of anti-inflammatory drugs and her ginger, garlic, and curry-infused chicken stock, I'd live into the afternoon. Maybe I could even finish reading those papers.

I patted the air. Nothing. No bed stand, no phone, no lamp. No dog pushing his wet nose under the blankets to wake me up with "Feed me, feed me" grunts and whines. No garbage truck banging down the metal containers outside my bedroom window. Swimming under the strangely heavy blanket, I turned around, trying to face the right direction. Somehow, I had twisted myself around, thrashing during the fever, which must have caused my hallucinogenic experience at the university's theater and then my imagined dream conversation with William Shakespeare.

I must have a terrible flu!

I swam, trying to right myself, and that's when I met up with his body. Him. Shakespeare. William. Will.

I was still there. Here. Or really in William Shakespeare's bedroom. Insane.

"Oh," he groaned as I jabbed him with an elbow.

"Oh," I groaned, but the sound gave me no relief, horrified as I was with my inhale of wet, hot air. A hug of dirt and sweat pressed me to the bed. Despite myself, I breathed in two reeking adult bodies exuding the worst of alcohols (something concocted of poisoned entrails, wool of bat, and toes of frogs by *Macbeth's* witches in their cauldron). Nausea gripped me. I spun in blankets that had seen better days or maybe decades. My throat tightened, and I popped out to find the chamber pot just in time.

After a few retching moments, I struggled back up to the mattress, a noun that really didn't fit what we were sleeping on. It was lumpy and had sudden sharp moments, stab under rib, punch under hip.

"God," I said.

"If indeed we have such a creator," Will mumbled. "Doubtful. For one, you are still in my chamber."

I rubbed my forehead, closed my eyes tight against the leak of sunlight coming in through the large window. "Let's move on. Stop your whining."

"Humph," he said.

We must have fallen back asleep because the next thing I knew, the sunlight beat against the middle of the window, the room filled with hot, stuffy air, as thick and appealing as fiberglass insulation. Will had thrown an arm around me and was snoring into my side. But my stomach had calmed down, the beat in my head only background noise.

I pushed him away and sat up to survey my surroundings. The room was bigger than I'd thought the night before, maybe three hundred square feet, with an alcove by the large window, the perfect spot for the desk. Diamonds of wavery sun flicked through the glass, illuminating his writing area, though it was clear his work hadn't been going smoothly, scraps of much-written on and tattered paper strewn on the floor. There was a dresser with a basin and a table as disorganized as the desk. Plates, mugs, knobs of animal bones, crusts of bread, empty bottles, one of which was ours from the night before. One long red hair ribbon. A nosegay, all the flowers wilted. A blouse that looked decidedly feminine. A small pipe tipped on its side (what had he been smoking?). The floor was littered with clothing (Breeches? Doublets?) books and straw. I scanned the corners for the creature that had been scrabbling about last night, but it was not in sight. Nocturnal. A rat. Rats.

Will snored, sunk deep into his hangover, his mouth open, his brown hair a whorl on top of his head. I wasn't dreaming. Not one dream in thirty-two years had ever reached this apex of clarity. In my dreams, time was disjointed, disconnected, and odd. People didn't act according to type. But now, even with all the impossibility of my being here, not to mention the heavy drinking, time moved in solid clicks of the wheel. And besides, after a dream, one usually wakes up in one's bed. But here I was in bed with a corporeal man. A hungover man who spoke in Elizabethan English. A man with a desperate need for a bath and a trip to the washerwoman with every stitch of his clothing and bedding. A man who seemed to accept the fact that Jessicas appeared in his room on a regular basis.

Every indication led to the truth that he was indeed William Shakespeare, and not my indigestion, imagination, or hangover.

My whole body slowed. I stared out the window until the light seemed fuzzy. Then I snapped to, plan in mind. I needed to get out of bed and make sure this was real. I needed to use my research skills. First things first.

One jittery limb at a time, I slipped off the lumpy mattress, my feet on the rushes. Without waking Will, I lurched to standing and moved toward the wardrobe I'd arrived in. Standing in front of it, I placed one hand on the wood, slowly, as if expecting to see it disappear, hand in one world, wrist in another. But no, my palm was there on the all-too solid door.

I pulled the knob, opened the door, breathing in the wet wool. Pushing aside the coats, I stepped in, turned, and closed the door, a slit of sunlight in my eyes. So I closed them, thought of last night at the play, how I'd run out of one door and time and into another. It was just that simple, right?

One, two, three. Without opening my eyes, I waited. For a moment, I conjured forth Shylock pacing across the stage as he plotted Antonino's debt.

But after a few clenched moments, I hadn't gone anywhere but inside a closet. The air. The smell. The ache in my head. And yes, as I opened my eyes and pushed open the cupboard door, there was Will in his bed, snoring.

What next? Maybe the portal was somewhere else, down the hall, as it had been at the theater. To get there, I would have to brave potential Gumble wrath and certain humiliation. So before grabbing the door handle, I smoothed my nightgown, my hair. There was nothing to do about my 150-proof breath. Toothpaste was likely a hundred years away from being even a glimmer of an idea.

A quick glance back at Will now starfished on the bed, one arm dangling off the side, I pulled the door open with a creak and then slipped out into the dark hall. My nightgown flapped. Cold air wrapped around my ankles, slipped up my shins, my skin a river of gooseflesh. I gritted my teeth as I closed the door behind me and looked around. I was on the second or third floor of a large building, a boarding house probably, a small window at either end of the hall. I tiptoed to the first window, the view nothing but sky and clouds swirled with grey, rain imminent. No surprise there. This was London, after all. I had no clothes, no umbrella, no boots. But hopefully, before I stepped out onto the muddy street, I'd have already magically popped back home.

My head spinning like a child's toy, my knees shaking, I walked toward the stairwell, desiring stealth, and the least amount of contact with the wooden planks under my pale feet. As I moved past every door, I hoped there would be a sign, a direction:

This Way Out!

Or *California, 5351 Miles.*

Or *Drink Me!*

Or best yet, *Home: four hundred Years from Now!*

All I had to do was take the correct turn, and I'd be back to what I understood. Things hadn't really met my childhood dreams and expectations—I was clearly not lecturing at Oxford—but I was able to read and write for a living. But all this mess? The dirt, the smells, the yelling? I needed out, no matter how appealing it might be to spend a couple more hours talking with Will.

Stealthy like the cat Will didn't seem to own, I slipped along the hall. At the stairwell, I grabbed the railing, ready to step down, when someone pulled me by the shoulder.

"Strumpet! Doxy! What are you doing in this house! I run a respectable establishment!"

I covered my head, my face, as something slapped me about the neck and shoulders. Opening one eye, I shot a glance down the stairwell. Two women were staring up from the floor below, eyes wide, mouths open.

"Stop!" I cried. One more blow would send me crashing down the stairs.

"Get out! This is a proper establishment! Master Gumble! Master Gumble. A doxy tarries in the hallway!"

I curled down, my head between my knees, holding on tight to the railing. There were footsteps, voices, and then someone hoisted me up.

"Mistress Gumble, pray, accept my apologies." It was Will.

"You pribbling ill-bred lewdster! I told you last night! No more strumpets."

"I'm his—" I slowed, knowing they might not understand me. "Cousin."

"Aye, she is," Will said, pulling me close. "My dear cousin Jessica. She arrived but late to my rooms from a long—a long journey from far, far away. Pray forgive me. She is overtired and perambulating in her sleep."

Ducking still as if expecting further blows, I turned my gaze toward the direction they had come from. Two short people with round moon faces glared at me, their eyes dark with disbelief. Mistress Gumble's entire head and forehead were covered in what I could only describe as nun-like headgear. Most of Master Gumble's head was covered with nothing but a shiny scalp. Bald with a whip of a ponytail, he wore an apron over his jacket and carried a broom, presumably to sweep me off the hallway stairs.

"Come, Cousin Jess. You need rest."

"Master Shakespeare," Master Gumble said, badgered forward by Mistress Gumble's meaty mitts. "The rent."

"Anon, dear fellow. Anon."

Then Will was half-carrying, half-pushing me down the hall, into the room, and onto the bed, flopping both of us down in a whoosh of dust and hay. Motes spun in the light, my head whirling.

"You promised not to leave the chamber," he said, the angry edge back in his voice.

"I'm sorry," I said, ashamed. "I hoped I might find the way home out here…" I pointed toward the door and then let my hand fall to my side.

"For future ramblings, pray wake me," he said in my ear. "It would be fiendish bad to have to save you from the Tower."

"Future? Won't I be gone soon?"

"As I have said countless times since yesternight, you are still here. But for the first time in so many weeks I cannot count, no other Jessica appeared. You have blocked the door of time."

"They never stopped before?"

Will sighed. "Your special magic made them cease."

"Why me?"

"I won't ask lest I break the spell."

Why was I different from all the other Jessicas? Because I studied Shakespeare? I couldn't be alone in that. Or was it the size of my butt? There I was, crammed into a wormhole, my ass stuck, a passel of Jessicas behind me. Literally. I started giggling. Will chuckled a bit, too. Who knows why? But we laughed, the dust spun, the sun moved across the dirty glass, and I closed my eyes and relaxed back against the mattress.

We must have slept again, but then Will sighed, stretched, reached out for me, his hand landing warm and gentle on my left breast, his fingers searching for…Wow! I jumped a bit and stared at his spread fingers, enjoying his touch, even though I shouldn't. Such a tender grasp hadn't happened in a long while.

"My left breast is not a perk of time travel," I said. "Besides, from the looks of the clothes strewn around this place, you have a woman already. And I may be going out on a limb, but it's likely not your wife."

Will removed his hand and turned on his back, sighing. "A fortnight ago. Mayhap more."

43

"Who was she?"

Will grumbled and failed to answer, so I poked him in the shoulder.

"Zounds, woman!" he said. "This is none of your concern."

Her identity was a mystery, even to him.

"Wonderful," I said, pausing, trying to remember my facts. If I were really in 1598 or whatever, I was in a horror show of illness. A hospital, such as it was, was more torture chamber than a place of healing. No anesthesia. Saws and knives, the types used in 1970s slasher movies. Rope restraints. Pools of blood. Viruses slicking the walls. Germs and bacteria everywhere. In everyone. Will. This woman who left her ribbon. Maybe a prostitute? A strumpet indeed. Maybe a man? What kind of STIs flourished in a sixteenth-century prostitute? Didn't everyone have syphilis in London? Crabs? Lice?

Suddenly, my shins started to itch. To burn, really. My knees. My thighs. I kicked off the blanket despite Will's swearing and raised my leg. I blinked, reaching out once again for the bed stand that still wasn't there, wanting my reading glasses. I blinked again. No question. Red dots. Bites. Lots of them. From ankle to waist.

"Oh, my God! Oh, my God!" I started kicking, trying to get out of the bed.

Will raised himself on one elbow and put a hand on my knee. "God's blood! Forbear your gyrations! Naught but bedbugs."

And that's when I finally started yelling. I jumped away from Will and the bed, brushing off the bugs that had long since scattered to their hiding spots.

"Or fleas." He started laughing, but I examined my arms and tried not to realize my rear also felt welty and itchy, though I didn't want to examine myself in front of Will.

"You have rats!" I sat down on the chair, tucking my feet under me, gripping myself with both arms. "We're going to die!"

The neighbor below began his ritual ceiling beat.

"Calm yourself," Will got out of bed, scratching his head and walked to the window, as he moved, I caught a glimpse of smooth bardly ass, but I was in no mood. "A rat can but chew off a finger. Not a head or heart."

"Are you kidding me? Seriously?" I felt horror and rage and fear in every bone. "Rats and fleas. The plague."

He turned, pale and stricken. "What did you say?"

"What year is it? Exactly! Tell me!"

"The year of our Queen Elizabeth 1598. The month of October."

I closed my eyes, rested my forehead against my knees. I was cold and shaking and chili-peppered with plague-carrying flea bites. Bed bugs were at this very second hiding in the folds of my nightdress. I was likely covered in typhus-carrying lice. I shivered. My throat tightened.

Focus, I thought. Plague years. Plague years.

All those weeks and months of studying in my small cubicle at Doe Library at Cal. Every single detail about Shakespeare. Everything that could have influenced or affected him. Any detail that might help me prove the ordinary man was in fact the man who wrote the most famous works in the English language. His friends, enemies, family, and lodgings—we must be in his rooms at Bishopsgate—his successes. 1598 wasn't one of his best years. But the theaters had been reopened. If I walked outside this moment, I wouldn't find the heaps of bodies, the carts filled to brimming, the Monty Pythonesque men calling out, "Bring out your dead!"

The plague was out there, somewhere. But not enough to shut down city life.

"What did you mean 'rats and fleas?'" he asked again, his voice urgent, strained.

I scratched my ankle to bleeding and glanced at him, ignoring the pound of my heart that told me I was looking at *the* William Shakespeare silhouetted against the late morning sunshine.

Trapped in the chair, the only safe piece of furniture in the room, I sat stunned. In my time travel fantasies—and as a scholar of the days of yore — I'd thought a lot about living in times not my own. I came stocked with a slew of antibiotics, soap, shampoo, antifungal cream, condoms (who knew?) tampons (please let me be gone before that time of the month), and toothpaste. None of this popping in and out naked as a jaybird time travel for me. In terms

45

of the rules, I was of the "you *could* bring it all with you" school of thought: clothes and a carry-on case. I'd prepare for my sojourn with a course of exotic inoculations and abatement regimes. Dengue fever, encephalitis, malaria, yellow fever, typhoid, rabies, Of course, my basics were up to date—even the hepatitis alphabet of A and B—but there were diseases still alive in the sixteenth century that had died by the time I was born. I had never had a smallpox shot. Did they even make that inoculation anymore? Didn't the germ only exist in a frozen test tube at some undisclosed CDC location?

"Rats and fleas?" he asked again, walking toward me, his hair a dark flower around his head.

"Black rats carry the plague and fleas," I said, teeth chattering. "Fleas carry the plague to us."

He scratched his chin, noticed what he was doing, and stopped. "The illness spreads in the multitudes. In the summers. In the swarms. The odors. The miasma—"

"Stop this medieval nonsense! More people, more rats. More heat, more fleas." I felt myself flush hot, as if I *were* hot, getting a fever. How long did I have after the fever started? One day? Two?

Will shook his head. "How then none understand this?"

"They won't! For centuries. 1603 will be a wretched year. Then there'll be another Black Death in 1665. There'll—"

"Do I die of this pestilence?"

I shot him a dark look and turned back to my ankle, a very undream-like ankle, red and throbbing. "We'll probably both die tomorrow! Maybe not from the plague. But look at how you live!" My eyes filled. Dying of a preventable disease. Me, who got a flu shot every year in September to prepare for the school year. The flu in 1598 would probably toss me up and eat me alive.

"You know when I leave this earthly plane," he said, a statement, matter-of-fact.

Of course I did. Every English major worth her salt knew the exact date of William Shakespeare's death. April 23, 1616, in Stratford-Upon-Avon, probably of typhus. But this knowledge had yet to be written in an unpenned biography. It was not information for the young man who stood in front of me, his dark eyes intense and worried.

"I'm going to die! Tomorrow! Look at all these bites!" I stood up on the chair, lifting first one ankle and then the next. "Look at this! And this! I can't believe I'm here without any tetracycline or Tamiflu!" Even though the plague was unlikely, I started patting under my arms, looking for symptoms, the bulbous growths associated with the infection. As I did, I must have been making noise because there was a hard *one-two* rap on the door. And then another set.

"Ho! Master Shakespeare! Cease the infernal racket! I've warned you!" We paused as Master Gumble beat on the door and beat again.

Will grabbed me under the arms and lifted me off the chair. He held me tight and whispered, "Silence, wench. I need not your infernal racket to make my life even more hellish."

I clutched at Will until the knocking and ceiling banging stopped. He sat on the chair and held me on his lap.

"Quiet," he said, looking around the room as he did, seeing, I hoped, what I did: piles of clothes, heaps of dirty rushes, caches of empty bottles. Only his desk seemed usable, and even that was strewn with stacks of books and leather folders.

"How long have I been here?"

"At my reckoning, twelve hours."

Statistics were never my forte, but based on prior evidence, my stay was an anomaly. What was I going to do if I were stuck? A woman without a husband or employment. My current "benefactor" couldn't even pay his rent. And what about what I was doing in my own time? Where was my body? My life? What about my dog! My students? My student essays! What would my sister think? My niece? Dan Gordon?

It was possible that my new life in 1598 would probably work out better than my old one. But at least at home, I wasn't going to die of the plague. At home, in my small apartment and clean college town, I would miss out on dysentery and typhus. Maybe at home I wouldn't have an abundance of excitement, but I'd be in control of my bowels, blood, and reproductive choices.

"It will be all right," Will said.

"Are you sure?" I asked, wondering how he could be.

"Indeed," he said. I wanted to believe him. Until we managed to undo the curse of the Jessicas, here I was. Sure, Will smelled terrible and lived like an animal, but he wouldn't die for many years. If I stuck by him, at least I'd have a chance of survival. I'd keep my boundaries and behave myself, which meant keeping my big mouth shut. Childbearing and radical feminist politics were out. No puerperal fever or beheading for me. No fortunetelling. I'd keep my future information to myself, lest I become branded as a witch. All this time travel ridiculousness was going to be my and Will's odd little secret. We'd be okay, unless other Jessicas started to show up and stay for a long time.

It might get a bit crowded. God knows, along with the blonde Jessicas, I might have to share space with the Fair Youth and the Dark Lady, Will's two great loves, the man and the woman to whom he addressed all his sonnets. For a second—even with my fear of painful death roiling on the surface—I was rocked by a tidal wave of academic excitement, my breath caught in my throat. What I could do with my time here! I could uncover the identity of William Shakespeare's muses, his greatest loves, and the people who inspired 154 sonnets. Two great mysteries solved, but only if I managed to return home and tell anyone the truth.

Humming a little, Will stroked my hair, a tangled brown mess in need of a wash. He murmured things would be all right, his touch reassuring. With a pang, it hit me that his son had died just two years before. Young Hamnet. His only boy. Likely from the plague. I winced at my earlier freak-out. What did I know about disease compared to Will? In *The Comedy of Errors*, Will had written, "O, grief hath changed me since you saw me last." Of course, I'd never seen him in the flesh before, but now, thinking about his drunken state, it was obvious that rather than a nightly string of bawds, he'd only been entertaining despair.

I breathed into his shoulder. Sorrow or not, this man needed a good bath. And I needed to get a grip. There was no special wardrobe or door down the hall that would shoot me home. No way to know when or if I could leave. Unlike Alice in her wonderland, I wouldn't find a magic cake or potion to save me. No rabbit hole. As far as I could tell, if I woke up—as I already had three times—I'd still be here in England in the year of our queen 1598.

Not even James Tiberius Kirk could warp drive me out of here.

But whether I remained fourteen hours or forty more years, we needed a plan.

"At least we can work on the bugs," I said, sitting up straight. "Let's clean up. I mean clean. Soap and water. Will, we have to—"

"Have to?"

"Must." I indicated the table, the floor, and—I cringed—the bed. "And after this, we have to live differently."

"We?" Will said, shifting under me. "So say you, we will have a life together?"

"Yes, we." I ignored his irony. "As you said, you created me. I'm yours. A *Jessica*. And I'm not ready to go out there on my own. I couldn't even make it down the hallway before being beaten."

"Plan we might, but there is no telling what will happen next. I might turn a corner to find you nothing but vapor."

"Or, on the other hand, this may be the longest dream anyone ever had. So attend and entertain my plans, sir."

Will laughed, the sound reverberating against my side. "Have you aspirations of employment or frolic?" He grabbed my sides with both hands. "Or maybe we first should settle on your identity."

I put my hands on his and moved them away from my waist. "We told the Gumbles I was your cousin. A long lost and never seen before relative. Perhaps a bit touched. Or just shy."

"That should suffice."

We were silent for a moment, nothing but our steady breathing. What if I didn't evaporate? I needed time to learn enough to survive on my own. William

Shakespeare wouldn't have time for me. He was about to go off and be himself, and I didn't want to stop him. How could I rob the world? So when he left these chambers as he must and moved on to fame and fortune, I had to be ready to earn my keep. I needed to find employment. But first, I had to figure out how to eat.

"I'm literate and smart and can learn fast. But I don't know where to buy an egg. Or to take a bath. Or how to buy a dress. I don't even have money *for* a dress."

"Being improperly dressed, stopped you not this morning." He shook me a bit, one hand back on my waist. "But worry not. I won't let you out the door again so unfestooned

"Clothes would be good. And I'll need a job," I said, looking around the room, wrack and ruin everywhere, both the landlords breathing heavily at the door, the rats in the corner, licking their little plaguey paws. The empty bottles. The mess and mayhem. I understood this state of affairs, the one where the bomb has gone off and all the survivors can do is walk around in the dust. My childhood home after my father left. My college apartment after Phillip broke up with me. The aftermath, whatever the *math* part was. Someone had to take charge. "All I can do is teach and write. But I can't even spell correctly in this century. I have actual handwriting issues."

"A trice!" he exclaimed. "A quill and some time."

"Really? That fast?"

"As *real* as anything is," he said. "Remember, you are sitting on my lap, talking to me from a four-hundred-year divide. All this might be, as you said, but a dream. Yet, in any case, I shall help you."

"Once you've shown me the ropes, I'll find a position. A lady's maid. A secretary. Worst case, to a nunnery. You have to show me how to live."

Will sighed and then patted my shoulder. "If you stay mired in this time, mayhap the Jessicas will forever cease. A fair trade. Penmanship for sanity. Besides, you are the only visiting Jessica to understand my speech. Strangely, also, I can understand yours. I can teach you, and you will save me from my nightly affliction. Agreed?"

50

"Agreed," I said. "Deal."

He pushed me to my feet and stretched. "First, a rousing cleaning. Then a meal. 'Tis well past twelve-of-the-clock. And then, we discuss the execution."

I paused, bringing a hand to my neck. "An execution? You're serious?"

"You wanted to be 'shown the ropes.'"

"But—"

"Water first."

William Shakespeare patted my rear and then walked out of the chamber door, calling for hot water. Flea-bit, bedbug-riddled, lousy-haired, dirty-footed, and shivering, I stood in the mess and waited for my lessons to begin.

Chapter Six — Dressing for Dinner

By the late afternoon, Will's chambers were clean, apparently an unheard-of feat in Elizabethan England. Already, my terrible influence was swaying history, causing a rift in the space-time continuum. Under my silent supervision (a supposed bad tooth—I patted my cheek and mumbled, so I wouldn't speak in my outlandish vernacular), two women came—one old, one young—carrying empty cloth satchels and fresh rushes. From their wide-eyed gazes, I figured they were the women who had been standing at the bottom of the stairwell during the Gumbles' frontal assault. But I forged on. Indicating my cheek and wearing my nightdress and Will's robe, I stomped around and pantomimed mopping and cleaning.

"Mad," the older one said to the younger as if the symptoms of a bad tooth included deafness. The young woman didn't say anything, but, she presented me with a tight, quick smile.

I took the rag from the older one's hand and dipped it in the bucket, squeezing out the water. Then I got on all fours and started in at the corner, coughing as I did, dust and a thousand other horrors billowing.

There's a method to my madness, I wanted to say. Yes, my accent would scare them into the Dark Ages, but the temptation to speak was strong. But I held back and kept at my teaching display until the older one said, "We won't get out of here till we do what she asks. Come on, Daisy. Move your hindquarters."

They got to work. I pointed to corners and tattered rats' nests and dust. I followed them around, barely able to refrain from saying, "Out, damned spot."

By the time the two women left, carting away bags full of refuse, reeds, rushes, bedding, hair, and dirt, the place smelled almost clean. I opened the window, a light afternoon breeze filling the room. As I mulled the notion of concocting and selling my own chemical cleaning compounds for a living, there was a knock on the door, and another woman—a water bearer with a steaming copper jug in each hand—clomped in.

"Hot water, mistress." Without a pause, she walked across the room and poured the water into a large pot, all the while taking in my unseemly attire, her lips pinched. The jugs empty, she riffled through her pocket and then pulled out a wadded looking lump of soap and slapped it on the table. "Can't comprehend the need, mind you."

I pointed to my cheek and nodded my thanks, wondering if I should have tipped the maids, charwomen, as well as this woman. But there wasn't a thruppence, tuppence, or ducat to be found. In fact, I was pretty sure Will was out spending what little change he had.

When the woman left, I took off my nightdress and actually stood in the pot, the water warm but not exactly smelling like spring brook. In fact, I was sure I should stick to the alcohol for my thirst issues. In the wide world of disease, Giardia was probably the least of my worries.

I grabbed the soap and made as much of a lather as I could from the miserly grey sliver. Soon I was covered in pathetic suds but feeling better already. Hair, face, underarms (ferocious scrubbing). Then I made sure to clean my bites, knowing I wouldn't be able to head out to the corner drugstore for Polysporin.

Shivering in my pot, I rinsed as best I could and dried off with the nightdress, slipping it on damp and stepping out of the pot just as Will burst in with parcels and a bundle of clothing.

Closing the door quickly, he smiled, his hat rakish on his head. "I came in haste to avoid discovery. Mistress Gumble would have commanded these paltry rags in lieu of rent." He held up his parcel and gave me the once over as if I were a contestant in a wet t-shirt contest. I crossed my arms over my chest, and despite the water on my skin, flushed.

53

Will shrugged and glanced around the room, taking in the Cleanliness Act of 1598. "Zounds! No rats. No bedbugs to sup on our wayward limbs."

"Let's hope," I said, glancing at the package in his arms. "What do you have there?"

"We have places to pilfer. Behold your costume!"

In a quick move, he pulled out a long, bedraggled cloak. A long woolen Elizabethan hoodie.

"I'm pretty sure Mrs. Gumble wouldn't have wanted that." I put my hands on my hips.

"Come now. We have but a pair of ragged shoes, your nightdress, and this long cloak in which you can hide as we commence on our travels."

"Just call me Mrs. Crone."

Will rolled his eyes and walked forward, cloak held out. "You will hide inside this as I take you where you can be dressed. But you will stay clutched close to me, only one eye to scan the crowds."

"But—"

"And not one word will pass between your lips."

Will pulled the cloak around my shoulders, his mouth set and serious but his eyes shining. We were enacting his favorite kind of scene—a hidden identity, a theft of clothing, potential arrest, or social condemnation. Or, at the very least, eviction, the Gumbles waiting for a chance.

Hunched over like a wise old woman, half-blinded by my wrap, I gripped his arm and we headed down the hall in silence, stealthy on the creaky wooden stairs, time stretching to the consistency of old gum. Then we were on the street and away from the Gumbles.

"Watch your step," Will said, escorting me around a thick stream of goo I smelled rather than saw. He yanked me this way and that, and finally, pushing aside the hood, I stared, gaping. Blood pulsed in every part of my body, a drum solo of *no damn way* in every cell.

Will paused, allowing me to take in the scene. The sooty sunset was completely visible—no towering buildings to darken the already darkening sky. The street was a road, part dirt, part clunky cobbles, the traffic made up of men on horses, men and women in carts, women with baskets and parcels headed somewhere, probably home. Everyone wore ruffs—rounded collars—but the women were dressed pretty much as I was. All this clothing, despite the dirt. A cow and two pigs followed behind a man carrying a staff. Children on a stoop, dirty, shoes untied (not like mine with their spiffy fabric laces), cats and dogs at their sides. On the corners, metal stands holding buckets full of fire, a woman or child tending the flames. Manure plops dotted the road, enough that between the sewage and cow pies, we were walking a crooked line. I lifted my brand-new dress and fluffy layers. With Will's soap and water aversion, I'd be hard-pressed to get my outfit cleaned any time soon.

Two carts thundered by, the drivers clutching whips. Waves of rich and horrid odors assaulted me, and I understood why sixteenth-century folk roamed the word with nosegays pressed to their faces.

"This is the church. St. Helen's." Will pointed to his right. I nodded, but then I stopped walking, yanking Will back to my side.

"St. Helen's Bishopsgate?"

"Indeed."

"It was a nunnery, right? Before Henry the eighth."

"True indeed. Know you this building?"

I stared at the church I'd visited several times before. But in my twenty-first-century reality, behind the church rose one of the most iconic buildings of the London cityscape—The Gherkin, located in the financial district. I was standing in the same spot where four hundred years later, London would rise, cold and concrete, towers of metal, glass, and money. This was no place of commerce, but a market town, the street lined with Tudor houses, painted white and sturdy of beam.

"I used to. But this place is so different." I looked up to the sky, imagining I'd see the shiny pickle shape of The Gherkin, the crosshatched shine of its exterior. But above me, nothing except sooty orange sky.

"My own parish," he said, lifting a hand to indicate the dirt road, the shops, and the inn.

"The church will survive the fire of 1666," I said, reciting the details. "World War II. The IRA bombings of 1992 and 1993. It will be here when I come to study it during grad school. When I came to study you."

I blurted out the last bit, my face flaming. What a fangirl.

But Will only laughed. "It nearly slipped my memory. You know my industry. My Shakespearean world." He held out his arms and spun around. "The majesty of the working folk, the noise of the inn, the dirt. Did you know not of the dirt and bedbugs before your impossible time travel?"

"Don't laugh! It's true, you know," I said. "First time I was here, I signed up for a walking tour. 'Shakespeare's and Dicken's London—The Old City.'"

"Pray tell who is this wretched *Dickens,* and how can he possibly share *my* London?"

"After your time. Not as important. But getting there."

Will pretended to be insulted, but I could see the slight smile at the corner of his lips. "Continue with your course of study," he said as we walked on. "Why came you here?"

"I came here to see your parish, such as it was in the year 2013. To see the church that remained. That survived the fire and war." The street looked like a movie set from a high-production value miniseries. Everything looked so real. It *was* real.

I was long past waking up.

"Marvelous strange. I can scarce believe it true."

"Maybe it isn't."

Will turned to me. "Think you so?"

"'Such stuff as dreams are made on.'" What a phrase. What a play. *The Tempest* written so many years from now, as dreamlike as my visitation. But how I wished for every second here to be as real as the play I'd read a hundred times since high school. It all had to be true.

"After the nightly string of Jessicas, how can I not believe what has befallen us? But what is real and what is not is confusing. No rhyme nor reason to it." He tightened his grip on my arm and picked up our pace. "Come now. We have a walk of minutes."

It was all I could do to hold on, my limited gaze stuck on everything I saw, felt, and smelled—animals, heat, the surprise waft of lavender, the thudding of carts and my own heart.

After a while, I tucked into Will's side, pulled down my hood completely, and let him steer, the world around me overwhelming. In about twenty minutes of jostling, walking, and yanking, we stopped once more. Without permission, I stopped and pushed back my hood. Yes. It had to be. Here I was at The Theatre, the place William Shakespeare got his start. The Theatre whose very beams would hold up the original Globe.

Whitewashed and rounded with tall walls, the building was imposing There was a large flag billowing from an outward-facing balcony. At any moment, I expected trumpets and maybe Juliet or the Princess Bride, to emerge and wave her kerchief.

I started to speak, but Will was clearly growing impatient of my lectures.

"Come," he said. "With haste."

Inside was roofless, open-aired, three rows high, a wooden stage in the center. At the back of the stage, a curtain, and behind that, darkness. Under my feet, hazelnut shells.

Bending down, I picked one up, my world rocking. Where had I been when I'd held the first shell? Here? Or there? In my time, or this time? No matter where I went, a play. In some other dimension, Dan Gordon sat watching Amber stumble through her lines, maybe finding her footing and owning Jessica.

Here? I was walking around London in a nightgown with William Shakespeare.

"Costumery is this way." Will pulled on my elbow, the joint about five seconds away from unhinging.

"Fine," I said, dropping the shell and walking behind the stage, into the wide open backstage.

With no candle, I wondered how we would find our way through the darkness, but Will marched us this way and that until we stood in a room piled high with folded, stacked, and hung clothing that sparkled and shone despite the lack of lighting. My eyes adjusting, the room opened up into shades of blues, greens, and the deepest reds. On tables and chairs were soft piles of stockings, caps, and scarves.

"You have a good selection," I said, running my hand along brocade and linen.

"Gifts from our benefactors," Will said as he riffled through the piles. "But first."

He turned, his eyes on me, drifting up and down in a way I could almost feel on my skin. Then he clapped once, the sound making me jump.

"Your first lesson of 1598 will be with clothing. But for my edification, what do you name what you wear? For a gentlewoman. From top to bottom, from inner to outer, in the style of the year 2018."

He winked at the word bottom, and I couldn't stop my blush. "Underwear. A bra and panties," I began.

"Panties and bra. I know not these words."

"Bra," I said, yearning for a whiteboard and brand-new pens. Instead, I indicated my general breast area and did the same with "panties" at the panty line.

He nodded, and again, that smile. "Drawers, but not often worn in England."

What aristocratic lady needed to deal with panties while wearing pounds and pounds of dress, petticoats, and a very restricting corset? I already missed my little cotton underwear, snug and so easy, no need for parcels or performance to put them on.

"Pray, continue."

"Shirt or blouse. Like this nightdress but shorter."

Will nodded. "More the male fashion."

"You have no idea how hard women had to fight to wear pants, which is what I usually teach in. Shirt and pants and a jacket. Leather shoes. Some jewelry. Silver."

"Silver. A woman of property."

I shook my head, not knowing how to explain even associate professors could wear silver in 2018. "From Mexico."

"Mexico?"

"The New World again." I almost stomped my foot, wanting to get some clothes on, no matter how heavy they were or what they looked like. "Listen, I know you don't want another lecture."

He turned and then pulled a garment from the pile and held up a smock-ish kind of thing trimmed with a tiny bit of lace.

"This is your shift," he said. "For everyday wear. A first layer. Against your skin."

"Can we get another?" I asked. "Or else I'll be doing a lot of washing."

"Cease this preoccupation with water!" Will exclaimed. "An unhealthy obsession. But yes, there is yet another."

I took the shift, a plain and simple gown. At home in organic vegan land, this garment, with its careful handmade stitches and the home-loomed fabric (pre-industrial revolution), would cost a fortune. I ran my hands over it over the surprisingly smooth fabric. Farmers growing the flax. Weavers weaving the linen. Seamstresses cutting the patterns and sewing the tiny stitches.

"It's gorgeous." I looked up at him, finding him looking bemused. "What?"

"Underwear only, as you said. Now..." He held up a fistful of fabric, and then unfurled two long gray stockings. "Hose. And you need these to keep them in place." He dangled two red-ribboned garters, which reminded me of the kind flung at weddings. But now, with these thick wool hose, they were truly functional.

I put down the clothing, anticipating the next reveal.

"As my cousin and as you will be accompanying me to the theater here and to engagements, so you cannot present as a charwoman. You listed not a binding garment, but this is necessary for the style."

Will walked to a shelf and pulled out something that looked like two wings with dangling laces. "A corset. Called 'a pair of bodies.'"

"Torture," I said as he placed the contraption in my hands.

"And a torture your body naught deserves, svelte as you are. But alack, fair ladies must obey the fashion gods."

I put aside the corset kite. "Next?"

Will smiled, his hair wild, smile wide. "I cannot see a farthingale. Must needs delay on that."

"A blessing."

"But you will not be without augmentation. To wear around your waist."

I took from him what looked like an airplane pillow, the kind that fit snug around the neck. But this white pillow was bigger, for someone with a neck the size of a waist. "Do you know how hard I have to work out to keep off the inches?"

"Work out? Labor out of doors?"

"You bet your Renaissance ass," I said.

"A donkey?"

"Never mind," I said. "What's next?"

"A partlet for over the smock and then the petticoat. Mayhap two."

The petticoat was like a giant apron, a huge skirt, this one red. Along the hem, the stitches were perfect and true. Again, I was struck by the attention to detail.

Will was digging another pile of clothing, talking as he searched. "Shoes. A doublet and a gown. Shoes and a hat. A coat to guard against foul winds. What a poundage of goods." He turned to me, handing me all. "Prithee, dress thyself lest I fall into slumber before we sup."

At *sup*, my stomach growled. I couldn't remember when I last ate. Throwing up, I remembered. Drinking, too. But then the thought of eating in 1598 England was probably the best diet ever. Gruel, scary roasted meats, lumps of dirty vegetables, like the kind some angry audience member threw on the stage at Shylock.

Will stood in front of me, arms akimbo, eyes alight.

"Turn around," I said.

"Oh, forsooth. I've seen your nakedness. No need for fig leaves."

"Had as lief—" I said.

"Well done," Will said. "Taking on the language!"

"Turn!"

He laughed, sat down on a stool, whistling with satisfaction. After his reveal of all things fashion, I took note of his garb for the first time, probably because he'd been barely dressed during our first hours of acquaintance. But here he was, Will Shakespeare as he appeared in the world. Sturdy black leather shoes with buckles. Black hose. Some sort of jacket or doublet, buttoned to the waist with large black buttons, and a puffy kind of skirty thing for pants (pantaloons?), the fabric dark and heavily stitched. A shirt instead of a shift but with a high neck with some frill at the collar. Thank goodness both he and I seemed exempt from the ruffs I'd seen in most Elizabethan portraits. I had always imagined the awkward, itchy things must have paved the way for cervical collar designs, best worn only for whiplash.

"Dress!" he commanded.

I took off the nightgown and slipped on the shift. Then, as Will had detailed, the other pieces in the correct order, tying and lacing as I went. If I hadn't been so hungry, I would have stopped to admire everything. The green dress made of a thick but detailed fabric woven into whirls of peacocks and flowers. The shoes sturdy leather oxfords tied with ribbons. How I wished I could take it all home, if I did, in fact, end up back in my apartment. Perhaps I could start a "travel home" hope chest, filled with all my purloined goods.

But probably, the time travel rules forbade taking home plunder. The joke was on me. Here I was, my big academic break. England, London, William Shakespeare waiting to take me to supper. And I couldn't tell a soul.

Once dressed, my roll tucked around my middle, I smoothed my hair back and put on the green hat, replete with feathers. Lumpy and ungainly with my padded waist and hips, tall, rolled shoulders, and enormous hat, I felt like some alien creature from a *Star Wars* movie. Thankfully, The Theatre dressing room didn't have a mirror.

"Okay," I said. "As good as it's going to get in these conditions. Or any conditions, really."

Will stood and turned. He cocked his head, walked to me, and fiddled with the high collar of my shift. Or, at least, I think it was my shift. He tucked a loose strand of hair behind my ear, his fingers warm behind my ear, my neck.

"You have left behind all those in your own timeline. A woman of 1598 solely. And now, you will beguile all at The Bull." He grabbed my new coat and helped me slip my arms through the sleeves.

"Sir, you flatter too much."

Will shook his head. "Now attend. Keep your words to nil. Your language is far from acceptable."

I'd spent the whole day quiet as a church mouse and as frantic as a mime, all hands, arms, gesticulation. "Why don't we say I'm from one of those islands above Scotland? Orkney. Shetland. I'm not sure what you call them here. Or now. Anyway, my dialect and accent will be so strong, no one will understand me."

He stepped back, hands on his hips. Little did he know tomorrow was his personal cleanliness lesson. Hair, beard, teeth. Oh, the English and their teeth. Some things never change.

"Orkneys, aye. But truly, your voice has no parallel."

"How many people at The Bull have been to the Orkney Islands?"

Will stared at me, nodding a little. "Some have traveled the English countryside on tour, but others have left London but once or twice mayhap. Your secret should be safe. Come, enough of this prattle. Off to sup."

"Also, I'm going to pick at my food. It's probably not washed—"

"Woman! May we eat without these infernal rules?" His voice raised, and his skin reddened.

Crossing my arms, I looked down at my shoes. Handmade, hand-stitched. They felt like gloves. Would they carry me out into a world I'd only ever read about? Once I left this building, would I ever find my way back, no matter how amazing the shoes?

I didn't belong here, no matter how well costumed. My heart and breath traded places, beating and pulsing in wrong rhythms.

"I'll say something wrong," I said, fear at my throat. "I'll insult the wrong person. Someone will cry 'Witch,' and I'll be thrown in jail. I'm going to be the one executed tomorrow."

Will's face softened. His brow unfurled, and he reached out and put an arm around my now much wider waist. "I will protect you," he said. "I will introduce you as my cousin Jessica from the Orkneys. 'Aye, what an accent! Barely English. But also, a bad tooth. She's mumbling a little. A lovely woman. Educated rightly by righteous, renegade nuns armed with strops. Literate indeed.' Then I'll inquire of all, 'Need you any clerical help? She can write like an angel.'"

I leaned into him, holding on to his upper arm. His coat smelled like alcohol, sweat, and just a tinge of manure. No dry cleaners on Bishopsgate Street. Nowhere to leave all his clothing for a good delousing.

I shut my eyes, breathed. Then I opened them again, cleared my throat, stood straight, adjusted my fine new hat.

"All right, fine sir. I'm ready for our outing."

Will donned his own feathered hat, and without another word, we left The Theatre and dove back into 1598.

"Say you the church survived fire and war?" Will asked as we headed past the Gumbles and St. Helen's on our way to The Bull.

"That's right," I mumbled.

Now fully able to look around, I was barely listening, watching ordinary 1598 people as if they were unicorns. But I heard the words *fire* and *war*, and Will's own poetic lines came to my lips, but I swallowed them back, thinking only, *"Nor Mars his sword nor war's quick fire shall burn/ The living record of your memory."*

His poem was penned out of love and for the Fair Youth (Will dedicated his sonnets to a "WH"), whoever he was, his identity still argued about in small, arcane, self-important circles, all of which I aspired to. Here were the WH choices: William Herbert, Earl of Pembroke, Henry Wriothesley, or William Hall, all with a "W" or an "H" in his name.

My educated guess had always been the first, William Herbert. Titled, rich, and handsome, Lord Pembroke had been Will's patron, and then some. The obvious choice, though I didn't think I could ask Will. Not yet. Maybe never.

As Will opened the inn's door, taking off his hat, and giving me a gallant swoop.

Maybe tonight, I'd meet "WH." But as the bawdy noise, heat, and din of the dining room hit me, it wouldn't be tonight. And it would never be at The Bull.

Beside the pluck and twang of the fluid lute (parts banjo, pianoforte, and guitar), the best news of the evening was Will had brought two forks with him. In 2018, people carried knives in their pockets for various ordinary and evil purposes. But in 1598, what you wanted was a fork. Otherwise, it was a knife and spoon at a meal out, if you were lucky.

After we sat down on a bench, Will handed me the utensil and then banged on the table, calling for meat, his voice strong and clear. I craned my neck to look at the platters the women swung past us like pewter spacecraft. Maybe I didn't need a fork or spoon. I was frozen, pressed next to Will and his friend Richard Burbage, who acted at The Theatre with him and—next year—would invest with Will in The Globe, unbuilt as of this moment but fervently dreamed of and hoped for. Eventually, the new theater would make Will so wealthy, he could retire and move back to Stratford.

"Beer!" Richard cried. More table banging. I sunk back, stunned into silence at the historical bounty before me. Across from me were Harry and John. I'd been unable to eat my piece of brown bread as I stared at them, two of The Chamberlin's Men, actors in Will's company. Henry (Harry to us) Condell and John Heminges, the two who put together and published Will's First Folio of plays and who were each mentioned in the will, bequeathed twenty-six shillings, eight pence. I recognized them from drawings and descriptions and hundreds of essays and papers, but it was easy to forget their historical significance as they sat chewing in front of me, their mouths open, their mustaches covered in mustard and beer foam. And out of those mouths! Curses and slurs and laughter. Then more food. More beer. The men drank a lot of beer. Two mugs full, it seemed, with every course. With each new round, a toast to my visit, my health, Will's health, their health, the health of the Queen, the success of the theater, the actors, the playwrights. And England! *O, England!*

If this went on, they would soon be toasting the table, which was strewn with bones, cores, and peelings.

Next to me, Will was warm and solid. Now and again, he reached out to pat my arm, as if to convince both of us I was still there.

Between courses and after the toasting, they shared a pipe with a very small bowl, filling it with tobacco, the thick, pungent smoke swirling over us. This new world discovery had taken hold, though the men treated the flaked leaves as if they were gold, arguing over who had the last puff and whose turn it was next.

Both Harry and John were attractive, pale-haired, very English looking with white skin and a certain rabbit reddishness around their eyes. They also had darkened teeth, and I could only imagine what my dentist at *Smile* dentistry would say about their flossing.

I scanned the long wooden table. It wasn't their fault. I couldn't blame them, even if my dentist, Dr. Becker, would disapprove of their oral choices. Will and I had just finished a platter of fruit tarts and pies, both sweet and sticky, and tasty. I'd snagged one with my borrowed fork and then another. I ate more of the sweets than the roasted turnips, beets, carrots, and roasted beef with mustard. Something had smelled too real about the meat, as if I could still see the cow walking on the field, dropping cow pies as she passed. The swish of her tail, the wet of her nose.

One tart had been filled with cherries and spices, cinnamon, ginger, and, I could have sworn, mustard.

"You lot love mustard," I whispered to Will. "It's everywhere. Every single course."

"Covers the tastes untoward," he said. "And it is delicious! Pray, eat!"

The strawberry pudding was awash in red wine, sugar, and cinnamon, topped with cream that tasted like roses. Rose water, probably, something I hadn't tasted since eating Persian rose water pudding. There was also shortcake, the rounds of dough baked to a perfect brown and crunchy lightness.

"You will be round and white as a pillow after your dash through 1598," Will said in my ear.

"Be quiet," I said, my mouth full. "I'm starving."

"Nay, but you are ravenous," Will agreed, putting another shortbread on our shared trencher.

"Will's cousin, is it?" Richard said, crunching down on a radish he'd rolled in salt. I couldn't get a good look at him without turning on the bench, but he was a thin man with a receding hairline and a large, compelling voice, one of the top actors in all of London town. "Never heard tell of you."

"You are in your cups so fully," Will said. "It's a wonder you heard a single word. But yes, my fair cousin Jessica, from the Isles of Orkney."

"Luck shone on you, Will." Richard turned to on the bench, and his eyes and voice took over. "To have such a comely lassie as family."

"Knave," Will said. "Listen not to any of his words as they be lies and slander."

"This is true." Richard nodded, crunched down on another radish. "But not about your fair looks. If Will fails you—and he will—come to The Theatre for bolstering."

Some form of kicking and violence happened under the table because Richard wobbled and Will swore. But then they both laughed and raised a cup, downing more beer and raising their cups for more.

There was a casual friendliness between them, and it would be a long and prosperous friendship. At this moment, Richard and his father owned the current theater but not the land. Soon, Richard, Will, Richard's brother Cuthbert, John Heminges, and a couple of other actors would invest in The Globe, building it from the very bones of The Theatre. This meal—with all its indulgences—was really a working meeting.

"You must have grown of age surrounded by cows." Harry eyed me over his roasted leg of something.

Rather than answer him, I raised my eyebrows in question.

"All that milk. Splendid teeth," he said. "Quite blinding."

"Hyperbole," John said. "But white enough, it is true. Long these many years, I imagined the Orkneys filled with onion-eyed maltworms."

Before I could start to ask when a maltworm was, the serving girl, sweaty—her hair captured in a kerchief-type hat—clunked down a platter of cheese and fruit. I eyed the mound of washed-rind yellowish cheese. Oh, my. I could smell it

67

from here. Whole unpasteurized milk. All those 1598 microbes shocking my intestines. I needed to line my insides slowly with all this new flora and fauna.

"Delicious," Will said, cutting me a wedge and putting it on the trencher. "With some bread."

"What about a wee apple?" I pointed.

"Apples cause more trouble than a triangle of cheese," he said, indicating his front teeth. But he handed me a small, tight apple, hard and reddish. I bit down on the thin flesh, a punch of flavor, tart, acidic, sweet, on my tongue.

"So good," I blurted, my mouth partially full. "Like it was just picked."

"Such a language," Richard said. "Such a sound. We needs must capture it for the stage, Will. Jessica can school the players."

"My fair cousin is searching for employment, but as a scribe, no less. Accounts perchance. Translations. Letter writing, mayhap."

The serving girl came back to fill their mugs with beer, John raising his now full one. "To fair Jessica and her gainful employment!"

"To Jessica!" they all cried, and I raised my barely sipped mug with theirs.

"To the Orkneys!" John cried.

"To me!" I said. "Whenever I am!"

Impossible to believe, but Englishmen can drink hard and still walk home. Good thing. No cabs. No metro. Will might have leaned more on my arm than I on his, but he made it all the way down the street, passing beggars in tattered rags who called out for coins.

Up the creaky wooden stairs in silence and by candlelight, into the room where a fire had been lit, burning low and red, and onto the newly stuffed and hopefully bedbug-free mattress, Will and I lay on our backs. Completely sober, I didn't comingle my body parts with his this time. After all, I was his fair cousin from the Orkney Islands, taught by nuns.

Outside on the street, the sounds of other revelers on their way home. Next to me, Will's light, even breathing.

"I don't even know what day it is," I said to the ceiling.

"Sunday eve," Will said in reply.

"Shouldn't we have gone to church? Isn't it mandatory? Won't you be fined? Or put in jail?"

"Aye. Next week, if you are still in this foul century," he said, his voice alert.

"How can you possibly be awake after all those toasts? To the clock! To the table! To the fork and spoon of my worst enemy!"

"Don't be ridiculous," Will said. "We never toast a spoon."

I snorted, but under my laughter was something else, pinched and nervous.

I clutched Will's hand. "Let's talk some more. Tell me more about the Jessicas."

"Why don't you ask about my friends?" He turned on his side, his breath sweet and clean because of the concoction I'd learned about that afternoon.

"Might help you with the pain, Mistress," Nan, the older woman had said, the one who had finally given me a sympathetic nod due to the rumor of my toothache. On her way out, she pressed on me a handful of mint. "Steep this in the vinegar I will leave behind. For half an hour. Then rinse apace."

I had mumbled my thanks, and that was when I really wished for a tuppence or whatever. But I steeped the herb in watered-down vinegar (also used for cleaning the one window), and before we fell into the bed, we rinsed with it, Will gagging and huffing as we spat. Then we wiped our teeth with clean linens Nan had left as well. It wasn't perfect. I didn't feel like I'd spent a leisurely hour frothing in front of the bathroom mirror with Colgate, but it was good enough for now. I just hoped my teeth (and every other body part) made it through my visitation.

The question—one I could scarcely contemplate—remained: Was my same body in both time zones. What rules held forth on corporeal placement in split timelines? If my body was here, was it there too? What was I doing back there, anyway? Had I graded all my papers and shown up to class, ready to teach? Or had time stopped in 2018 and moved forward in 1598 for the sole purpose of allowing me this experience? But how could I imagine any part of any time frame would bend for me? Or were we back to the dream explanation? A very long dream. Intense, detailed, realistic. A sensory extravaganza. A one-off, never to be repeated? Perhaps, it was merely spiked Snapple. And finally, there was the sanity question.

It was too much to think about.

"The fellows are full lively," Will went on.

The whole evening had been full lively. All of them talking about the construction of The Globe, as it would be, a great center for drama. Their motto: *The whole world plays the actor*. How armed with swords, daggers, axes, and such like, they would dismantle the very beams of The Theatre in the dead of night and reuse them in tribute (and because they were just really good beams). And then they would be rich! Fortunes for the whole lot of them! More toasts. And then their ideas took off, so unrestrained I had trouble following them, translating as I was their English into mine. Eventually, I'd just sipped at my beer and nodded.

"John and Harry will be your strongest supporters. And Richard! Well, I read one story."

"Which?" Will said, his voice encouraging. He reached out to touch my wrist. "Pray, do tell."

I smiled into the darkness. "Legend has it one performance, your friend Richard played Richard the Third so intensely and well, that a woman in the audience invited Richard to her chambers after the performance."

Will started to laugh. "I can construe the finale!"

"I bet," I said. "So the story goes you heard this conversation and showed up yourself instead. You got to work, so to speak, and were *en flagrante delicto* when Richard finally arrived."

"Oh, a wondrous tale. A marvelous tale," Will said. "But of all the yarns involving Richard and me, all our long work together, 'tis hard to imagine this the one recounted."

"Probably because the tale is like your plays. Switching roles. Who loves who. One being called, another showing up. Thwarted love. That kind of thing."

Will patted my shoulder and turned on his back, sighing softly. "Thwarted love. True enough. In plays and life."

I watched his silhouette in the darkness, his eyes open, blinking. Was he thinking about WH? Or his wife, Anne? Or the Dark Lady, whoever she was or would be, the woman to whom he dedicated the last twenty-seven sonnets? His love was thwarted on so many fronts.

"So now," I said instead of going into a touchy subject. "Tell me about the other Jessicas. You said it began just after *Merchant* was performed. Maybe there's some kind of pattern that might lead me home."

Will spun back toward me. "Attend. One night, due to a player's illness, I was thrust into the role of Shylock. Oh, I bit into that role, and the audience bit back. I was pummeled by objects, hissed at, and cheered for, my actor eye fierce on the audience as he enacted his revenge."

I conjured Shylock, the one from my hallucination. The actor with those tired eyes. Could that have been Will?

"Go on. Then what?"

"The performance was exalting, the applause profuse. But that very night after much celebration, I was awakened by a scream. My first response was madness. I flung myself in horror from the bed, trying to wrest myself from a dream. At my gyrations, the first lady screamed and pranced and jumped about the chamber. Most did the same frightened dance. Even you."

"What do you expect?" I asked, slightly embarrassed. But really. What *did* he expect?

"Now there is clarity. What other action after having been yanked from one life to this? Zounds. But every night. The yells and howling. First, it was but once a night. Then twice. Of late, I had not slept a wink."

"Do you know where the Jessicas come from?"

"A dozen came and went before I began to ask of them their locales. Most, England. A Scottish lass or two. The Orkneys, mayhap." He chuckled a bit. "Then,

71

more. They appeared all in the same white shift as yours, so no clues to be had in the garb. After my fears of ghostly visitation and death dissipated, I managed to ask: 'Where are you from, lady?' and then, 'What is your name, lady?' Those who stopped screaming oft times managed, 'Jessica' before disappearing."

"No Rebeccas or Sarahs or Tiffanys in the mix? No Maeves, Cristinas, or Zoes?"

"Jessica. Each and every. Despite the varied hues and shapes. Of late, many from the Indies and African shores. Most who held not back, but threatened bodily harm and arrest and worse, with language I still know not. Most verily I was hit and pummeled about the face and shoulders. But even without English, cried all, 'Jessica!' at some excited point."

"It seems chronological," I said, blinking into the night as I calculated. "First, the British Isles. And then elsewhere. Also, as they began to become more vocal, they were coming from later. Post-1850s. Women's suffrage. Women's lib. ERA. Modern times. I'm pretty sure Jessica, as a name, topped out in the 1970s. Just about the time I was born in 1986. You might be through the worst of it. Maybe."

What I didn't tell him was that on every roster, I had one to four Jessicas. The name had legs.

Will yawned. "I know not suffrage, lib, or ERA. But normal times these are not. And I refer not to time travel alone. Have you not noticed we are sleeping in my newly stuffed and cleaned bed? In my sparkling chambers, talking oft of time travels and repeated Jessicas? But oh, those women. I became so weary of their howls. The gods have deemed I created you, so it is mine to bear. But verily, two nights of blessed peace with simply one Jessica— however abnormal—is a welcome relief."

"Hey, Mr. Shakespeare, you calling me abnormal?"

A laugh in his throat, but I mostly heard his fatigue. In a minute, he was asleep, his hand on my shoulder. But his touch was light, friendly, his breathing heavy with beer, leaving me to think about the list of Jessicas. And then of my other self, asleep or ill or maybe even dead back in 2018. I thought about my students and their valiant attempts at interpreting Shakespeare. Of Horatio; of my sister, who, despite our disagreements, had always been my protector and friend. Then my thoughts landed on my niece Shelby, her braced mouth and sudden, frequent laughter and moved to my mother with her judgments but deep concern. Dan Gordon, Sherry Maita's play, and all her players. If I stayed here, my life would be a dream come true. But it wasn't right. Time was, as someone very wise once wrote, out of joint.

I turned on my side, staring Will's sleeping profile, thinking of the nightly Jessica cascade. Somewhere in that surprising string of visitations, I hoped, I could find my way home.

Chapter Eight – A Public Hanging

Before it was light, Will whispered, "Wake up, cousin Jess. Time's slipping past."

He got out of the bed, taking his warmth with him. I rolled away from the sound of his turn at the chamber pot, a horror I had yet to grasp. As he dressed in the corner, I stumbled out of the bed (no new bites) and took my turn, eyes closed, as if not seeing Will made me (or him) disappear. At least an unfortunate chambermaid would dispose of it while we were gone. As in any time: out of sight, out of mind.

After a sip of beer, a bite of bread, a splash of water, and swish of the grumbled about vinegar and mint solution, Will and I were out the door into the gray dawn morning of Bishopsgate. The road was wet and smelled of dirt and sewage. Monday already in full swing. People carried their baskets, merchants opened their doors. Rickety carts rumbled by, and as I squished into muddy road, I yearned to be in one. My poor new shoes wouldn't make it until I vanished.

I wore the same outfit from the night before, minus the fancy hat. Instead, I wore a head covering that reminded me of a handkerchief. But Will assured me I was the height of fashion.

I clutched my coat as we headed south. There was a chilly breeze, and for a second, I wished for one of those huge ruffs to ward off the cold.

"Where are we going?"

"To the hanging." Will gripped my arm tightly as a coach barreled past, spraying watery mud in its wake.

"I know that," I said. "But where does it happen?"

Will nodded. "The Tyburn Tree. It's not but three miles."

I winced at the familiar name. What had Will himself called it? "Love's Tyburn" in *Love's Labour's Lost*.

"You mention the gallows in every play."

"All writers have habits."

"But hanging? What does that say about you?" I asked.

"Death is as birth. From one state to the next. All's drama and spectacle."

"And a lot of dead people."

Will stopped and looked at me. "Pray, can you state that in your time no one swings the rope?"

I wished I had a more convincing argument. "Not like this. They are convicted, spend about ten years on Death Row—"

"Death Row? They wait for ten years in a row?"

"A metaphor." I batted down my impatience. Who was I to get irritated with him? "Listen, we have a weird legal system. Lots of appeals before we pull the switch—"

"Switch? Such as one is whipped with?"

"For—" I began and then paused. "Another method. Involves something not invented. Maybe I'll tell you later. So yes, we do kill people. But we don't execute people for buggery, at least legally. Or arson. Or witchcraft, for that matter. In fact, witchcraft is big. An industry."

Will rolled his eyes. "Your society has industries for all. Come. A cart awaits at Lothbury."

I let him pull me down the streets. He greeted some passersby, introducing me to a shopkeeper or two, but I mostly kept my eyes down. The Tyburn Tree. A romantic name. A blooming tree, an apple or pear tree in spring but with horrible fruit. The gallows used to be set up at the corner of Hyde Park, the present-day Marble Arch on Oxford Street, a place of shopping and boisterous crowds. Respectable, business-like, the US Embassy right there on Grosvenor Square. But that was in my time. Now, Hyde Park was farmland and faraway, the home of the famous gallows. Oliver Cromwell was hanged posthumously on the tree. Dug up and hanged to make a statement.

Time was crazy. One century a terrible place of death. In another, a slightly swanky area and Tube stop. We people of the future covered up the brutal past and went on, forgetting as we went along.

When we reached Lothbury, a cart driver wearing a large gray hat waved at Will.

"Hugh! Good morning, fine fellow. Let's make quick time," Will said. "Needs must procure a seat."

"Aye, Master Shakespeare," Hugh said, turning to me, his face a sunrise of freckles and smiles. "Mistress?"

It was impossible not to smile back at Hugh—large, soft, friendly. I trusted him immediately. My twenty-first-century self wanted to ask for Hugh's card or cell number so he could pick me up during times of crisis and need, a carted Uber. But really, where would I go?

Hugh stood waiting, hat in hand, smile wide as his brim.

"My cousin Jessica from the Orkney Islands," Will said as we sat on the wooden bench. "Here on a visit."

"To see the hanging," Hugh said as he sat down, the cart lurching and rocking as he did, and took hold of the reins. "A fine entertainment."

My stomach roiled, the beer swirling in acid and fear. "I know this is your thing," I said. "But why are we really going?"

Will looked down at his hands, one on each knee. I felt more than heard his sigh. "A true friend has a stake in this particular punishment."

"He's not being hanged, is he?"

Will shook his head and seemed to want to say more, but Hugh hit a pothole, the cart bouncing down the road, both of us momentarily airborne. I gripped the seat and focused on the road as well as the landscape, both familiar and completely unknown. How many times had I climbed to the top of St. Paul's Cathedral? Five, six? But the cathedral I knew so well wouldn't be built until after the fire of 1666, yet the spire from Old St. Paul's rose high. If I could shimmy up, what would I observe? In 2018 from that vantage, nothing but houses, apartments, buildings, traffic, pedestrians. The view in all directions a thriving, bustling London. While Will and I passed by buildings and houses, they were interspersed with stretches of land. Green. Trees. Actual cows and the ripe smells of manure, hay, and heat.

After a few minutes, we turned west on a larger road, full of carts and coaches headed the same direction.

"Tyburn Road," Will said. The cart rolled forward, and I plummeted into overwhelm. So much coming at me. Familiar names—Holborn, Tottenham— villages, hamlets, really, but names I associated with two Tube stops on the Ealing line. There was a lurching bustle as carts rumbled forward, people eager for spectacle. But this Monday morning, the excitement wasn't for a concert or blockbuster film but for death. I could only hope no one hanged today committed treason. The punishment for that crime was first drawing and then hanging and quartering. Overcome, I shut down, staring at the green fabric of my new dress.

"Jess," Will said after a long stretch. "Are you ill?"

"Not yet," I said, though the up and down banging of the cart wasn't making things better.

"Should I not have brought you?"

"It's possible I didn't need so much enculturation all at once."

Hugh turned around, smile bright. "I cannot understand a word she says!"

"Fortunate man," Will said. "She's but complaining of the roads."

Hugh waved a hand. "Ah, but a glorious day." He turned to me, his smile reassuring. The cart jostled, and Hugh focused on his horse and the journey ahead.

"You said you needed to learn this life," Will said, his voice low. "This is our spectacle and truth."

"What about things I need to know on a daily basis? Market day. Penmanship? And there's always laundry."

"More water," Will said, taking my hand. "But you are here. So much to see. Besides all else, it is a full entertainment."

"Despite your friend, maybe you need to take a break from the gallows."

Will patted my hand and looked away. "Aye, I surely might. But we are on the way."

The noise of another cart blared past, whiffs of horse and dirt, the bugle of voices. I pressed a hand to my stomach, my meager breakfast on the move. Clenching my teeth, I held it down. Perhaps I could handle a hanging. After all, hadn't I witnessed every form of murder and torture during my nightly Netflix binges? And I lived in one of the most brutal, gun thirsty countries in the world. How could I complain about a hanging when sometimes—my time, the more advanced future—it wasn't always safe to step foot into a movie theater, go to high school, or even drive a car to the grocery store.

Who was I to pass judgment on them when it was ever possible some wingnut had a gun?

Will pressed closer to me, his voice near my ear. "I will shield you from the horrors."

Another squeeze of my hand, and then he nudged Hugh a little, made mention of a bad stretch of road ahead. Watching the strange but familiar English landscape bump and chatter by, I thought about his words. *Shield you from the horrors.* Yes, this would be horrible. In period piece plays and film, I'd watched treasonous dukes and knights, Civil War soldiers on the wrong side of the Mason-Dixon, varmint cowboys, cattle rustlers, and convicts hang. The little wooden door opened and bam! Necks snapped. Hooded figures dangling like scary rag dolls, limp and lifeless.

Also, hanging was my first irregular verb.

"People are hanged," my mother told me every time I made the error. "Pictures are hung."

It made sense the act had a special conjugation. Irregular indeed.

I started as Hugh flung us across a bad stretch, bumps and divots. I breathed in and held on. Will pulled me close, and I felt his solid presence.

The body left terrible evidence the living had to clean up. Living was, too. There was no escaping it, even though I'd tried to stay away from all the mess, hangings and life. I never wanted to live in the mess, hiding away somewhere, either literally or in my heart. Even now, in a past I had never lived, with a man I only knew from his work, I was ready to be shielded from the horrors in front of me.

Was what happened here, now, today, real? If I hid from it, did it count?

"Jess?" Will put a hand on my knee. "How fair you?"

I closed my eyes, trying to be in this moment of my very unreal life. Hard to hide in a bouncing cart, not with William Shakespeare and an impending hanging to contemplate. But I was practiced. Hadn't I always been tucked away from everything? Not simply my English major introversion; not merely as an English professor, standing in front of the chalkboard, my back to my students. Not just the working in the middle of a fog bank thing, where the middle of the day seemed like dawn, everything obscured, including me. But the real hiding, the kind where I went home and read essays and watched movies and socialized mostly with my sister and my niece. Where I didn't try to find a dating pool to swim in. Where I made sure my heart couldn't be touched. Not after Phillip.

In those days, Phillip's blows to my heart had been constant; his broad and all-encompassing excuses the theme songs to our relationship. Even now, I could still see him sitting at my desk bent over a book, his dark curly hair falling over his face as he concentrated on an essential passage, probably something by John Milton or Alexander Pope. He scratched his cheek, rubbed his forehead, mumbled to himself as he scribbled notes in the margins.

At first, I thought he was brilliant, immersed in language and beauty. A true scholar. Then I thought he worked too hard. Finally, I thought he was using my apartment as an *ad hoc* library. Maybe in irritation, I asked, "Can we go out to dinner?"

Or maybe I wanted to go to a movie. Or on a walk.

He'd looked up, blinking, forgetting I was there or that he was in my apartment and not his own, the one he shared with Emma, the real person in his life.

"Must read through this," he'd said, his mind back on the words before he'd even finished speaking.

As the years went by, he didn't even bother to bring over a book, an academic journal, or even Chinese takeout, his stops impromptu and of a physical necessity. As I sat up in bed watching him put on his jeans, mismatched socks, and shoes, Phillip would explain why we were reduced to swift sneaking. According to him and in a rotating order of importance, he'd been miserably unhappy for years, his marriage to Emma a college mistake, and/or he and his wife didn't have anything in common. If I could just hold on one more week, month, year, he'd leave Emma; Emma and their first baby Claire; Emma, Claire, and then Sam; Emma, Claire, Sam, and then MacKenzie, who'd been born by the time I argued my dissertation. Graduated. Got a tenure-track job. Time was always of the essence, and the time was never now but when. *When* I was granted tenure. *When* I got a job. *When* Phillip could leave his family. Always when, and then when again. At the same time, child after child was born. Then they bought a new house, moving to the suburbs.

"Just for now," he said.

Then the story changed to, "We're at different places in our lives. You're just starting. I'm the father of three children. I can't just leave when you get on faculty somewhere. This is for the best."

When became *never*. Phillip got everything he wanted: bread buttered on both sides, the cow and the milk, the cake and the eating of it too.

But Phillip was four hundred plus years away. Maybe now, ironically, it was time to change. Of course, I didn't have to go to a hanging to start my metamorphosis. I didn't have to wake up in 1598 either. Though, nothing else had ever worked. I laughed, the sound yanked from my heart.

"Are you in distress?"

I wiped my eyes. The good news was mascara hadn't been invented for the likes of me. "How can I not be, Will? I'm four hundred years separated from my own life that might be going on without me."

"A conundrum for the spheres. But naught can be accomplished here by wondering." Will paused. "But a hanging may not be the thing."

I took it, and again, I laughed. Who would think it? Here I was, in a one-horse cart with William Shakespeare, holding his handkerchief. The fabric was stained, of course, and smelled slightly of tobacco and beer. It wasn't white and embroidered with strawberries in the way of the key and crucial handkerchief in *Othello*.

I was in a story. A play. Jessica for real and Jessica on the page, too.

As we got closer to Tyburn, the roads filled, enough that Will tapped Hugh on the shoulder. Hugh pulled up on the side of the road, clumping off his seat to offer me his hand.

"After the event is over, we will meet you here," Will said, slipping Hugh some coins. Hugh tipped his hat and turned his kindly beams on me.

"I thank you," I said, trying to work on my syntax. I had to start somewhere.

"'Tis nothing, my lady." His freckled smile flared.

I adjusted my head covering, took Will's arm, and we followed the crowd. My heart beat in my forehead and stomach, the rest of my body tingly with nerves. I could barely look up, but I also couldn't stop staring. Here they all were, Queen Elizabeth's subjects. Dirty, somewhat bedraggled, and most living their lives in squalor, these working people made do with little, much less than I expected for myself on a bad day: food, water, shelter, shampoo, and Cabernet. They had a short life expectancy, their children died young of diseases my sister never had to worry about with Shelby, and they ate food we put in the recycling bucket. But this event seemed to exhilarate, men and women smiling and talking as they forged on. Only this grisly scene—death by hanging—might be worse than the lives they were living. They might be hungry, but at least they weren't swinging.

Ahead of us and surrounded by elms were stadium seats. Actually, the structure looked more like rickety junior high seating, bleachers to the left and right of the contraption that could only be the Tyburn Tree. On the top of the structure was an enormous beamed triangle, supported at its points by thick wooden columns. On each beam, three or four nooses at the ready.

"Why is it so tall?" I asked Will. "How do the prisoners get close to the nooses?"

"Carts," Will said, pointing. "Portage the prisoners to the tree."

Mouth open slightly, I stared at the open space under the triangle. "And then they pull the carts away?"

"It is how it's done."

Flecks of gooseflesh erupted under my new clothes. Will gave me a quick glance. "Each time you ask a question, I hear in it the opposite of your time. But I fear to ask, knowing in your answer will be information I dare not know."

"Probably a smart idea," I said. "Besides, my theory of hanging is suspect at best."

Will shook his head and was about to say something when an exquisite coach jangled up, shiny and black, pulled by two equally shiny and black horses. Inside, I could see the poof of dresses, women who were clearly wearing farthingale petticoats, all suspended in the carriage by the wires under their gowns.

Something hitched and lurched in Will's gait, and then we stopped to view the splendid disembarkment. Three shiny footmen jumped off the back of the coach, one opening the doors. Two women emerged, lacy and glamorous, though their hips barely made it out the coach door, their enormous under-carriages impeding every step. But eventually, they popped free from the coach, followed by a young man, who, when he saw Will broke into a smile, unbidden. His smile—for that tiny second—was as wide open as Hugh's. He couldn't help himself, his body fighting against his desire to laugh and rush forth to greet Will. But he also seemed to be moving away, drawn closer and back at the same time. Uncomfortable with his own reaction, straining against it, trying, it seemed, not to run toward us arms wide open, he finally managed to shut down his joy. His expression fell, his brow lowered. His female companions stared at him and then us. His coach driver waited. Next to me, Will stood ramrod straight, barely breathing. His hands shook.

This was undoubtedly the friend of whom Will spoke. The one interested in the hanging.

One, two, three, the young man quelled his impulses. His full bedazzled gaze shut down into a pinched, habitual superiority. Earned, mostly likely. If the clothes, carriage, servants, and companions were clues, this guy was loaded and used to everyone doing his bidding. With his feelings in check, he was still handsome if not dazzling. As sleek as the coach and prettier than the two women beside him, he was tall, thin, graceful, and exquisitely formed. He turned to address the coach driver (his backside just as fine as his front) and then turned slowly back to us, eyes dark and blank.

In that instant, if I hadn't been a time traveler, I would have said time stopped. In the young man's sharp gaze and in the sudden stillness of Will's body, time was locked.

Will's own lines came to me: "A woman's face with nature's own hand painted/ Hast thou, the master mistress of my passion."

Holy smokes, I thought, a sudden notion almost pushing me backward. My heart skidded to life, my breath high in my throat. This wasn't just a guy with a legal problem. Not just a *friend*. Who else could he be but WH? The Fair Youth. And fair indeed. Large dark eyes, curly hair, pale, perfect skin. I'd seen him before in portraits by the Dutch painter Daniel Mytens. This lovely man was William Herbert, the third Earl of Pembroke, my perennial favorite for the "WH" role.

Glancing at us one more time, Lord Pembroke spoke to the women and then made his way toward us, his expression firmly dialed to channel *I'm The Only One*: satisfied, confident, clear. Will pulled me closer.

"My lord," Will said, bowing. As he did, he yanked a little on my arm. All the Jane Austen film adaptations I watched nonstop after Phillip dumped me paid off; I curtsied, dropping my head a little.

Peeking up, I noted the women in their huge dresses staring. The wide wafts of fabric almost rattled with buttons and beads and maybe even some kind of machinery underneath keeping their skirts aloft. Who were they? Neither was the earl's wife. In 2018, we called folks like Lord Pembroke's spouse a "little person," but in Will's time, a dwarf at best, a monster at worst. Poor Lady Mary Talbot, the woman the lord married out of spite.

You want me to marry? his betrothal said to his family. *Well, here's my beautiful bride.*

It was possible the couple weren't married yet. As I kept my eyes cast down, I tried to count back the years, suddenly too confused to remember Lord Pembroke's exact timeline.

These slight, pale, fine ladies might be cousins or friends, but I couldn't ask, Lord Pembroke only a foot away. His lavender perfume preceded him, the flowery scent wafting toward us.

"Master Shakespeare," Lord Pembroke said. I dared to glance up. Perhaps not yet out of his teens, he could have been one of my freshman students. Smooth-faced save for a sleek mustache and beard, his dark head of hair contrasted his imposing white ruff. Wearing the puffy short pants/skirtish thing Will outfitted himself in, Lord Pembroke managed to look attractive and manly. Puffy, but handsome.

Lord Pembroke's eyes traveled over Will, in a way no one had ever looked at me, his gaze like a brushstroke. His eyes captured—possessed even—Will's face, chest, torso, enough that I felt my face flush. Lord Pembroke permitted himself to linger, to savor, to almost taste. His glance was slow and filled with loving ownership. Familiarity and possessiveness. If this examination made my whole body shiver, I could only guess what it was doing to Will.

"May I present my cousin, Jessica." Will's voice was shaky, but he turned toward me, and I curtsied again. My right knee creaked.

"My lord," I said, keeping my gaze on dirt and grass. In front of us, the nooses whapped.

"A cousin?" Lord Pembroke said, his voice icy. "How convenient to have a companion."

I glanced through my eyelashes, noting the challenge. Maybe challenge wasn't the right word. Perhaps it was anger. Jealousy. Lord Pembroke put a hand on his hip, then removed it. Behind him, the women held glacial court.

In my Jane Austen movies, Lizzie or Emma always said something they shouldn't right about now.

"How do you know Will?" I might say. "And why are you acting like such a stuffed shirt? Wait. I mean douche bag."

"Horrid girl! Forward girl," a dowager would exclaim, negative opinions ensuing. But one slip here, and Lord Pembroke might think I was a strumpet, or—what had Will called me? A saucy nut-hook.

I kept my mouth shut. So did Will.

"So, you see, I brought my own companions." Lord Pembroke lingered on the last syllables, making *panions* almost sexy.

Will and I simultaneously bowed and curtsied again. My heel thrummed where I had the beginnings of a blister.

"Ladies." I could feel Will's way with words come back to him. "An excellent day for a hanging. The rogues who killed your hawks are to be dispatched? Paying handsomely for their crimes."

The ladies curtsied only with their heads and nodded. Lord Pembroke took off his gloves, slapping them rhythmically into his right palm, the sound a slow *crack-crack*.

"Had to see the ruffians go, though they both tried to dispute the law. Pretended they could read. Declared they were simple brothers from the monastery who but loved falconry. Said they should be pardoned. But only God can forgive them now."

Passersby were staring. I wasn't sure why. Maybe because Lord Pembroke shouldn't be talking to anyone, much less William Shakespeare, the down-on-his-luck playwright from Bishopsgate.

"Only God," Will said, meeting Lord Pembroke's gaze. Brown eyes locked, a story in that gripped gaze Will had only written about in rhyme.

I tried to back away, but Will's tight grip held me still.

"Enjoy your revenge." Will's voice was low.

"Aye, marry," Lord Pembroke said, as if not hearing Will's first statement. "'Tis little else to interest me here. Good day."

He gave one of those *pro forma* head bows and left, his walk half swagger, half invitation.

As the three bedecked and beaded aristocrats strolled toward the seating area—the women's skirts a fantasia of sway and swirl, their servants trotting behind them—Will and I stood quiet, numb, and watched them go. The crowd pushed past, noise and dust billowing around us. He let go of my hand.

"God's blood!"

His face was red, and he pressed the back of one hand to his mouth. "Pray, in your future world, tell me you know him not."

His right hand was curling and uncurling. A fist and then a hand, ready to touch, reach out. I nodded, looked at my own hands, dry and shaking. "I know who he is. And not because of his family. Or his wife."

Will turned to me, his face pale, eyes wide. "Wife? He married? After all—"

He took off his hat and ran a hand through his hair. Despite the morning air, he was sweating. Will was in Lord Pembroke's thrall. I glanced at the receding party, followed the lord's booty-call gait. Without breaking all the rules and destroying the line of history I depended on, how could I tell Will everything? That Lord Pembroke's mother hired Will to write the first 17 sonnets to convince her firstborn son William to marry Bridget de Vere? Will knew these facts already. Yet he didn't have any idea about tiny Lady Mary Talbot, not to mention Lord Pembroke's later affair with his first cousin Lady Mary Sidney—maybe one of the fine women with him today—with whom he had two children. Besides all this, how to let him know this love triangle—with the hitherto unmentioned Dark Lady—was the stuff of BBC miniseries and Modern Language Association conference breakout sessions: *The Fair Youth: Controversy and Confluence* or *Passion in Form: The Anti-Love Sonnets of William Shakespeare.*

With my current obsession with ancient and now curable illnesses, all I could think about was syphilis. Supposedly, Lord Pembroke had it. So, maybe, Will did or would contract it.. But from whom did he catch it? From Lord Pembroke, the Dark Lady, or various and sundry women of ill repute?

"They know of Lord Pembroke. What must they think?" Will hissed in my ear. "What wrongs I have committed with my mind alone. No wonder the Jessicas haunt me nightly."

A world of thought caught in my throat. Before I could even read, my mother had opened up that worn copy of Will's sonnets, reciting,

"My mistress' eyes are nothing like the sun;
Coral is far more red than her lips' red;
If snow be white, why then her breasts are dun;
If hairs be wires, black wires grow on her head.
I have seen roses damasked, red and white,
But no such roses see I in her cheeks;
And in some perfumes is there more delight
Than in the breath that from my mistress reeks ..."

When I was four, I had no idea what a *mistress* meant, much less *damasked*. But even I understood something odd was going on. This mistress, whoever she was, wasn't being described very nicely. A wiry-haired, sallow, stinky woman. And those words, hard and ugly: *Dun. Wires. Reeks.* As my mother usually said, "If you can't say anything nice, don't say anything at all."

Now, also, I wondered what the hell my mother was doing reading me Shakespeare's anything (probably had to do with the divorce soon to come and all her sad longings). Despite the odd words and the meanness, I could tell how the writer felt. The man in the poem loved the wired-haired lady more than anything. "...I think my love as rare/As any she belied with false compare."

A throng jostled us out of our mutual but separate melancholies. Later, I thought, I would tell him how fully he understood love. How many might argue he discovered it in all its permutations. And I was also pretty sure Lord Pembroke wasn't the reason for the Jessicas, though I had no proof or idea what was.

Will pushed a fellow or two out of our way and took my arm. We followed the regular folk, clomping up the wooden steps to a seat that overlooked the Tyburn Tree and the currently criminal-free nooses. People packed in on either side of us, and I pulled out my bundle of marjoram, rosemary, and lavender and brought it to my nose, breathing in the sharp green fragrance. Nudging me and laughing, the other spectators chattered, some in a dialect I could barely understand. They spit, sipped from flasks, belched and hollered, laughing as others staggered up and sat down beside them. Their gaiety was more in step with a hockey match than a hanging.

The only solemn note was a man standing before the bleachers crying out, "Repent! Repent! Christ Jesus has come!"

If he wasn't careful, he and his reformation would be swinging next.

I breathed in a waft of herb and said, "Was one of the women with Lord Pembroke Lady Mary Sidney?"

He shook his head. "Nay, but the lass is a wench."

"A wench? How—how old is she now? She can't be more than—"

"A strumpet!"

I turned Will toward me. "She's a talented woman. A writer."

"That is not what she is," Will said, his voice a throaty rumble.

"Hold on there! I know 'stuff' happened later with... well. Anyway, she wrote a potentially unreadable but seminal study of gender in her novel—"

"Harpy!"

Ignoring him, I pushed on. "She completed a sonnet sequence! A rule breaker! In fact, many scholars imagine she was your..." I stopped. I'd already mentioned the work that wouldn't be published till after Will's death. Why bring up the mysterious Dark Lady now?

"Vile little creature."

"Don't hold back, Will," I said. "Clearly, a sore subject."

"Why do you inquire after that oyster wench?" Will held out a hand as a man before us leaned back in laughter. Thank god, I thought, we weren't at a football game clutching beers and mustard-covered hotdogs.

"I told you, I've studied it all, not that I remember everything clearly. But I'm pretty certain about your associates, friends, and your foes."

Will stared at me, and for the first time, he seemed to understand I was serious about him. His writing. His industry. His legacy.

"Zounds," he said, about to ask more when a cart rumbled past, a single man lurching in the back. Instead of quivering on the bench in terrified contemplation, the man was standing, yelling out to the crowd, waving what looked like a handkerchief.

"What's he? A clown?" I said, my mouth close to Will's ear. "A fool?"

"A fool perhaps, but not a clown. A criminal playacting but ready to swing," he said. "A knave at his final performance."

"One of the hawk stealers?"

But Will wasn't paying attention anymore, looking left, craning his head. Toward the end of the bleachers, there was a special covered seating area, likely for peers or knights or just better and much fancier people. I couldn't see who was ensconced there, but based on Will's intensity, it was probably Lord Pembroke and his girl posse.

"You love him," I said, but the noise of the crowd tossed my words to thin air.

The cart with the standing man came to a sudden stop in front of the Tyburn Tree. The criminal tossed out trinkets—a glint of shine and ribbon—and bowed at the applause and laughter. All around us, the crowd stood and called back, beckoning the man to throw his goodies. When he had exhausted his supply, the man took a final exaggerated, theatrical bow. Only then, with that last move, did I see his nervousness, one knee buckling. But then three other carts rumbled forth, each with a man, though these fellows were seated. They weren't making any kind of show, and I slumped. This morning's outing wasn't just an adventure with Will or about unearthing the identity of The Fair Youth. The weather was fine, people happy, but the criminals in the carts weren't actors in a play. They were the real thing. This was the real thing. I was here to see people die.

Will shook out of his reverie and took my hand. "My apologies for this mad spectacle," he half-yelled into my ear. "I was a fool to come for but a glimpse."

"You mean of Lord Pembroke?"

Will didn't meet my gaze. "Alack, there is nothing for us here but endings."

I will be brief about what came next. The men—comatose with fright in their cart—were forced to stand, just like the fool who had rolled in first. Now the four carts were in a row under the nooses, the men shaking in their boots, hands roped tight. None were laughing or throwing trinkets or goading the crowd into applause or laughter. The crowd quieted as each man was fitted with a leather hood over his head and then a noose around his neck. Made anonymous, they seemed more human, vulnerable, defeated, and hopeless against those that would kill them for stealing hawks.

For a moment, the audience was rapt—still and quiet—birdsong filled the air. Overhead, the sun broke clear of the clouds and shone, yellow light flickering in the elm leaves. All around the bleachers and the Tyburn Tree were fields, acres and acres of rolling emerald-green.

I could have turned away and walked into the picture of the world that best suited me. Sun and nature and beauty, but I forced myself to watch, gripping hard onto Will's hand. Then the men shook, stumbling. One cried out. The cart wheels turned slowly, creaking as they lurched away. The men stepped and jigged to regain their footing, boots scrabbling in the carts, but then they were forced off-balance, lunging and then dangling. The crowd stood and began to shout and stamp their feet.

It was a bullfight. Bear baiting. It was WWF wrestling or kickboxing but with a *fin* outcome. It was terrible and painful, and the audience wanted more.

The carts surged forward. The three men who had rolled in second were lucky. They had friends to pull their feet, to help provide a swifter death. Each had a man on either foot, all pulling hard to force the rope to do its work. But the man who had thrown the trinkets was alone in these last strangled moments, suffering longer and harder. Inside and out, the man had to be in agony. My insides pulsed and spun.

Finally, someone from the stands rushed out to pull his feet as well. The man yanked hard, the trinket man gasping and twitching. I turned and pushed my face against Will's shoulder just as the noise from all around us built a wall between us—the living—and them—the soon-to-be-dead.

I'd seen too much, but before I'd turned, I couldn't stop watching. I'd lived my human life in a world where people were put to death for crimes, but I'd never really understood what it meant to exact such punishment.

"Come," Will said, pushing past other onlookers, who were still seated.

"Is it over?" I whispered.

"Not by half," Will said as we stomped down the stairs, heading back the way we came.

"What else? More hangings?"

"Drawing and quartering," he said. "Then the bodies hauled back to town for public display."

His body was tense, probably with the effort of not looking back at Lord Pembroke. But unlike Lot's wife or Orpheus, he didn't move a neck muscle. Will Shakespeare made it to Hugh and his cart without stopping to search with his wide, sad eyes.

Hugh tipped his hat and beamed at us as if we'd just been picnicking, which a few people actually were in the fields near the bleachers. Seated, back we went, away from the crowds, past the fields and trees and cows, past the Holburn green, quaint houses and buildings now lining the road. A fairytale setting was whizzing around me, but it was one with an evil queen and maybe a wicked witch. It was a tale of nooses and knives. It was the ordinary world of the people who lived here.

As we headed into town, I found my breath. My heart rate slowed. I blinked away the images, at least for now. Soon I would be in Will's clean chambers. After what I'd just witnessed, though, I had to face the facts. We'd beat the dead bodies back to London, but we hadn't outraced our own problems. Mine was I was here in this violent, dirty, and dangerous world, William Shakespeare or not. Without talent or skills, I was living in a place where an ordinary man could be killed for trying to scrounge a living, honestly or otherwise. For stealing a hawk. Will's problems? His financial woes, whatever they were. The Globe and its construction. His writing. But mostly, his heart. His desire. His need, and want, and sadness. His grief for his small dead boy. I thought of Hamlet, my old morose pal, so full of grief and pain.

"'Tis not alone my inky cloak, good-mother,
Nor customary suits of solemn black,
Nor windy suspiration of forced breath,
No nor the fruitful river in the eye,

Nor the dejected havior of the visage,
Together with all form, moods, shows of grief
That can denote me truly. These indeed "seem,"
For they are actions that a man might play;
But I have that within which passeth show—
These are but the trappings and the suits of woe."

Here Will was. Firm, tall, strong under his coat. Maybe he drank too much, and he certainly needed a hygiene routine. But he was in his true, handsome prime, some of his best work ahead of him. Despite all these riches of talent, he was depressed and didn't know what to do about it. He couldn't hide his feelings. If the ladies or I hadn't been there, Will would have fallen to his knees and offered Lord Pembroke everything.

And the truth was, Lord Pembroke was out to steal Will's heart and then chuck it in the trash. There might have been longing in the lord's eye for Will, but there was also a glint of power. The sheen of manipulation. A glow in his face, pulsing with the knowledge of all he could do. Lord Pembroke could make Will spin and twist on a rope as easily as the court could make criminals hang on the Tyburn Tree.

At the thought, I shuddered.

"Something amiss?" Will asked.

I swallowed. "You were there, right? The part where four men were killed?"

Will rubbed his chin, shook his head. "My mistake, this wayward journey."

"If you ever come to 2018, just wait for the tour you will get," I said.

"But is the place becoming familiar? Did not the journey hence prove fruitful?"

"More than I ever needed to know."

"Pray then, stop this beating of your sorry drum. An instrument you play too often. I will not take you to the tree again," Will said. "But what else have you learned thus far?"

"To clean my teeth with vinegar and mint."

Will gave me a disgusted look. "Truly."

92

"This is hard living," I said. "You are dealing with parts of life I've never had to. So much is easier in my time. Washing. Eating. Getting around. Yet so much is the same. Same hurts."

I put my hand to my heart and held his gaze. After a moment, Will sighed and turned away.

"But also." I raised a finger. "I've met your buddies and learned to toast to the entire universe. After today's visual, I promise not to steal anyone's hawks. Or copper pots. Or bread. Whatever. But there are about a thousand lessons more important. Don't you think?"

At my long speech, Hugh turned around, grinning under his broad-brimmed hat. "I still canna make out a word!"

Will patted him on the shoulder. "Aye," Will said to me. "There is much to understand. And I've not taught you what you truly need. To be a woman in town, you must know the daily tasks. Money and the exchange of goods. Foodstuffs. Homewares. We will start with those."

What I needed. I'd always wanted to learn what that was, and until a couple of days ago, the William Shakespeare on the page was who I thought could teach me. But not like this. Real and sitting next to me in a cart, his shoulder against mine, his leg pressed tight, his hand a comforting pat, a one, a two, on my knee.

Chapter Nine – Two Very Different Visitors

During our ride home in Hugh's cart, every bump and pothole shuddered up through my body until I thought my bones would end up in a pile on some street corner. With each rut and jostle, Will's mood turned ever darker. Now in his chambers, his upset filled the stuffy room until, finally, he grabbed a quill and scratched down a few lines on a piece of paper. Without looking up at me, he grabbed his coat and hat, dug into his pocket, and scattered some coins on the desk, saying, "I've no time for such nonsense. With grace and luck, you will vanish before my return." Then he slammed his way out of the chamber, headed off to *Richard II* rehearsals at The Theatre.

As I listened to him stomp down the stairs, I could no longer swallow past the tightness in my throat and ignore the prick of sadness at the corner of my eyes. Sitting down on the window seat, I sobbed and shuddered, finally sniffing and blowing my nose as I stared out the window, hoping to see Will rush back. But he didn't. I was alone, stuck in this violent, horrible world, and William Shakespeare was angry at me. Maybe he'd run away. Now that the Jessicas were bottled up, he was free to roam. He'd left me here like a cork with the remaining bugs and a few coins.

But I couldn't even count them, much less spend them.

"Fine," I whispered, holding Will's note and staring at the small pile of copper and silver. Wiping my eyes one last time, I tucked my kerchief in my pocket and sat down at the desk.

Pounds, shillings, and pence. Twelve pence make a shilling. Twenty shillings make a pound.

A sovereign is worth one pound, but Will had no sovereigns to show me. *Twenty shillings made a pound.*

Both gold and silver, a crown is worth five shillings.

A sixpence is worth... Six pence. Even I could figure that out.

A half crown is worth two shillings and six pence. A silver penny is worth a penny.

Two "p" coins would make it confusing at the market. *A halfpenny is called a ha'penny.* No ha'pence existed.

The farthing. Not worth anything. I fingered the useless coin. I was worth less than a farthing right now. Maybe I could go out and sell my shoes and survive into next week.

I arranged the coins in stacks, took stock of what Will had told me about money etiquette. Tip staff a few pence. Maybe a penny. A *vail*, he called a tip.

But as I scanned his note and the coins, I realized that I couldn't get by on borrowed clothes. It would have cost a fortune to buy my outfit. Possibly close to a pound.

How would I survive? Sighing, I stared at Will's desk, running a palm on the wood, feeling crumbs and dried ink. So much work, much of it done here. With two careful fingers, I plucked several sheets from a towering stack of loose pages. Unbelievable. A miracle. The first page of *The Merchant of Venice.* Despite the ornate detail of the handwriting, it read as though written by someone with a speech pathology: "In footh, I know not why I am fo fad."

Fo fad, indeed. Ss in the shape of Fs. Not a lisp at all. A style. Thank God my students never saw this spelling. They would never crack a book.

I riffled through and found the title page:

The Excellent Hiftory of the Merchant of Venice. With the extreme cruelty of Shylocke, the Iew towards the faide Merchant, in cutting a iust pound of his flefh. And the obtaining of Portia, by the choyfe oif three Caskets.

I let the page flutter to the desk. In my time, I could write and read. Pretty well, actually. I had published enough to have not perished. Here, I'd have trouble reading or writing. Anyway, I couldn't even count coins without a cheat sheet. I had a hell of a learning curve ahead of me before taking my role in society as a scribe. While I'd read all of Will's work in Elizabethan English, I'd never transcribed it.

After all those years of reading and study, the old language and flowing script had to be in my brain somewhere. I picked up Will's pen, a true quill. A feather. A swan's? There were enough floating white and slow on the Thames. Or maybe the homely goose. I wasn't into birds. Robins, crows, magpies. Pigeons for sure. Maybe sparrows. The rest? Morning noise.

I dipped the pointed quill in the pot of ink on the desk, a black and slightly oily substance, and made a couple of scratches on the edge of a piece of paper. The letters blurred as I wrote: *Jessica Randall*. I dipped and tried again, having a slight success. I penned: *Jeffica Randall*, creating the letter s like an f, as it had been on the play's title page. Again and again, the words more fluent and clean with each stroke. I started to write down my unnatural history in London when I noticed the side of my right hand was entirely black.

As I raised my scary claw to assess the damage, there was a knock on the door. I startled and turned, wondering if I should answer it or hide. I needed to fit in and give 1598 a go. If I were, in fact, Will's cousin, I should act like it.

But I was only wearing my shift. After the horror of the hanging, I'd wrenched off my new dress because it pulled on my shoulders and made it hard to breathe. So now I grabbed Will's dressing gown off the bed and put it on, pulling it tight. I slipped on my shoes, too, just in case I'd be making some terrible *faux pas* by opening the door in bare feet.

Steeling myself, I took in a breath, grabbed the wooden knob, and opened the door.

"Good day," I said, even though I'd spoken with her earlier about the water. I would have to ask Will for a better word, an Elizabethan, "Hi."

The chambermaid gave me a little curtsey and handed me a bunch of dried sprigs. "Master bade me hither to give you herbs and flowers."

I cocked my head and stared at them. What were they? Marjoram, thyme, rosemary? For a vase? My hair? For my person? Did I smell already?

"To strew the floor, Mistress. Mark, thus." She reached out for the bouquet, and I handed it back. One by one, she dropped the fragrant springs on the rushes, the room filling with sweet, sharp, herby tang.

"You are called Daisy?" I asked, enunciating each syllable.

"Aye," she replied, her face bursting into blush the way only truly fair people's cheeks can. I wanted to tell her I wasn't like the other lodgers. But that would do nothing than confuse her further. Not only did I sound weird and have no clue about dried flowers, I also made odd conversation.

"Many thanks, Daisy." I went to the desk to get her a vail, two pence. Three, an extra for the water. When she was done, I handed her the coins. "I will see you anon."

She smiled, her crooked, dark-toothed smile so unlike Shelby's, those pale porcelain petals Kate tended to with massive insurance payments and nightly vigilance. "Did you brush?" she'd cry out. "Shelby! I can't hear you brushing?"

In her nighty, Shelby would walk down the stairs, toothbrush in her mouth, her lips white and frothy with foam.

"I'm brushing," she would say, flicking us with spray. "Can't you *seeeee?*"

For all her eleven years, Shelby had been treated like a princess, protected, nurtured, tended to. Not this girl standing next to me. Daisy was what? Fourteen? Fifteen? What I could do for her and others with tubes of toothpaste and floss. Fluoride. Calcium tablets. I could set up shop, offer up suggestions, be arrested as a witch, and burned at the stake or hung like those poor fellows this morning. But what I could do with the feminine hygiene world. What a mess it must all be. And birth control, though surely that wasn't a safe topic now. I had no choice but to figure out this writing thing.

Then something horrifying struck me. Blinking, I started counting days. I swallowed. Less than two weeks until my period. But wait! For a second, I relaxed. It was impossible to imagine I'd still be in 1598 two weeks from now. And *still* presupposed I was actually here, and not, instead, in a coma in some California hospital, having the dream of my life, this whole experience just blips on an EEG.

Maybe this is what happened. Driving through the fog on my way home from the theater and Dan, I skidded off the road and struck a tree. Head injury. Brain swelling. Getting better, yes, now awake and alive and in 2018.

But what if the coma was not the case? Tampons were centuries away, as were the huge bricks of cotton my mother supposedly wore all through high school. It was going to be a constant checking of skirts and kirtles) and shifts, worse than eighth grade and the imminent disaster of the sudden period before lunch.

"Daisy, one more thing," I asked, my face flaming. "I'm in need of something. Cloths, maybe. For my... my monthly... flux." I slid through the word flux. There was a bloody flux, but that was dysentery, a disease I did not yet have, though it was only a matter of time.

Daisy smiled, curtsied again. "Of course, Mistress. I will bring some with the washing."

Off Daisy went, and I closed the door. How kind. And how kind of Will to send the herbs. He must not have been totally furious with me for being a simpleton, with coin and otherwise. For being stuck in his time. For not knowing how to spell or talk or do anything of use. For freaking out about a hanging. For seeing his pain over Lord Pembroke. For not being Lord Pembroke.

I walked back over to the desk, staring at my name. Jessica Randall. What were they thinking about me back home? "Jessica's MIA," my department chair Susan Franklin was saying right now at our weekly meeting, Dan trying to stick up for me. Susan would swat away his explanation with a harrumph, his excuses about the late hour of the rehearsal and all the essays I'd mentioned.

Sitting down at Will's desk, I snorted. If I managed to survive these brutish conditions and push my way back through wormholes, continuums, and time warps, I could blow up Shakespeare studies as we knew them. I'd be the toast of the Modern Language Association Conference for years to come. My forthcoming and heavily anticipated book would be so crucial, the title would have only one word. *Known.* Or, *Truth.* What about *Facts*? Or it would be so entrenched in meaning it would have a colon and a dash. *William Shakespeare's Erratic Writing Process: Quill and Ink and Spirits—From Haze to Meaning.* I'd be a distinguished chair at Oxford or Cambridge. I'd solve at least three ongoing Shakespeare mysteries simply by returning to my own timeline.

But what if I returned without remembering a thing, this entire extravaganza forgotten? Once I bought a slinky red, black, and purple dress online. Two days later, the dress showed up, smelling like cigarettes and perfume, smudges on the back. After calling the site and getting a ten percent discount, I took the dress to the dry cleaners. It looked great on, this dress, so it was worth the effort.

When I told the clerk the story, she nodded and printed out my receipt. "Too bad this dress can't talk. It probably has quite a story."

While I'd had big plans to wear this dress to the English Department Christmas party, I imagined the dress's better party, it slinking around a hotel with a view of San Francisco Bay, sashaying through the crowd, tossing back one cocktail, two, laughing at a shared joke in an adoring group of friends.

Both the clerk and I stared at the dress that went to a party without me. Now, it was possible I could return home as silent as the dress, a world of story caught inside.

There was another knock at the door. I clunked over in my shoes, wondering what else Will sent as a peace-offering.

But it wasn't Daisy holding out two lemons or the coveted comb.

Startled, I stepped back, caught Lord Pembroke's eye, dropped it, looked up and then down again in some kind of gaze game of catch. Then I curtsied deeply, flushing because of my shift and Will's dressing gown. I kept my eyes down and pulled the collar tight under my chin. Last thing I needed was to be arrested for lewdness.

"Is he not here?" He strode in as if he owned the place, which he very well might. The whole block. All of Bishopsgate. He'd changed his outfit, too, his doublet sleek, black, tiny red threads glinting throughout the fabric. His jerkin was gold and gleaming. Over his shoulders, an embroidered black cape. His hat in his hand, his hair was clean, combed, and dark with thick curls. His black silk hose taut and held up with golden garters, unsnagged, his shoe buckles bright. He smelled like Spanish orange groves and crushed allspice.

"Nay, my Lord," I said, eyes still downcast.

"Cousin, you say?"

I nodded.

"Oh, come, come. Forswear the gentle behavior. You have naught to fear. I am but Will's honest friend." Unlike at the hanging, he sounded honest. Gentle. "Will would want us to be fast friends, but you must tell me the truth."

"Aye, my lord, it's true. I am Will's cousin from the Orkney Isles."

Lord Pembroke pulled out the desk chair and sat down, his every movement fluid. He was like a pitcher throwing a ball in slow motion, every ligament, muscle, tendon, bone working together perfectly. He put his hat on the desk and then pulled the page I'd scribbled on toward him. I stiffened, hoping he wouldn't read: "I appeared in Will's room in the middle of the night . . ."

But perhaps the paragraph was just too sloppy to comprehend. He focused on my name, saying, "Jessica Randall. Not a Scottish surname. But Jessica? One of Will's cunning inventions, or so I thought."

"Family name, my lord," I said.

"Peculiar," he said.

He stared at me with his wide caramel-brown eyes. He was a man impossible to refuse. His face noble. His expression entitled. His features, even, strong, perfect. And yet. Under a certain hardness, I saw something else. A question? A worry? Could it be jealousy, my proximity to his lover? And all those concerns brought lines, tiny fans of time at the corner of each eye. He was older than I'd thought before, well into his twenties. But still a boy despite all his wealth and title. Chin and jaw hairless, cheeks smooth. Will wrote it best: "A woman's face with Nature's own hand painted/ Hast thou . . . ."

"Will has mentioned my name?" he asked, interrupting my thoughts.

My body trembled, whether from my lack of clothing under Will's gown or sudden fear of being trapped in a room with this guy. One wrong word here and off to Tyburn for knowing about their maybe love affair. And since my first Shakespeare class in college, I'd known about Will's longing for the man sitting right in front of me.

"Really?" we gasped during our professor's introduction to the sonnets. "He wrote these poems for a man?"

But what went down between Will and Lord Pembroke was none of my business, even though every particle of me wanted the details.

"I just arrived in town, my lord," I said. "We've not had much time to talk."

"Prithee, repeat. I understood not one word of what you said."

"Nay," I lied, my words careful, deliberate. I spoke as I would, stupidly, to someone hard-of-hearing. "Before this morning, I had not heard of you."

Lord Pembroke didn't look relieved.

"He admires you a great deal," I said. "He told me this very morning, my lord, after we first met."

Back came the shining black peacock who'd strode into the room. I could almost see him preening.

"Certainly," the lord said. "That's why he's here in London and not in Stratford," Lord Pembroke said, his words forced and light.

This was true. In the country, away from town and all its expenses and diversions, Will could be living large in a real house with servants, water, kitchen, and family. But he was here because of whatever there was between the two men. The Lord smiled, his secret safe inside him and certainly with me.

I curtsied for good measure.

Lord Pembroke leaned forward, pulling the same page of *The Merchant of Venice* I'd looked at earlier.

"Splendid trifle!" In his expression, the vestige of that happy man who looked upon his beloved at the hanging, his face full of what? Pride? Respect? Ownership? "The audience loves the play full well. The fellow Shylock quite the entertainment."

"I don't think he's funny," I blurted, moving closer to the desk. "Not anymore, that's for sure."

The page in his hand, Lord Pembroke shot me a dark look. "The audience roared when Shylock sauntered on stage. His every action shows Will's genius."

"But Shylock's a gross stereotype—"I began and then stopped. What was I doing?

But Lord Pembroke interrupted me, thrusting the page on the desktop. "Will could do no better with the creation. Each word was exact and right. As are all his words. Only ignorance could say otherwise."

He leaned back and stared me down, his strong feelings about Will's play now repacked. And for so many obvious reasons, I shut up.

"Of course, my lord," I said. "Pray, forgive my boldness."

Lord Pembroke stood and stepped toward me, reaching out a hand. I closed my eyes, clutching Will's gown to my sides, fearing whatever it was he wanted to do to me. A touch. A slap. A yank of hair. I was alone and in Will's room, both things suspect. I was an interloper, a contender for Will's attention, if not interest. Lord Pembroke could do whatever he wanted and get away with it. So I was surprised by his soft fingers on my face. I sucked in a breath as he gently stroked the angles of my cheek, my jaw. I shivered (and not in a good way) at the coolness of his fingertips at my lips. I tried to squeeze shut the world. But then there was space and air between us, his touch evaporating. Everything inside me hushed, waiting, waiting. I opened my eyes, blinked. He'd already turned away.

"Nay." He picked up his hat. "Go back to your scribing."

Nay what? I wondered, unsure of what I'd just escaped. And that awful pause on the word *guest*. "My lord, I need much practice with the quill," I said, looking at my slightly shaking but thoroughly blackened hand.

There was a pause as he took in my words. "Your writing is quite fine. Surely Master Shakespeare will put you to work on the plays. Or attend to this excellent notion. Most excellent! You might pen for my cousin Lady Mary.

She is a writer of some talent, a daily scribbler of her own imagination. Not to mention her letters and other written mischief."

"I'm honored, my lord, but I—"

"I shall send you word. Pray tell Master Shakespeare I called."

He bowed, leaning forward as if he might kiss me on the cheek, and then stopped. He reached toward me again with his hand. Every single part of me wanted not one part of him, so I reared back a little despite myself. Anyway, was kissing goodbye normal in Elizabethan England? The French maybe. But the English? My only excuse could be I was from the Orkney Isles. Passing strange, for sure.

But Lord Pembroke didn't seem to notice my *faux pas*, pressing into my hand a small bag, heavy with coins that clacked and jangled in my palms.

Rent money, I thought, knowing I had no right to refuse it. I didn't want to. If Will was safe in his rooms, so was I.

I curtsied again, my face burning. "My lord," I said.

And then with a nod, he and his spicy scent were gone.

I watched the door, hoping he might come back to rescind his employment offer. But no step outside the door. Hopefully, his wacky idea of me helping his cousin would disappear once he jumped over the sewage in front of Will's lodgings. And maybe tonight, I would disappear, waking up in time to phone Susan with yet another apology, grade a few papers, and slog to class. My students would think I had the worst hangover ever, but at least I wouldn't be caught in some strange love vortex. Will and Lord Pembroke. Lord Pembroke and his cousin Lady Mary Sidney, the cousin I would be scribing for. It was all, too, well, Shakespearean. He loved him, and he loved her. But he was married, and he needed a wife pronto to carry on the family lineage. And she? She loved him, but not in the way he did. And the other she? The Dark Lady? Maybe they all loved each other.

Me? A wild card. How could I possibly find a place at this table, not that I wanted to? I was the Farmer in the Dell's cheese, standing alone at the end of the singing game.

"Hi-ho, the derry-o
The cheese stands alone"

Working for Lady Mary was a bad idea. If I was trying to stay on the down-low and not wreck the continuum even more than I already had, mucking about with two people important to Will's history was wrong. Will had to sort it out. But just in case, I sat down at the table and picked up the quill. A heaviness settled on my shoulders like a terrible rolled shouldered dress, the enormous kind Queen Elizabeth wore in every portrait I'd ever seen of her, a small woman trapped by her own garb. The air in the room was heavy, stuffy, and smelled like the sprigs of marjoram and rosemary Daisy had strewn. I breathed in and out, each breath still finding me here half-dressed and confused beyond measure.

I know not why, I scratched out, my blackened hand smudging the paper with each letter, *I am fo fad.*

Chapter Ten – The Bath Interlude

Eventually, I snapped out of my bad mood and put on my kirtle, just in time for Daisy and the boy who helped her to drag into the room an actual cauldron of hot water.

Despite a slight waft of soil and sulfur, the heat and steam felt wonderful on my face as I helped them settle the cauldron in the middle of the room and took the large folded piece of cloth Daisy handed me.

"For drying, Mistress," she said, giving me her gentle look once more. She was kind and wholesome, her cheeks pink, a slight sheen of sweat on her forehead. But her big blue eyes said, "Dunce!"

I held it up. Coarse and yellow, it was a far cry from the cushy Four Seasons towel variety. Or even Target's bargain bin.

"Thank you," I said. Daisy lay a stack of washing and the comb I so desperately needed on the table and then turned toward the door. "Mistress, he's coming up the stairs."

I heard Will's slow *clomp clomp clomp*, and Daisy and the boy scooted out the door just as Will came in. After the hanging, Lord Pembroke and his entourage, and my idiocy with learning money, I expected the hot water to royally rankle him. But after he closed the door and turned to see the steaming water and the clean towel, Will relaxed, his shoulders slumping. He took off his hat, tossed it on the table, and started to undress.

"I won't rend the air with a tirade on your fastidiousness. For today," he said. "it is the perfect answer to my current agony."

I paused, wondering whether it was work or love that caused the most anguish. "Daisy bought some Mediterranean soap. It's made of olive oil. I hope you don't mind."

Will picked up the smooth bar and brought it to his nose, breathing in deeply. "Superior to our dirty wedge of fat and ash. Better even than the soap made of hazelnuts."

"I can get more. She's going to take me to the market tomorrow."

"Such an adventure will prove your mettle with the coins. I'm sure you are an expert by now."

I walked over to the desk, sat down facing the window, and picked up the quill. Swan. Once white. Now stained with words. Outside, the foot traffic had slowed, evening filling the sky with oranges and grays. I heard Will undressing and then the splash of water. His sigh. His *Ahhh*.

I dipped the quill in the ink, trying to write without leaving a swath of black smudge in my wake. Will splashed, I scratched. The room filled with the smell of clean suds.

"How was rehearsal?" I picked up the paper and stared at my Q. Not bad.

"A raving band of bawdy knaves. But the play's the—"

"Thing," I said.

There was a pause. I kept forgetting he hadn't written *Hamlet* yet. The witty line before "To catch the conscience of the king" wasn't even a twinkle.

"Very well said." He seemed to mull a bit. "Could be an excellent title."

There was some splashing, and then he sighed. "So how goes the counting?"

"My fortune will be made in writing, not counting," I said. Then more lightly, "I did get a job offer."

More splashing. "Employment? Pray, how did this offer arrive?"

I dipped the quill again, writing, *Lord Pembroke* in slow. deliberate strokes.

"Jessica?"

"When you were at The Theatre I had a visitor. It was a little weird."

Will must have dunked his head under the water, for then there was a sputter, a shake, and a muffled, "Weird? Such a telling word. So, pray, who?"

106

"Lord Pembroke." I put down the quill, grimacing into the window, happy not to see Will's face. "He—he bade me tell you he called. He also left you a bag of money. It's here. On the desk."

All was silence. Or at least all I heard was whispered cursing. A pause. A sigh.

"It's a lot. I didn't count it or anything," I said, though I wanted to tell him I *could* if I needed to. I reached out to touch the soft bag. So fraught. Money for what? To keep Will bound to him? And why wouldn't Will maintain their, well, connection? He was broke. He was a year or two away from his fortune.

"You can pay the rent," I said, trying to keep my tone light.

"This is how he dangles me."

"You could send it back," I said.

"I have long wished to snip the strings that yank my performance."

"Really?" I blurted, but Will did not reply. I fingered the smooth quill and said, "The bad news is it gets worse. He wants me to work for his cousin."

Will didn't reply but kept bathing, the rhythmic sounds of water filling the room. I waited for him to comment, but he was mum, the bath taking all his concentration. Not a lot about bathing in Shakespeare's work. One reference to a bath in *Julius Caesar*. Clearly, not the ideal situation: "And let us bathe our hands in Caesar's blood/ Up to the elbows, and besmear our swords."

Yikes.

During one unfortunate local production of *Othello*, the director decided it made sense to have Othello take a bath, Iago giving his lord a very good scrub down as the actors delivered their lines. The interaction surely proved some underlying homosexual inclinations (at least on Iago's part), but sadly, that was also the *Othello* I took Shelby to.

As Othello began to choke Desdemona and deliver his awful lines, I held Shelby's head against my chest, whispering, "She's still breathing. See? She's alive. She's an actress. See? It's all fake. See?"

Shelby whimpered into my side.

"Do you know how much her therapy is going to cost?" Kate asked after Shelby explained the plot to her mother. "Or should I say *you*?"

But Shelby seemed fine, despite the almost murder and the naked man.

But the point was bathing in the plays was an add-on. Washing was not on the top of Will's mind. But now it seemed easier to bathe than talk.

"Want some water?" he asked finally.

"Are you decent?" I asked, pushing back in the chair.

"Never decent. But come. The water wants his due."

Will was mostly dressed as I walked toward him and the cauldron, which was more of a bucket. When were bathtubs invented? Maybe that should be my trade. Will could invest the pile on the desk. We'd make millions of sovereigns. Or maybe we could just go right for showers. A shower hut. Two pence a pop. Clean as the whistles that weren't yet invented.

I pushed up my shift sleeves, picked up the smooth egg of new soap, and dunked my hands, lathering up. I washed my face, my neck, behind my ears.

"You said *weird*? Pray, how so?" Will asked when I was done.

Here he was. The bard. Wet-haired, opened-shirted, loosely panted. Big brown eyes bright in all senses. Smart and sparkly, deep depths of light. Okay teeth and a wide, easy smile, the kind that took up his whole face. And now, he smelled clean and slightly of olives. And to think I'd just bathed in his bathwater. I could bottle up the rest and sell it at the Renaissance Faire for a hefty profit. Create a stall. It would be like Lourdes for the Shakespeare fanatics.

I picked up the comb and sat on the edge of the bed. "A lot of this isn't going to make sense, and maybe it isn't even true. But I have to tell you."

He collapsed back in the chair, and I paused, using the comb like a piece of chalk.

"There is a space-time continuum." I moved my hand to form a line in the air between us, using the comb to make an imaginary end. He stared at me, nodded. "We are all moving ahead in time. People are born, they live, they die. What they do in their lives affects those who come after, but it's a natural causality, right? I'm a bad mother, and my child ends up a criminal. I spend all my days working hard, providing for my family, and they don't starve. The next generations don't either, living well in the city in the house I bought. You see?"

"The nature of things," he said, taking the comb from me and smoothing his hair. "What's the novelty?"

"We've got a situation here, right?" I motioned again, the line forming once more. "I've come from here at the end of time to here, the middle somewhere." My hand jumped from the end of the line to my imaginary 1598. "I'm bringing a whole bunch of causality that doesn't belong. Worse, I happen to know a lot about your life and this time period. I'm poised to screw up this line." I turned the line into an infinity symbol, a squiggle, a series of hashtags, a whirl of imaginary balloon animals. "What I say to you may alter what comes next. Or what is supposed to."

I drew the line straight again. "So I mess with the space—here. And time, there—when we are—continuum."

Will smiled. "A philosopher! Where did you learn such?"

Where had I learned it all? School? Then I smiled. "*Back to the Future* movies on Netflix. Romance novels in high school. And Einstein," I said.

Will lifted both his hands, a question on his face. "Try to remember I know not your world."

"Never mind. This stuff is mostly theoretical but very possible. Maybe true. If I'd been smart, I wouldn't have gotten drunk and told you what I already did. Today when I met Lord Pembroke, I should have pretended I had never heard of him. Probably I altered your relationship's course."

"You truly say our relationship is known to the world at large?"

I pushed my hair back off my face, felt my pulse beat hard on one temple. "Here's the thing. I want to make you feel better about all this. But I don't want to screw up the line either."

Will gave me a glance, eyebrows raised. "The line will stay in place. Tell me what you have concealed."

"Okay." I took in a deep breath. "You wrote 127 sonnets to him."

Will paused with the comb and stared at me. He then looked past me, seeming to count. Then he shrugged. "Twice that."

A buzz filled my body. "You're telling me you have 250 poems about Lord Pembroke?"

"William," he said, meeting my eye. "I call him William."

"And what about those written about the 'Dark Lady'?"

He looked up at me, confused. "No Dark Lady in my work other than worry."

"I'm sure you edited before putting out the collection. Editors' choice and all—"

Will held up his hands. "Collection?"

"Oh, well," I said. "You'll want to put it all together sometime, right?"

But Will didn't put out his collection—someone made all the choices for him and without his permission.

"Of the newer poems, I would never publish half. Not for the public eye. I will destroy them." He shoved himself up and walked to his desk, searching until he came upon a battered leather folder.

I must have yelled out because he turned to me. "Pray, why the foul noise?"

"Don't do anything with those." I rushed to him, putting my hand on his. "You just don't get it, do you?"

"Get what?"

"How important all your work is. *You* are. Haven't you been listening to a single thing I've said?"

"Jess, attend. We two are in but a confabulation. All these words, they matter not but air. Hope only. Wish. Memory. We whirl in a dream that started the night of the first Jessica and has not since ceased. To Hades with your continuum and Shakespeare festivals. What is real is this." He moved a hand to indicate the room, us, the world outside the window. "Is nothing but what dreams are made of."

"But you love Lord Pembroke," I said. "He's the Fair Youth. The man you write to. He's read them, right?"

Will shook his head. "I endeavor to show him, but I cannot."

"He's the reason you aren't living in Stratford right now." I held on tight to the leather folder, his fingers strong and warm under my own, but he did not let go.

"Naught has transpired between us but looks and meaning. His touch I have had not."

"But you want it."

Will gave me a look I can only describe as soulful, his heart beating in the dark well of his eyes. "I know not."

"Let me read them."

"They are . . . wrong," he said. "Words that go against God and the law. No self of mine—future or past—would let them see the light of day."

"Do you think the world in my time would care? That those of us who have spent our entire lives reading you would disparage this dear love of yours? Will, you jest of the festivals, but I'm not kidding. Here I am at your mercy in this time I should understand but don't. All I have is your best interest and your history at heart."

Under my hands, I felt his relax. I pulled a little, and he released the folder. My heart beat hard in my chest as if I'd saved a precious child from a terrible fall.

"May I?" I asked, polite at last.

"Please forgive the stories inside," he said.

We stared at each other, me with the folder clutched to my chest, he with his hands at his sides, his eyes on mine. In his gaze, fear, sadness, and something else. I wasn't sure what, but I was about to ask when Daisy called and knocked.

"Dinner. Or supper," I said, sitting at the desk, not caring now about the roast of beef, a meat day. Whoo-hoo! Who needed meat (wormy as it probably was) when in my hands were Shakespeare poems read by no one but Shakespeare. The air in my body turned to fizzy bubbles. My hands tingled, and I located my breath fluttering somewhere in my left eye.

"Enter," Will called.

Daisy opened the door and brought a tray filled with the awaited meats and savories. Will turned to address her, asking Daisy to take the water and wet towel away. The same boy from earlier came in to assist her in the task.

Despite the thumping and banging of plates and goblets, I couldn't look up from the folder. A true treasure. I swallowed. If I could, I'd selfishly evaporate back to my time with all the poems, leaving Will to deal with his love life and the ensuing stream of relentless Jessicas.

But would I? Will could have already kicked me to the curb with the sewage. Or rented me a room located next to the overflowing privy, a fetid, rat-infested dump where I could die of the plague. Or he could pronounce me a witch and bring all his beer-drinking pals to Tyburn to watch me swing from the tree, no one to pull my legs to help me out of my misery.

What he'd done was accept me from the future, dress me, feed me, teach me. Then he took a bath, despite the fact Elizabethans thought water was the devil's spawn. He had handed me this very precious work, the folder that held his heart. Probably because he imagined any second I would vanish, he'd told me his deepest secret.

It couldn't be just his fear of the Jessicas? Or could it possibly be that for no reason at all, Will trusted me? Without cause or reason. He believed.

I nodded at Daisy, barely smiling at the girl as she headed out the door, closing it behind her.

"Some mutton pie?" Will asked. Food seemed to bring a welcome relief from the talk or untoward love and sonnets.

"I want to read these. If that's okay."

"O K?" he questioned and then seemed to understand, nodding.

My back to him, I opened the folder, touching the parchment gently, noting the script. First, I riffled through—oh, very gently—the pages. Some of the poems had obviously been revised. Others were hurried, the ink smudged, the print of *his* right hand on the corners. At least even professionals suffered from the black claw. Some poems seemed unfinished, five lines and a couplet short of a sonnet.

"Sonnets are so predictable," at least one of my students would say. "Like Dr. Seuss, you know? All that rhyming. But it doesn't make any sense."

How they passed their SATs was still a mystery.

Before I started, I turned around to look at him. Will seemed content with his mutton pie, his goblet of wine, his custard tart. He glanced up, smiled a little, and speared a turnip with his knife. "Formidable," he said.

"Yes, you are," I said.

I turned back and started at the beginning, a play on Sonnet 18. But instead of a summer's day, we were deep in winter.

"Shall I compare thee to a winter's night?
Bare and bright and cold on my uséd bed.
Our tussle of skin and hair and meaning
Do waken prick of heart and hand and head.
Soft, thou stir, eager touch, caress, and sigh,
And I jump into thine open, new…"

The poem ended in the middle, eight more lines (including the couplet) to go. The scansion seemed okay, the rhythm of the lines clear, if needing some tweaks. Mostly iambic pentameter, the rhythm of pairing ten syllables for each line into five pairs.

But there were Shakespeare's double meanings. The double entendre of *prick*. The use of the verb *stir*. The address to a person. The heart. The *thou* on the uséd bed—maybe the very bed I slept in with Will. Used as in, well, used.

Without thinking, I looked at the bed, nicely and newly stuffed with feathers, made up by Daisy earlier in the day per my instructions. No tussle going on there. But how could there be? Why would there be? Will was smitten with another, and I was encouraging it, making, as usual, a muck of things.

I turned another page and began another poem.

"If hot desire were subject to cold reason
My yearning dare not reach so hard and high
To want what shouldst not some may call a treason
But that I burn in truth I'll not deny.
Not gold crave I but greedy for thy love
Wilt stoop to love so low from far above
That treasure hid within thy graceful form.

And grant this feeling flood its rightful bourn?
Yet that thou flam'st alike in love tis true
As day greets night at sweltr'ng noon so too
Doth should youth meet age to melt at hot midway.
Thy outer cold thy inner heat can't stay."

Oh, my. *My yearning dare not reach so hard and high.* I glanced at Will and then back at the page. The sonnet was unfinished, a space, and then the concluding couplet:

"Of heav'n, perchance of hell, I beg but this
One fiery night with thee of manly bliss."

Tonight was not that fiery night. He sat back in his chair, a lit candle on the table, a book on his knee. My supper was waiting for me on a pewter plate, but I couldn't stop reading. In every line, Will spoke what he felt. With every poem—bungled or perfect—he was as wise as ever. Parchment after parchment of the kind of love two centuries later, Lord Alfred Douglas would call the "love that dare not speak its name." But a love unconsummated. Unrealized. Unrecognized.

Later that night, the poems, books, quills, and food cleared away, Will and I lay in bed, the candle snuffed, the chamber silent. Outside the window, the moon skidded soft across the sky, casting her blue glow.

As we prepared for sleep, I'd hoped Will would drop off into an immediate slumber. I was juggling too many images of bare skin with a slight sweaty sheen, legs as muscled as Jupiter's, and general, all-purpose lust to engage in normal conversation. As a student might say, I was in "total wow." How long had it been since I'd had sex? Noteworthy sex? That tiny relationship two years ago with Boris, the speculative fiction expert and visiting writer? A month or two of dinners and dates before he left? A couple nights in his bed? One or two at mine?

A dozen sexy sonnets and my heart was beating between my closed eyes (not to mention other squirmy places). I tried not to imagine Will and Lord Pembroke together or anyone and anyone together. Not me and Will. Too dangerous right now.

I needed a new sonnet diet. One a day. Max.

Will shifted onto his side, facing me. I heard his breath pause as he began to speak. I closed my eyes against the night, not knowing what I would tell him when he asked me about the poems.

"Tell me," he began, reaching out and stroking my arm. "About the dream of your time. You had so much to say earlier. Net-flicks. Ein-stein. Teach me what I do not know without worry of breaking the line."

"Where should I begin?"

"Always at the beginning," he said.

I put my hand on his, holding it between us. I could smell our comingled breaths, vinegar and mint.

"I can't tell you everything tonight."

"Choose then," Will said. "Pick a fancy. Something to bedazzle and amaze."

In the darkness, I lit upon a topic. "What about electricity," I said.

"Electricity. A fine word. Heat and sizzle."

"I don't actually know how it works. I never took physics. I barely got through chemistry. But someone invented a way to harness the energy all around us. It's here now. In this very room. But it's going to take a couple hundred years to be of use."

"Electricity is in my chamber?"

"It's in our bodies," I said. "In fact, a human being can power a light bulb."

"You have left me behind already."

"Sorry," I said, taking a breath. "Here it is. Someone learned how to harness electrical currents and contain them in wires made of metal and rubber. We run these wires into our houses and build in electrical plugs. We have machines we plug in, and they work."

I tried to draw this with a hand, snaking the wire into the imaginary house and then plugging the imaginary machine into a wall.

Will was silent for a moment but then said, "Continue."

"So to do all your writing, you have a swan's quill. At my home, I type on a computer powered by electricity. I use a keyboard that has the alphabet and numbers on it, and words appear on a screen. Then I can print out the page."

Will was silent for a moment. "A printing press at home."

"Sort of. Smaller and a lot less work."

"What else do you plug in?"

"Lights."

"Electric candles."

I turned on my side to face him. "Imagine there were lit candles on the wall. Two on the table. Two on the desk. That kind of light."

He nodded.

"In my apartment—chamber—I walk in, flip a switch, and the entire place lights up as if there were one hundred candles."

Will took in a breath. I went on. "Then I walk into my kitchen and open the refrigerator. All my food and drink are in there, and everything is cold. I have milk and eggs in there. A chicken."

"You keep chickens in a contrivance in your home?"

"Not alive! A dead chicken. Cut up. Ready to cook. I can keep all I want for weeks in there. Vegetables and fruit. Not that I actually do."

"Go on."

"And this is what I love most. After working all day, I go into the bathroom and turn on the shower. The bath. The water comes heated into the pipes. I can stay in there till the hot water runs out. Then later, I can take my dirty clothes and towels and put them in the washing machine."

"Marry, I understand. A machine that washes."

"Right! And then I dry them in—"

"A drying machine?"

"You're getting it," I said.

Will laughed, moved closer. "This apartment. You arrive by horse and cart?"

"By car. Most people don't ride horses except for fun or sport."

In the dark, he was staring at me. I could almost hear him not blink. "Let's talk about cars later."

"How can you not say all?" he asked. "To tell but a piece is cruel."

"I shouldn't have told you anything."

"Aye, aye. You have made it clear the world's fabric would shred to pieces should I know the secrets of your future."

Now I blinked, waited. I'd not wanted to admit it to myself, but as the hours of my stay here turned to days, as I settled in, as I got a job, it was obvious I was not going home. There was no answer to the question of my departure. I could tell him everything, and it wouldn't matter. We could talk to each other about the future as we lived through the past.

"Oh, cousin. Do not give up hope. Trust me on this, too. Hope is the raft I float on daily."

He pulled me close and hugged me tightly. "You are my favorite Jessica of all."

I laughed through the tears in my eyes. "I'm the only Jessica who stayed."

"No matter," Will said into my hair.

We hugged for a while. His nice warm, strong body next to mine, it was difficult to suppress my sexually carnivorous thoughts. After my evening's reading, the fact was truly thus: I wasn't his type. At least, not now. So there was that. I was about to ask something inappropriate about sexual orientation when I heard scufflings in the corner. I shuddered and prayed it wasn't a black rat, but a small white one with red eyes. Or a tiny grey mouse. A shrew.

"You have to promise me something," I said as we disentangled and settled back on the mattress.

"Within reason, I promise."

"Tomorrow," I said, listening to the rattle of rushes as the evil creature who shared the chamber with us scuttled the perimeter. "We have to get a cat."

Chapter Eleven – To Market, To Market

In my dream, I was home in my bed, contemplating the book I'd written about Will's new poems. The president of Harvard had emailed the night before, and I was Skyping with an Oxford dean in the afternoon. Cambridge had messaged my New York agent, and the University of California was ready to up my salary. Later, I had a date with a handsome colleague who accepted my past, all of it, including Phillip. Best of all, my mother had forgiven me for my derelictions of daughterly duty and had promised to pay to fix my transmission.

"Thanks, Mom," I said to her over the phone. "I've got it covered. And then some. My book advance was huge!"

But then light shone into my eyes, forcing me to blink into the 1598 morning. There I was, pressed up against Will's back, his breathing regular amid all our irregularities of time, space, and intimacy. I held my breath, listening. Last night's furry rat friend was finally asleep. At one point, I was sure he was nesting in bubonic happiness under the bed. Outside the window, I heard the cries of people, the clomp of horse hooves. I breathed in rushes, dust, and cold air.

Fine. 1598 it was.

After our breakfast of beer and bread, and then our new ritual of daily ablutions, Will dashed off a note to Lord Pembroke, while I cleaned and organized the room.

"We must say yes," he said, sealing the letter with a blob of thick hot wax and a big S stamp. "To refuse would be a slight."

"But I can barely write in your fashion. I don't have curlicues and odd letterings."

"All in the practice. If you are unsuccessful, William and his cousin will let you go, but gently. No shame in that."

Will stood, adjusted his black doublet, and took the comb to his long hair. He looked quite dashing.

"The best way out is through," I said.

Will turned to me, eyes keen. "A turn of phrase I quite like."

"Please don't use it. Someone else will need it in the 20th century."

He held up a hand. "I will not tread on the continuum line. So today, while I go to The Theatre and various, off you will go to Cheapside to purchase sundries, ink for one. Your scribing sorely vanquished the pot, and I have much writing to do. Take some pennies and Daisy. Hugh will be downstairs to convey you."

"But I don't—"

"You have seen a hanging and lived with bedbugs. You have read my scandalous poems and explained electricity. A trip to the market is nothing. You cannot fear where you live. For better or worse, you are my cousin Jessica. And besides, the best way out is always through."

"Funny," I said.

So by eight of the clock, I sat with Daisy on the cart bench behind Hugh. Daisy was oddly silent, her face aflame. Hugh, on the other hand, was downright garrulous, chatting away as we headed through the London city wall and west. I spun on my seat as we passed through the actual Bishop's gate. I'd been too nervous to notice it on the way to the Tyburn Tree. In my time, there were only tiny chunks of the wall left. But now it was functional, though, at this point, it wouldn't keep out rogue Saxons, Celts, or Picts.

Hugh chucked the horses, and we rattled onward.

"Where are we now?" I asked Daisy, who grew redder still but did not answer me. She sat on the bench as still and hard as a garden gnome.

"Daisy?"

119

Hugh turned around. "Bishopsgate Street. Now to Cornhill."

He looked expectantly at Daisy for a comment or at least a shrug, but she kept her gaze ahead, avoiding Hugh's eyes and mine.

"Cornhill," Hugh repeated, imploring Daisy once more to no effect before turning around.

The cool air on my face, I was yanked wide awake. The morning of the hanging had been—as Will suggested—a dream. But today was as real as any day I'd lived, this town as lively as any in 2018. But there was a quiet I couldn't place, spaces between the noises of carts, horses, and hawkers.

What wasn't I hearing? What was missing amidst the voices and cart clatter, the horse hooves and donkey braying? I looked up. For one, more London sky than ever. No skyscrapers. No power lines. No planes overhead. For that matter, no buses. No cars. No messenger bikes. No zebra crossings and flashing lights. No hum of the motors and gears and turbines that powered the great city beast day and night. And that was it. No machines.

"Where are we now?" I asked again, feeling like my niece Shelby, her "Aunt Jess? Are we there yet?" a joking family refrain.

"Onward to Poultry Street," Hugh called back, his eyes and face as bright and shiny as the sun overhead.

Daisy continued to simmer and stew, tugging and yanking her cape around her as we jostled down the road. After how she saved me with the period cloths, I wished I could make her feel better. I reached out and took her hand and squeezed. Though she didn't look at me or say a word, she squeezed back.

Down Cornhill to Poultry we went, passing pedestrians, carts, water carriers, and coaches. Just before we reached a large market square, Hugh pulled the cart over. The horse stomped and shat great weedy clomps.

"Cheapside, Mistress," Hugh turned to say, anticipating my next ridiculous question. All around us was commerce at its most essential. Boys called out, "What do ye lack? What do ye lack?"

I wanted to cry, "Hair conditioner! Tweezers! Chewing gum! Tampons! Coffee!"

I wanted a huge foamy latte. A giant cinnamon scone. A big plastic cup of chilled orange juice. A straw.

Also, a burrito. Maybe a pizza. Mounds of Chinese noodles. All the food I'd eaten without appreciating any of it, throwing half away or saving the leftovers for "lunch," and then tossing it all out a week later in its moldering box.

"Tarry not, Mistress," Daisy said, indicating Hugh's proffered hand, though she didn't meet his eye as we both got out of the cart.

Hugh helped me onto the paved road. On the north side of the square were plain houses from which signs hung: *The Hedgehog, The Slippery Eel, The Green Dragon.* With each, a hedgehog, an eel, or a dragon swung in the morning light.

Taverns that people could find without having to read? I wondered. As I stepped forward to investigate, Daisy passed me a basket and took my arm, yanking me away from Hugh, his horse, and the menagerie of stores.

"Many thanks, Hugh. We shall return," I said as we headed south toward milk and fish stalls, booths for bread and soap. And ink.

"Daisy," I said as we dashed away from the cart. "What is the matter between you and Hugh?"

"Pffft," she muttered, seeming more crone than maiden, hunched over as she was in indignation, her cloak a dowager's hump.

"Stand up straight!" I wanted to say.

Instead, I asked, "Do you know each other well?"

She turned to me, her face flushed and vivid, eyes gleaming.

"Daisy?"

She shrugged a little. "He came by Mistress Gumble's house daily for a month in the spring. To stand by the door to pass a few words about his business and his Kentish family. Not only to take Master Shakespeare to the theater. But by summer, it was certain I was no more than a passing fancy."

Daisy adjusted her cloak at her neck irritably, enough so I thought she might tear it off and start running. But she sighed and stomped forward, pulling me toward a store. Once there, she began to fill our baskets. Soap (the kind I liked, slick with olive oil). Ink. A new quill (not swan. Maybe goose? Or old swan.). For my practice. And maybe it was customary for a scribe to arrive at her place of employment prepared with writing supplies. I held the feather in my hand as Daisy bargained for ribbon, thread, and a length of linen.

As she talked with the proprietors, I tried to listen and take in everything, but as seemed to happen in a crowd, I got overwhelmed. Everyone spoke fast, with accents and vernaculars that sounded like Middle English. Heavy words from the bottoms of guttural throats. Sounded out silent Ks. A Norwegian twang. I floated over it all, letting Daisy steer us from store to store. We passed a perfumer, the air thick with rose, lavender, and musk. I pressed my hand against my nose, eyes watering. Fabulously arrayed but stiffly dressed people walked in and out or stood by the windows peering in. They stood poised like mannequins at a clothing exhibition at the Victoria and Albert Museum, though with a lot more mud on their hems and shoes.

Big skirts, padded shoulders, puffy trousers, it was a miracle anyone could pass by the multitudes bashing around, especially the women in their farthingales. And though my bolster made me seem less than genteel, I was glad to slip and slide easily through the crowd.

Call me a slatternly doxy. A common strumpet. A lowborn farming wench. Not worth the pence or penny in her pocket. At least I could walk side by side with Daisy. If push came to shove, I could run home without slamming into everyone or thing.

Finally, our baskets full, Daisy popped into a store and came out with two warm pasties. I noted the number of treats. Only two. Poor Hugh.

Near Bread Street, we found a barrel both of us could sit on. Our baskets at our feet, we ate. The pasty was delicious, the crust flakey with butter, the meat savory and slightly sweet, the carrots toothsome. Taking small, careful bites, I watched the crowd shove past, their words starting to make more sense. As I bit and chewed, enjoying every morsel, I noted a stone cross on top of a fountain.

I stopped chewing. "Daisy," I asked. "Is the cross over there 'Charing Cross'?"

She stopped chewing but not out of awe. Then she seemed to remember I was from foreign climes. "King Edward built it for his poor dead wife, Eleanor.

He lugged her a far distance. Had to stop. The cross is one place they took a rest."

The English major in me wanted to run to the fountain, prostrate myself on the tower. A holy relic of the English culture! My heart thumped to its new "I can't believe it" beat. But then the English wench in me wanted to eat. I was so hungry, I could have eaten a mountain of pasties at every meal, I put my stomach at risk.

"It's not right," Daisy said.

I glanced at her, her pasty half uneaten, her body slumped again.

"Daisy, this upset won't do."

She looked at me, blinking.

"It's not—seemly," I said, reaching out for her uneaten pasty, which she happily handed over. "Not on Hugh's part. Talk to him. Fast—in a hurry. Tell him what you told me."

"Not my place to tout my own wares," Daisy said.

"Hugh is the sweetest of men. This must be a misunderstanding."

"Think you so, Mistress?" Daisy turned her wide open, trusting face to me, and I wondered how two people full of sunshine could be at such odds.

"That I do." I finished off the rest of Daisy's pasty and brushed off my dress and robe. I might die of an extinct disease, but it would appear I would also die fat. "Come. Our goods are purchased. Let us go home, and when we arrive, you shall speak with Hugh. Understand?"

I reached out my hand to Daisy, and after glancing up at me questionably, she took it. Together, we walked through the crowds, back to the cart, back to Hugh.

But we didn't get to the cart right away. In a determination of strides, Daisy had us taking a left, a right, and then we were in a back alley, maybe behind goldsmith's row.

"We have missed the cart by a bit," I said, strangely certain about my location for a change.

Daisy reached out her free hand and pulled me along. "It will be but a trice. Come."

Finally, in the middle of the alley, we reached a small brown door. Without knocking, Daisy entered, and we followed a path through a tunnel that opened up into a small courtyard and then into another passage that led to another door, this one small and reddish.

"Where are you taking me?" I asked, gripping and re-gripping the basket, which was getting heavy.

Daisy shook her head, put a finger to her lips, and knocked once, twice. After a moment, the echoes of the market flying up over the building and then slinking in muffled and distant down the passage, the door opened slowly. I caught my breath. What was Daisy searching for? This was suddenly not Elizabethan England, but a television show, circa 1985. A drug deal in a tunnel, money and drugs exchanged without a word.

But the door opened into a bright room, a small, gray-haired woman of about seventy smiling at Daisy. I almost started. She had all her teeth, white and clean. Blinking, I breathed deeply as we walked in, the air in her rooms different somehow, softer, familiar. The house smelled of soap and lavender and herbs, everything tidy and dust free. On a stool in the corner, an orange cat was curled tight. One small open and brilliant shined window let in every bit of available light and breeze. On the pot over the fire, a soup bubbled, steam rising and carrying the smells of chicken and sage.

"Mistress Meade," Daisy said. "This is Mistress Randall, cousin to Master William Shakespeare."

I turned to the woman, amazed. She studied me for a moment, eyes thoughtful slits, and then asked, "Open your mouth."

I stepped back, feeling my face protest into a grimace, eyes wide.

"Open your mouth," she said. "Wide."

"Pardon me?" I asked, knowing how my years of dentistry would aid me in this era. No fillings. Brace-straightened bicuspids. Solid molars. Extracted wisdom teeth. I would be free to chomp my way through the decades pain-free.

"Come! I cannot hurt you thusly. No tools of the trade to pull a prize."

Daisy nodded, clearly wanting to get on with it.

I smiled, but it did not reach my eyes.

Mistress Meade gave me a quick once-over and then nodded. "Welcome to our time."

"What?" I asked, but Daisy plunged on.

"Mistress," Daisy said. "I'm in most dire need of your advice."

Mistress Meade indicated the chairs at the small table. "How about some soup?"

Still full, I shook my head, but Daisy nodded, and as we both sat, Mistress Meade brought over two steaming bowls and two spoons. "Just in case," she said, putting one in front of me. The soup smelled delicious, better than anything else I'd eaten in this century. So even though I'd eaten almost two pasties, I started in on the soup. At my first spoonful, I gasped, looked up. Chicken broth and herbs and spices, a glimmer of fat in tiny bubbles on the surface. Turnips and potatoes. Shreds of tender chicken. I almost giggled. *Chicken soup for the soul.*

Daisy only picked up her spoon. "I told you of Hugh, my beloved," she said. "But it is not to happen."

Mistress Meade sat down with us, her own mug of soup in her hands, smooth and strong, the nails clean and cut short. Her face was lined but still beautiful, her eyes light, clear, and sharp. Her dress was simple but clean and unwrinkled. "Eat your soup," she said to Daisy.

Daisy nodded and took a tiny spoonful. It took her forever to swallow, but then each dip of spoon and taste and swallow went a bit faster, so much that she suddenly seemed absorbed in eating and only eating.

"Are you from..." I began, trying to figure out how to say this without being reported to the authorities. From all evidence in this room and on her person, Mistress Meade was different from anyone else I'd met in 1598. "From the area?"

Mistress Meade sipped her soup. "Born in Shropshire. Here now. Making soup and listening to those at their most unhappy. Such as your Daisy here, who knows not that her unhappiness will come to a swift end. But now, all is her love for Hugh. Hugh and his inattention. Hugh and the answer he already has in his heart."

Daisy ate on, forgetting, it seemed, it was her idea to be here.

"But what of you," Mistress Meade said. "Are you from the 'area'?"

I sat up straight, glancing at the door. What was I supposed to do now? Daisy seemed to be in a food-induced eating coma. And if I admitted when I was from, what would Mistress Meade do?

"Of late," I began slowly. "From Bishopsgate."

"And before?"

I glanced into the fire, the flames a whirl of wild fingers. "Not really from here before that."

Mistress Meade nodded and sipped her soup. Finally, she put her mug down and looked at me. "I will tell Daisy to be patient with the questions in her heart. Hugh must find his own way. She can say her piece, but then she should take care to go about her business until time brings them together. In emergency, mayhap. When there is great need."

I turned to Daisy, who was almost finished with her soup but still not listening.

"And you," Mistress Meade said. "All I will say is to bring it back with you."

"What do you mean? Bring what *it*?"

Mistress Meade stood up and attended to her soup pot, her back to me. "If you do that, you will have a long, happy, and prosperous life."

A long happy, *prosperous* life? While I hadn't admitted this negative morsel to anyone, note even Kate, *long* was all I'd hoped for. But maybe that had just been the recent sunless, dank, foggy central California winter talking.

Daisy's spoon clacking in her bowl made me jump. I wanted to ask Mistress Meade more about "it" and "take." As far as I knew, nothing came with me from the past. Maybe a nightgown. How to bring more than that back home?

"Can I come again to speak to you?" I asked, but Mistress Meade had left our conversation, turning to Daisy, her bright and shining eyes on the girl.

"Many thanks to you, Mistress Meade." Daisy stood, took a few pennies from her pocket, and put them on the table. "As always, your soup is a fair relief from Mrs. Bunting's watery stock."

At that, I stood and bowed a little, my eyes on Mistress Meade as we walked out of the warm room. Before I could ask a thing, we were outside, winding through the passage, the courtyard, the passage again, and by the time I turned around, I couldn't see the way we'd come in.

"Who is she?" I asked Daisy, striding fast to catch up to her. "How do you know her? And what was the rush for soup?"

"Like my own mother's," she said, ignoring my first two questions. "In nasty times, it is what I crave most."

"Did you hear what she said?"

"Concerning what?" Daisy gave me a "loon" look. "The soup?"

"Happy," I began. "It."

Daisy stopped walking, put a hand on my arm. "Are you well? The pasty! Has it upset your stomach?"

Clearly, I'd missed something big. Hadn't Mistress Meade been giving me instructions about how to get back to 2018? But Daisy hadn't heard anything. The moment of getting-home divination had passed. Or was it past? Past. I was stuck in it.

"Never mind," I said.

"I'm going to say my peace to Hugh and be done with him."

We had just visited a soup witch, I thought.

"Hurry on," Daisy said. "The milk will not keep."

Once back in Will's chamber, I put away our purchases of the day. Soap, ink, paper. Then I stood in front of the window, watching the new old world pass by. It was hard to shake Mistress Meade's messages, especially the ones about Daisy and Hugh. What emergency would bring them together? It took all my self-control not to open the window and lean out to eavesdrop on them as she and Hugh talked by the cart. I wanted to employ my super spy techniques learned as a younger sister with a popular sister. How many times had I listened in on the end of her dates? Hiding in the downstairs bathroom or sitting on the stairs, my ear to the shared wall, waiting for the kiss and more. Kate had gone nuclear when she found me on the kitchen floor behind the island when she and Dylan Tucker did whatever they did on the table. Kate beat me into silence with her evil eye and choice swear words, and then bribed me with a dinner at Chipotle and an R-rated movie.

Okay, so old habits die hard. I glanced out the window once. They were talking, Daisy with her arms crossed, her head down. Hugh gesticulating. Oh, I hoped it all worked out.

With my new quill at the ready, I sat down at the desk. I dipped it in the open ink bottle (the new ones lined up on the desk like shiny schoolboys) and pulled out my scrap of paper from yesterday.

"*To be or not to be*," I wrote, channeling from memory my beloved *Hamlet* and his famous existential crisis.

"*That is the question.*"

"Whether 'tis nobler in the mind to suffer

The slings and arrows of outrageous fortune,

Or to take arms against a sea of trouble,

And by opposing end them."

I put down the quill and blew on the paper, the ink fading a tiny bit as it dried. Not bad. I picked up the powder pot used to set the ink. "Pounce" Will called the stuff. It made me sneeze, so I put it down and waited the ink out. Then I went on:

"To die: to sleep;

No more; and by a sleep to say we end

The heart-ache and the thousand natural shocks

That flesh is heir to..."

Sitting back, I stared at my work. If Lady Mary Sidney dictated, maybe I could do it. I knew enough about the spelling and punctuation to form the words correctly. But I needed to work on my technique. Some of my capital letters were a bit fuzzy. Too long a pause. Too heavy a hand. And what to do with the half-moon smudges in the margins?

There was that unfinished sexy sonnet I'd read, but it was unwise to work on. I would end up reading them all. As I dug around on Will's desk, I found the *Merchant* manuscript I'd read before. I flipped through the pages to Act IV, Scene I, the most horrible part of the play. Every time I read or saw it performed—even with Sherry Maita's underwhelming cast—I felt the same roiling disgust. Just days before, I'd covered my eyes at the university production, Dan whispering, "It's over now" when it was, court adjourned, lives saved and ruined all at once.

Of course, I wanted Antonio to live—to not have to give up his pound of flesh and his melancholy heart. But the truth was, I also wanted Shylock to have his money. He loaned it fair and square. And then in struts Portia, dressed as a judge, and twists the man to bits.

I dipped my quill and wrote the name Portia, focusing on that capital P. What about Portia? Unlike Jessica, she has a compelling backstory. Since her father's death, she's been treated like property. In his will, he created a terrible test for her suitors, none of whom have passed muster or given the right answer to win her hand in marriage. She's alone and lonely in her kingdom, just waiting for a match. Plus, she's rich, so the parade of suitors never stops. Antonio gives his borrowed money to Bassanio so the dolt can woo her, but what does Bassanio have to recommend him but youth and beauty? He is poor and not so smart (for instance, he doesn't notice the judge in Act IV is Portia in drag).

Bottom line, she's a character looking for her own play. But she's stuck in this one, and here she comes, the only one wise enough to argue Shylock can't take the flesh as his bond and, at the same time, not shed Antonio's blood. It's hard to cut out a heart and not spill any. Murder of a Christian Venetian comes with a death sentence. So Portia traps Shylock in his own agreement:

"Therefore prepare thee to cut off the flesh.
Shed thou no blood, nor cut thou less nor more
But just a pound of flesh. If thou tak'st more
Or less than a just pound, be it but so much
As makes it light or heavy in the substance
Or the division of the twentieth part

Of one poor scruple, nay, if the scale do turn

But in the estimation of a hair,

Thou diest, and all thy goods are confiscate."

What a treacherous passage, Portia manipulative, self-righteous, eager for justice for her new husband's best friend. Shylock's crime? Obliviousness. Selfishness. Stubbornness.

Like most people.

And really, wasn't I like Portia, too? Wasn't I sitting here in costume, waiting for my own play to start? Will had been waiting for me to disappear. So had I, not really jumping into this life because, at any moment, it might vanish. And yet, that was the same way I'd lived in my own time. And I'd never believed I could disappear, at least until I did.

But now I had a chance to actually do something. A real job. So again, I dipped my quill into the inkpot. And with my eye on the original language, I reworked the end of the passage, leaving Shylock's options open. Fine. He can't take his bond. But he will get his original loan back. Not exactly fair, but he will keep his way of life.

"*Thou canst have flesh but instead thy money take.*"

If Portia had been a bit nicer to Shylock, the play might not have been such a success. But later, if Will weren't so harsh, the world would have imagined Shakespeare empathetic, kind. Farsighted even. And that was the problem. I knew what I knew because of when I lived. How could I expect Will to jump out of his own time and culture?

I flipped through the pages in front of me. With the original lines, Shylock sees he has been trapped and asks for his money. Bassanio, ever the fool, ever more dim-witted than his bride, says, "I have it ready for thee, here it is."

But then Will turned the screw. His Portia says, "He hath refus'd it in the open court; He shall have merely justice and his bond."

I dipped my quill and shook off the excess ink. What if Portia said instead, "Though he hath refu'd it in the open court; He shall have more than justice. His principle, hither, Bassanio."

In my version, Bassanio ambles forward, gleeful and with a naïve smile on his face, and gives Shylock what he is owed. Shakespeare could still make his point about Antonio's devotion, but at the same time cast a smarter, better eye on Shylock, who would be allowed to go back to his life. Daughterless, true. Alone, yes. But free to live and pursue his business.

There. Cruelty solved. And furthermore, my handwriting looked pretty damn good. I held up the paper. No lady would be offended. And once I was in her employment, I'd be employed. I wouldn't have to count on Will for everything. I could buy my own farthingale. And a ruff, for those very special occasions when no neck movement was required.

I stared at my work. Dan Gordon hadn't been one bit wrong about revising the play. If Will wanted to, he could shift the whole story. He would have to go back to the beginning, work on Antonio, the poor lovelorn bastard. But for now, Will didn't have to see my changes. If he did, I'd simply call it practice, which it was.

About to rework a few more lines, I heard a clomping up the stairs. Oh, no, I thought, putting down my quill. The talk hadn't gone well. Daisy was walking like her old unhappy crone self, slumped over and angry at the world.

Anticipating her knock, I walked over to the door, pulled it open. But it wasn't Daisy. It was a cat, suspended in the air in the open door. Old with one missing eye. Held by a hand, and arm, and body. Will, emerged from his hiding spot behind the door jamb. In this moment, his face was as friendly as Hugh's.

"A gift," he said, plopping the old pirate into my arms. The cat struggled, gave up, and hissed, his one eye averted from my gaze. With effort, it pawed at the dangerous air of his new home.

Will took off his hat, closed the door, and walked in.

"Get you dressed. Off to the theater we go."

Chapter Twelve – The Show Must Go On

"Pray, how will ladies of any number sit to watch the show?" I walked with my arms forward, my legs stiff, mimicking a robot, which I could explain to Will later.

The good news for me—at least in terms of my 1598 disguise—was that while Will was out, he purchased me a few more items, thanks to Lord Pembroke's donation. While Daisy and I shopped, one of the house servants had placed a couple of boxes on the bed. For Will, it was a day of expense. After learning the coin and being out in the world, I was beginning to understand what things cost.

"I scarce believe we will all fit in a stall." I stood in front of my reflection in the wavery window, examining the cage of my brand-new farthingale. Not to mention the stiff and total ugliness of my new ruff.

He smiled.

"What?"

"You sound of the age, cousin mine. Keep up to the task, and you will raise nary a glance when you go to meet Lady Mary."

"Do they reside at Wilton?"

"The Pembrokes have a house in town," Will said. "Baynard's Castle. But you know Wilton?"

"Drove by once when I was in Salisbury while on a tour. So many great movies were filmed there! The grounds are beautiful. So Jane Austen."

Again, I'd gone too far. After my lecture on electricity, robots I could explain. But movies? Lord knows I couldn't explain those. Jane Austen, easier.

Will raised his hand, his now signal for *no more*. "Cease the future ramblings. Tomorrow on our way to meet with Lady Mary, you can try to explain."

How to explain the future, one going on without me? Horatio! I shuddered, pushing away the thoughts of my abandonment and dog abuse. But there was more. My books, though, of course, I could read here, too, and in the original. I could read a play before it was even officially performed. My students, their faces opening up as they suddenly understood iambic pentameter or the guile in Iago's speeches. My life in 2018 was tidy and neat, packaged in a way I could open it. Few surprises. No rats. No cages to wear other than the occasional high-heeled shoes. And no hangings.

For a moment, I fussed with the farthingale, but then I plopped on the desk chair, tears coming in a surprise attack. Like a play that went on and on and on with no intermission. I was acting my role and then some.

"Jess," he said.

"I can't help it," I blubbered, feeling his hand on my shoulder.

"How not, dear cousin? How tremendous to go forth in this world? What strange opportunity. Dream, nightmare, warp in your mystical continuum, living without rules. A magic trick played by God to arrest and suspend us in mighty disbelief."

"Things are happening here that never happened at home," I sniffed, "But no matter how strange and wonderful, I know I shouldn't be here. I don't know where I belong anymore."

Will kneeled and held my hands between his. "It is quite the conundrum. But I will tell you that since your arrival in my chamber, unasked for, my life seems to be overshadowed by brilliance. Amazement. Why I the one to receive such visitations when countless other scribes before me penned unusual names? Jessica. Why Jessica?"

"We need to figure it out," I said.

"There is no figuring magic," he said.

"I'm just tired," I said, wiping my eyes.

"You have come a far distance. But soon you will have work to energize you."

"I'm scared of Lady Mary," I said. "She's smart. Also, she ends up—"

Will kissed my fingers and stood. "Not now, cousin. No information unfairly ripped from whence it belongs. Or for another day. Or maybe never if you don't last the night. Lady Mary is but little. But now, the theater. I will tell you this a time or two: We cannot but go forward. So put on your cage and whirl your way to the players. Aye?"

I pushed my hair back and looked for the comb. On the desk, Pirate stared at me with his one eye. I reached out to pet him, and he dipped his head to accommodate my strokes.

"We need to get him a bowl of water." I stood, strapped on the cage around my waist.

"Zounds!" Will said. "With you, even cats will swim."

As we did the night Will purloined my outfit, Will and I turned north, up Bishopsgate Street with a crowd of people all headed toward the performance. I held onto Will's arm as best I could, but the farthingale kept us a good foot apart.

"I feel like a canary," I said. "Rattling around in my cage."

"Make thee dance canary with fire and motion." Will gave me a little twirl, a man passing us cursing under his breath.

"That line is in—" I began, counting down through my memorized list of plays. *All's Well That End's Well*, unpenned, unplayed. A week in, I was more confused about the prime directive, feeling as transgressive as Captain Kirk always was, breaking every rule in the book. To tell or not to tell? Forget Hamlet's existential pondering about being or not. What to say and what to hide was really the damn question. "A good line."

"Some have told me I can indeed turn a phrase."

This time, I could stare at everything, no longer shrouded in my hoodie. And with each step toward The Theatre, my heart ticked away on the edges of fully content and totally gobsmacked. How I'd always longed to talk with

William Shakespeare, but I'd imagined he'd show up in my office. I'd have a list of questions he'd answer in order. He would tell me what an excellent job I was doing interpreting his work and then disappear, reminding me he would be on call for all my students.

The crowd began to clump and slow, so I assumed we were getting closer. People pressed up against our shoulders, and I looked down at the swaying skirts and plodding shoes. Mud splashed with every step. The space filled with body heat and odors. Two fingers pressed to my nose, I looked up and over the moving crowd. Near the buildings, men stood at the sides of the cobblestone street smoking pipes; the women, fancier than those I saw at Cheapside, wore tall hats, towers of shiny fabric and beads perched on their heads, their dresses wide, stiff, and formidable.

The crowd queued to get in through two sets of large doors. As Will pulled me by my elbow, I stared up at the audience. A thousand people at least, enough to make modern theater directors weep with envy—all laughing, talking: a stirring, restless animal waiting to be fed. Will ignored the commotion, leading us around to a side area to a set of stalls close to the stage. As we walked, I felt the heat and air of that strange night at the play with Dan when I popped into that other magical theater. Even now, I saw Shylock, his dark eyes on me.

"A fair prospect," Will said, his eyes straying from me and up into the crowd. "Stay you here. I will be but a moment backstage to counsel the players."

Too stunned to move or reach out and grab him back to sitting, I blinked into the crowd, staring at the empty stage in front of me, as broad and wide as the imaginary one where Shylock wrung his hands. But if that had been a dream, this was a full-on phantasmagoria. Our seats were not too far from where the Penny Stinkers stood, shoulder to shoulder, a mass of hot, sweaty, unwashed theatergoers, all drinking beer and relieving themselves, right here, on the dirt and—yes, there it was again—hazelnut shell floor. On top of the urine and dust floated the smell of garlic and cloves, both chewed to stave off the plague. The chatter and periodic screams of laughter swelled up and over those who stood in front of the stage, a whirl of noise and smell I'd never experienced at a rodeo, much less a theater. For the first time in my entire life, I wished for a fan, Scarlett O'Hara fashion. Instead, I pushed my face into my handy nosegay. I'll never, I thought, leave home without it.

So I studied the stage, the platform where *The Tragedy of King Richard the II* would unfold. Poor pompous, arrogant King Richard. Soon to be killed, murdered in prison, his crown taken. But he's mostly killed by his own bad judgment, treating his family, courtiers, and England, treating everyone and thing like play toys. By the end, his cousin Henry usurps him and causes Richard's murder in prison.

Not the happiest of plays. Or even one I liked much. Written in verse, it lacked the loose prosy spots I loved in Will's plays, the sections where the language opened up and released the audience from the intensity of the tightly controlled meter. Because of this, I never taught *Richard the II*, appeasing my students, who loved the more popular and film-adapted. *Othello, Hamlet,* and *Much Ado About Nothing.*

As I waited for Will to return, three musicians sauntered in from backstage—men, of course—carrying their instruments, one a violin, maybe, though I knew nothing about the history of instruments. A viola, perhaps. Also, a lute. A flute. They began to play, and then several players gamboled across the stage, making a mockery of the music, performing somersaults and cartwheels. Two men dressed as women began screeching like fishwives.

"She claims she smells like a pansy! A pansy?" The large fishwife staggered at the thought of other woman's particular and private odors. "More like a trout! A salmon! Just fancy that garden of terrible horrors!"

The audience roared, the Penny Stinkers stamping their feet. Someone tossed a cabbage onto the stage. The other fishwife chased the first across the stage, lifting her skirts as she did, besieging her compatriot with her garden of deathly delights. In front of the stage, The Penny Stinkers became embroiled in the show, more players running around, hats waving. I saw Richard Burbage flash by, dressed in a pink-and-green fool's costume, bells on shoes. At the sight of me, he stopped, took off his large floppy hat, and bowed.

I waved, called out, "Richard!" but another player booted him in the rear, and they both ran off, pell-melling through the musicians.

Something else was stirring to my right, others near me shifting and shushing each other, but I was caught up in the simultaneous wonders and absurdity of the preshow and thoughts of the horror of the play itself, King Richard in his cell, waiting to be murdered. Henry Bolingbroke had made his move, angling for and then obtaining power. Wasn't it the way? Someone always wants the place of another. But then the hush and murmur surrounded me. Jostled and pushed by those sitting next to me, I glanced up into the keen eyes of Lord Pembroke and his entourage who stood before me and the stall. The brightness behind him blazed golden, sharp, and glimmering. What was with this guy, always turning up like a bad penny?

Will's sonnet images of skin, flesh, and mouths came unbidden. Apparently, Will knew something about Lord Pembroke that Lord Pembroke didn't even know—or wouldn't let himself. Those poems could only exist if there were a passion burning inside both of them. As I scanned his face, looking for clues about why Will could love him so, those terrible, vulnerable spots in me shuddered, so I stood quickly and curtsied. "My Lord," I said, head bowed, hat wobbling, my legs trembling inside my farthingale.

"Nay, pray repose," Lord Pembroke said, the man next to me leaping away to allow the lord to walk to my bench and sit. "I'll stay but a moment. We have our own box."

He pointed to the lords' boxes above the stage, a perfect place to be seen, and if not see the play, hear it.

Nodding seemed my only recourse, my tongue a twist of nerves. I averted my eyes from the glare of his gaze. My breath hummed in my mouth; my body shook from all the mistakes I could surely make in this instant.

"So you will see the play?" I asked simply.

"One of Master Shakespeare's most brutal."

"The ending especially," I said.

"You know it?"

"Very well," I began, about to tell him my thoughts about the cycle of power, the former rule tumbling into the new generation via violence. But I was a woman in 1598. Not a scholar. "He has told me much."

I turned to smile and play possum, but when I saw his expression, I stilled, noting the glare in his amber eyes. It was as if he knew I were from the future and had nothing but lies up my puffy sleeve.

"I can but imagine," he said, the sarcasm flowing.

"He has long been a storyteller," I said.

"What stories has he told you since your arrival? What fine tales has he concocted? What artful lies?"

I looked at my hands in my lap. "Not but the general," I said. "He's been at rehearsals."

"His spirits seem much improved since you have come," Lord Pembroke said, his voice taut and sharp. "What might make him so happy?"

He raised an eyebrow as if to give me a nudge and a laugh. But nothing in him was smiling.

"I am unaware, my lord," I said. "His prior mood has been subdued?"

Lord Pembroke waved an arm. "Of late, his mood is melancholy. I have long told him he is over fond of his own suffering." The lord glanced away, and I felt the understory, the one I'd read about in the secret poems. Just as I was formulating a generic retort, Will strode back toward our seats, his face a kaleidoscope of emotions: relief, upset, irritation, excitement. Lord Pembroke and I stood, the three of us looking at each other.

"Lord Pembroke," Will said, bowing. "An honor to see you."

"I could not but accept your invitation."

They stared at each other, maybe a beat too long for propriety. I looked down at my hands, wishing I could evaporate. But Will had made this awkwardness occur. He invited Lord Pembroke today, as he invited me. Discussing the poems must have affected him, too, made him remember what he'd been trying to forget. But why drag me along? I wanted no part of this unrequited love triangle. No one seemed to be getting what he—and maybe she, me—wanted.

Cue the violins. So as they talked, I turned back to the stage, letting myself drift away. The play. The play! I was at *Richard the II* with William Shakespeare and the Fair Youth. I pressed my nosegay to my face to hide my smile. Who cared who or what was here? This wasn't some reenactment at a facsimile Elizabethan theater. This was the *bona fide*, one hundred percent real thing.

"Attend," Will whispered into my reverie.

Startled, I curtsied as Lord Pembroke and his group of sleek men and women turned to head toward the staircase that would lead them to their seats. Both Will and I followed their progress, watching them disappear and then reemerge in the lords' box, all of them artfully arranging themselves. I couldn't stop staring at Lord Pembroke's immaculate profile, sharp beard, and aquiline nose. But then he turned to us, to me, and I sat back, lowering my gaze.

"Oh, my," I said as the audience around me swelled with voices and noise. "Were you trying to make things more awkward?"

"Mayhap no wise thought at all," he said, his voice sharp.

"Then why? Just to get a glimpse?"

Will stiffened next to me, pulled his shoulder from mine. "Even as he walks away, it does me good to see him."

Really, what type of good did he mean, I thought, but then the trumpets sounded. The audience hushed, shifted, and settled. And then started up talking again, swilling beer and laughing. Then out onto the stage came the characters Richard the II and John of Gaunt.

"Recognize Richard?" Will whispered.

A play on names, Richard the II was played by none other than Richard Burbage, as you please, striding across the boards as he addressed John of Gaunt, who had brought his wayward son, Henry, to court.

Standing at the very edge of the stage, with his arms held wide, Richard was transformed from his earlier fool to flat-out magnificent. His costume was white and gold, his cape a rich red velvet, his crown agleam even under a cloudy London sky. It was clear why the woman called to him from the audience for a chamber visit.

"...time-honored Lancaster,

hast thou, according to thy oath and band,

brought hither Henry Herford thy bold son,

here to make good the boist'rous late appeal..." Richard as Richard asked.

"Brilliant," I murmured. "Beautiful."

Will pressed against my shoulder, the rest of me unavailable in its cage. But I felt his warmth as the words spun on, the players, the play, the true, the very, the only thing I'd ever dreamed of.

It started with a curse. The sound of someone tumbling down a stair or two. A terrible laugh, heedless of landlords or fellow tenants. Awakened, I grabbed the blanket, eyes wide in the darkness. Pirate tensed at my side and stopped his purring.

The cat might not know, but I understood what these sounds meant.

In Will's plays, there are many references to losing all to drink, as his father John did. During his lifetime, John Shakespeare went from mayor to tax evader, drinking away his family's money. I could relate. My father used to love martinis. Two drinks after work, the glasses frosty, the pimento-stuffed green olives big, a bowl full of those pretzel sticks (woe to any who ate them without permission). After dinner, we learned to tiptoe around the house to avoid waking him from his post-drink state. If we dropped a book or plate or accidentally turned on the television too loud, he awoke in a roar, called us out on all our cumulative misdeeds. We were banished to our rooms or, worse, spanked, despite our mother's pleas and our closet hiding.

After an episode of yelling, glass throwing, or spankings, Kate and I turned into silent mice, scurrying around the corners of the house, much like the rats in Will's chamber. Unseen, invisible, we could cause no problems. Until we did.

Later, a therapist or two recommended Al-Anon meetings. So I went, learning that Kate's and my adaptations to my father's behavior were almost textbook. Kate bust out of her shell, a social and sexual diva. I took my shell with me to college and then grad school and into life. It was at home in 2018, on top of my dresser, just waiting for me to wake up from my long coma.

Now, I wanted my shell back. Will thumped against the stairwell, whapped against the door, fell into the room with a curse and in a waft of ale, bad rum, and the acrid smoke of self-pity, a smell I remembered well.

"God's blood," he cried, the neighbor below us commenced to yet again pound on his ceiling. "Infernal and damned evening."

I sat up, clutching Pirate. "What's wrong?"

Will staggered to his feet, holding onto the desk, slipping, and then clattering into the chair. My hard-won practice pages of an hour before fluttered to the floor.

"I will not undertake another day of this torture."

At first, I thought he meant me, the curse of the Jessicas. But as he muttered and swore some more, throwing boots and clothing as he yanked off items and flung them around the room, it was clear this upset was due to Lord Pembroke.

"Did he do—"

"Don't you dare ask," Will cried.

I sat up, crossed my arms in front of me. "Don't talk to me like that," I said. "I haven't done anything."

Will shot me a hard glance. "Don't you say a word. Ha! *Entranced* says he. Unmatchable beauty. *Mesmerized*."

"What the hell are you talking about?"

Staggering as he pulled off his shirt, Will mimicked my accent. "What the hell are you talking about?"

Pirate tensed as I pulled the blanket over us. "My behavior has been above reproach. I've managed not to get caught at anything, despite the fact I'm four hundred years removed from this cesspool. So don't dare me to do nothing."

"Silence, woman!"

"I—"

"Keep your mouth from moving." Will thrust himself close. I blinked into the flickering candlelight.

Under the covers, Pirate hissed.

But Will didn't want to simply vent and whirl. He pushed me back against the mattress, Pirate shooting out and cowering under the desk.

Will's mouth against my ear hot and angry, he hissed, "He does say he's interested in what's between your ears. And your legs."

I gripped my knees, clenching every muscle closed and still.

"He said I am a selfish man to not share my bounty." Will pushed at my shoulders, grabbing at me. "Look at me, strumpet!"

Tears clogged my throat, beat at my eyes. I shook my head, feathers shifting as I moved. "Stop it. Leave me alone!"

"You have!"

"He's the one who touched me!" I blurted, flashing to Lord Pembroke's lazy fingers on my face. The intimidation in his touch. The message. "I don't want anything to do with him."

"So there's truth to his words! You want to take him!" Will pressed closer to me, his hard breathing at my temple, his hands on my back.

"How can I take what neither of us has?"

"In my mind, a hundred times," he cried, his voice ready to break, even as he pushed me hard on the bed, my breath shocked from my lungs.

"So go to him, then. Leave me alone." I tried to yank myself away from his grasp.

"I am torn asunder."

"Clearly." I pushed back at him, the heel of my hand against his shoulder, chest, and then stomach. "Look at what you're doing! How can you be with me when it's not me you need?"

I pushed him again, and he backed off. I shifted position, inching away.

"How know you what I want?"

I sat up, clutching the blanket to my chest. "Then what, Will? Who?"

"You," he said, leaning in, his mouth at my neck, his voice hot and wet.

"I know the sonnets," I cried, scooting farther away. How could he mean it? I'd felt the longing and love for Lord Pembroke. "I read them all. Twice!"

Will put his head in his hands, smoothing his hair. "I am drunk, more than I have rights to be. I did listen to him talk and swill, concocting a story about you. When before, it was about me. And then he said—" He paused. "What he said about you and your beauty. I felt something break through what had been. This week. This time."

He moved closer again. "You," he said again, his body fully on mine.

"No," I whispered into his hair.

"You with your dark hair and artful prophecy," he said, but as he spoke, he pulled me closer, his hands on my shoulders, neck, cheeks. "You who know who I am more than I." His mouth was at my ear, my eyes, asking, asking. His breath turned to lips. His lips to mouth to tongue. William Shakespeare slipped off my shift, his mouth on my throat, my chest, his hands on my breasts.

Something loosened in me. Despite the fight in my mind, my body uncoiled and opened, arms around his shoulders, legs opened under his body. He wasn't angry William Shakespeare, he was just Will. He pressed me back, his face wet, his angry, over-rummed body warm and ready.

I kissed him back, letting my hands feel his body as his did mine. I pulled him close, hard enough I felt my breath caught under my ribs, under my tongue. I tilted my head back and was floating on the shiver of every nerve. Each second passed too quickly. In the pause of us, I closed my eyes, stunned by him and the fact that sex in any century is sex. But I'd never felt this willingness in any time zone.

"You do beguile," he said, a question in his voice. The question, though no one had ever asked like that, with words and touch and taste. Not ever. Not Phillip. No one.

His hands became the beginning, middle, and end, meeting mine, squeezing, releasing, holding. Our mouths spoke of loss and love, arcs of conflict, struggle, and surprise. Of what we wanted. Our bodies locked together on the bed, we were every scene, every setting, all the parts of every play, all night until it was night no more.

In the muted dark of the room, my head on his chest, I listened to his breathing, my hand over his heart, which beat on. I wanted to relax into what had happened, but he must be in a twist of emotion. Or maybe I was projecting, a bad habit. But here he was, holding me but in love with Lord Pembroke. Writing sonnets to Pembroke, but me naked in his bed.

As if hearing me think, Will pressed me close. His skin smelled like the olive oil soap I'd bought at the market.

"Stop this pondering," he said. "Perhaps it is your penchant for time travel that keeps you from being in the moment at hand."

"This time is unbelievable." I held his hip, his skin soft and warm in my hand.

"Your time is unbelievable," he said. "This time makes much more sense. What you tell me could not be born here and now."

"Back home," I began as I did at night, telling him the stories of the future. "Two men or two women can get married."

Under my head and hand, Will's whole body seemed to still. "Let us speak not of this."

I went on. "They get married, adopt or have kids."

"Adopt." He was silent and then breathed out. "It's true? But how—"

"The women find the means. The men sometimes have a surrogate. A woman who has the baby for them. They are just families like any other."

"Never in these times," Will said. "The noose."

"I know. Some of England's most famous writers will have conflicted and often terrible times of it."

"What knows the world about my loves?" He shifted, turning onto his

144

side, stroking my hair off my face and tucking it behind an ear. "When they know not of you?"

I kissed his palm, breathed in the scents of ink and paper. "I wasn't here before. The first time. But maybe it doesn't matter who you are writing about. It's all your writing about love. You saved a lot of people."

I felt his confusion. "People not acting to type. Portia, for one, even though she's beastly. Dressing up as a man in a position of power. To decide life or death. And then, make it a young man, playing a woman, playing a man. All the plays where people weren't who they were expected to be gave people who couldn't be who they were hope."

"Tragedies give no one hope," he said. "Mayhap, show what *not* to do."

"Some of your characters survive. Maybe they're even better for it. Horatio, for one." I bit my lip, wishing I hadn't let Horatio out of his *Hamlet* box. I rushed on. "Maybe not better. Alive at least. But you were pretty harsh on so many of your women. Brutal, really. Hanged, drowned, poisoned."

"It is clear in my dotage, I grow angry and resentful. I live here wizened and bitter, scribbling out the worst of plays."

I kissed him. "Some of the best of plays come next. *Pericles* is in there, but some of the most wonderful."

"I vow to never write that infernal play. Or if I do, I will make sure to include messages. When you return to your time, make certain to read carefully."

His eyes shining in the dark, I kissed him again. "And the sonnets, Will. The ones to Lord Pembroke. They are lovely. You bring forth every joy we need to cultivate. That's what showed the world a side of love people didn't want to look at. The idea that 'Shall I compare thee to a summer's day?/ Thou art more lovely and more temperate' was for a man is astounding. Freeing. Hopeful. Will, it's nothing to be ashamed of."

Will closed his eyes and flopped on his back. "I lost my mind. But my anger tonight. It wasn't about him. It was my belief I was losing you."

"It is a fact universally acknowledged I am not going anywhere."

"But you understand how love makes monsters of us all?"

Yes, I did. In one way or another. And there was Phillip again. His brooding brow, his brilliant mind, his pantheon of excuses. My pangs of guilt about Emma, his sad wife. Who, I realized later, must have known something was not right. But back then? I didn't let her pain get in the way of my happiness, such as it was, which was about as happy as Will's was with Lord Pembroke.

"I wasn't ever lucky enough to feel that much," I said.

"Luck? Such torture is luck?"

"It is," I said. "I mean, unless you start stalking someone. Or go all murderous and rampage-y. But that feeling. Your feelings. All those sonnets? A gift."

"A pain," he said, "I turned into thought and then writing because I could not bear it otherwise. 'A man loves the meat in his youth that he cannot endure in his age.'"

Much Ado, I wanted to say but didn't. Much ado about nothing. And "nothing" in Will's time meant more. It meant everything.

Will shifted under me, kissed my hair, his body relaxing. "Too much pain," he said. "And you may be true, my dear Jess. Sometimes pain is all we have to remember love by."

"Sometimes we end up loving the pain because it's more real than the one we loved." Phillip's shadow was more constant than he ever was. My father's, too.

"My young son Hamnet," Will said, saying the name he had never mentioned before. Under my cheek, I felt the change in his body, his heart a slow beat of sorrow. "He died before I knew him truly. His life was mostly unknown to me, his death without my presence. All that remained was the shell of his being. Too late to say my final words."

How small my grief over Phillip. Even that for my father. Both still alive, just not with me. Both betrayed me, but I survived, days now without thinking about either. But the loss of a child. Hamnet, eleven, had been exactly Shelby's age when he died. Even at only eleven, Shelby was individual and unique, full of quirks and gifts and sometimes horrors (a rage machine at the end of road trips). How horrible to imagine her sassy incandescence snuffed out. No more dance performances, Shelby flinging herself around the living room in her leotard and new ballet shoes. Or her brace-filled mouth at my ear as she whispered her schoolgirl secrets about Braedon, the cutest boy in class. Or shopping trips or movies with Red Vine binges. Or just the sweet smell of her soft hair as she relaxed into my hugs.

From the moment she was born till the second I left 2018, she was the pulsing center of my life, and she wasn't even my own child.

Kate would never recover if anything happened to her. I wouldn't either.

Hamnet had been as alive as Shelby. And then he wasn't.

"You lived here in London." Tears clogged the back of my throat. "You couldn't have known."

Will snorted, though I could feel his tears running down his temple to his neck. "Could I not? Could I have traveled back to Stratford on more frequent visits? Could I have invested more love and hope in my own child? Could I not have been satisfied with life at home with my wife and family? Was my employment here in town and on tour more important than my child's life?"

I wanted to defend him, argue back, but Will pressed me still, his arm tight around me. "Hamnet died of the plague while I traveled to him. And then I left directly after the funeral, throwing myself into my work. Devoting myself to the verses for William. But no lines for my own son. My own son! And then I turned my gaze to William. Only William, who wanted naught and asked for naught but took all."

In his arms, I stilled, full of the evidence that could prove him wrong. His work pulsed with loss and despair. In *King John*, Will wrote: "Grief fills the room up of my absent child,/ Lies in his bed, walks up and down with me."

Why didn't he see? Or maybe he couldn't bear to look.

"It's not your fault," I said. "I told you about the plague. Rats and fleas. Not you."

"Mayhap," he replied. "But all the time since my dear boy's death seems filled with air and ridiculous yearning. Save meeting you."

He shifted so I could see his face. "Tell me, dear Jessica, that my child is still remembered."

I put my hand to his face and nodded. "He is," I said. "I promise. We who love you know."

We were silent for a while. All around us in the wooden building, the other tenants shuffled down halls, clanged in their chambers. The heavy wooden beams groaned, the floorboards creaked. Outside, as the moon dropped down behind the buildings, early risers called to each other.

I swallowed hard, holding him against me, kissing his face, his shoulder.

"You are the surprise of my life," he said, his mouth hot against my neck.

I laughed, thinking back to our first night together, me drunk and reciting a Shakespeare sonnet to William Shakespeare. "Only you have could have tolerated me. How lucky for me in so many ways to show up in your chambers."

"And not the constable's."

"Or the Gumbles'," I said, thinking about their wicked broom. "Or Richard Burbage's."

Will chuckled. "He would have proclaimed you a time traveler and put you on the stage to speak in your strange tongue."

"My story could have certainly been otherwise."

"A story can always change. At a moment's notice," he said. "This is my stock in trade."

"How will this story end?"

I could feel his smile against my face, the heat of his hands as he pressed me back against the mattress, the taste of his minty mouth. I had never loved and lost as much as Will. Maybe I never would. But right now, out of my time, in a time I loved so much, with a man (and not just a writer) I admired and loved and respected, I had more than any other time could give me.

I awoke first, Pirate purring next to my ear, Will spooning me, his arm thrown over my shoulders. The sun slanted a fan of light on the bed, dust motes whirling in the morning air. Feeling me stir, Will pulled me closer, his lips on my shoulder blade. Then a pause and his light snore.

This comfort, ease, and joy had never happened to me before. With Phillip, there had been some long, passionate nights, but I always held back knowing that every sexual moment was an assignation, an evil breaking of the rules, forbidden.

But this? With Will? Not William Shakespeare. With Will, the poet who loved too much, it was—to use a cliché—magic. Who knew? I'd thought time travel was all the magic I had in me.

I was wrong.

Chapter Thirteen – A Love Triangle Becomes Love Rectangle and Other Disasters

The next morning was far from Elizabethan. More Modernist. Dali, Picasso, maybe even Jackson Pollock. After spending the entire night and some of the morning having sex with my "cousin," he and I traveled to his erstwhile lover's castle so I could act as scribe for the lover's cousin, the very woman who would later bear him two illegitimate children. I was the only one to know all these dark and messy secrets. Crammed into my dress, trapped by my farthingale, crushed by my new fancy, decorative stomacher inside my bodice, topped with my ridiculous hat, I lurched and shuddered on the wooden bench as Hugh yanked us toward Baynard's Castle. Next to me, a warm and friendly William Shakespeare.

Will snaked a hand under our comingled robes, taking mine in his. My heart thrummed. Falling for a married but sexually ambiguous man wasn't a good idea. And on my way to work for Lord Pembroke's cousin?

He had the same train of thought. "Had I but known of the joys of last night, I would have never agreed to such madness."

At Will's voice, Hugh turned back, and I almost gasped. He wasn't the sunny man of the day before, but drawn, wan, dejected. He seemed thin, his former happiness leaving sad spaces under his coat.

"Hugh?" I said. "Are you well?"

"Aye, Mistress," he said, his voice dull and flat.

Will turned from me to glance at Hugh and whispered, "What is the matter?"

I waited for a large coach to rumble by and then whispered, "A love gone wrong. With Daisy."

"Our Daisy?" Will mouthed.

Hugh's slumped as he urged his horse forward. Pressing as close as I could to Will, I said into his neck (he smelled like the bath we'd had earlier), "He rejected her once. It is possible she returned the favor despite her strong feelings."

"More madness," Will whispered into my ear.

I squeezed his hand, unable to forget what that hand had been doing just hours before.

"Lord Pembroke may not be at home when we arrive," Will said.

"Of course he will. That's the point."

"How so?" Will pressed close to me, my heart thumping louder at his closeness.

"We're at his command. His beck and call."

"He's a lord," Will said, pulling back. "We all must do his bidding. There is no other option."

I tucked a loose strand of hair behind my ear, the cart jostling us around, my hat tipping. "What ho, Hugh?" Will called, but Hugh wasn't hearing anything now, too involved in his private thoughts as he guided us over the rutted road.

"Pray, continue," Will said after a while, the road smoother. I pushed my hat firmly on my head and sighed, wishing I'd never been involved in power plays. Or dating, online and otherwise. I never wanted to calculate my moves or watch anyone else do so, either. Mostly, I didn't know how to do it—and if I wanted to, I had to plan. Eventually, I learned to spot it in others. How often had I sat through a coffee date, watching a man run a hand through his hair, check his watch? Pull out his phone, decide it was suddenly time for him to go? After a few dates like this, I started asking Kate to call me at 11:37 am (an odd time, so as not to look obvious) so I could make my excuses due to an emergency at the college. So, if Lord Pembroke and I had been sitting across from each other at Starbucks, I wouldn't have a clue what he was up to.

"He wants something."

Will rubbed his face, fatigue settling under his eyes. "Aye."

Aye. Yes. Of course. What did I expect? Will to run away from his entire life because of last night? I came unannounced and uninvited. I was here and now, but based on how I arrived, I had to assume one illusive day, I'd leave the same way. No goodbyes. No farewells. Just gone. How could either of us hang on to something so intangible?

Will looked down, squeezed my hand, let go, one finger, another, another. We bumped and lumbered along down toward the Thames. All of London was outside. Coaches and carts, pedestrians with baskets. Raggedy dogs, stray cats, and homeless beggars slumped against walls. Hawkers and merchants crying out their wares. Cows, pigs, and goats. I noticed the hats, the doublets, the big black shoes. All of this, and my body still pulsed in places that hadn't pulsed in a long time. I looked at Will, closed my eyes, remembered his hands and mouth and smooth, lean sides, and opened my eyes again.

The sky above was blue and still, clouds only on the horizon. I craned my neck, searching for familiar landmarks. I could see St. Paul's—we'd come this way on our trip to Cheapside—but this time, we passed so many buildings, I was lost. Hugh made wide, silent turns, no tourist info, no jokes or rejoinders as the cart tipped up on one side and slammed down, mud spattering. As we got closer to the river, the breeze carried the smells of fish and foul (and I mean foul). I pressed my nosegay to my face as I studied the buildings. I'd never seen Baynard's Castle because it burned to the ground in the fire of 1666. I'd heard of it, of course, and in 1598, it was almost six hundred years old, one of the fanciest houses in London. King Henry the VII had lived here. So, for a time, did King Henry the VIII, that murderous lout.

I reached for Will's hand, but he'd moved it away. I glanced at him, and his thoughts were not in this cart. There it was. He was already regretting the night before. He must be somewhere in the vicinity of remorse and suffering, the intersection of worry and despair. Fine, I thought, collecting my writing kit: my quill and ink and paper. I'd gone into last night knowing about Lord Pembroke. I'd read the poems. Will's distance was to be expected.

We passed a large church and then rounded left onto a wide road that had a sign: Thames Street. We clattered along until we pulled into a turnout in front of a great stone castle, and castle it was, with enormous walls and turrets. Sitting in the claptrap cart with silent Hugh and Will, I felt like a child being pulled to school in the back of a little red wagon. In front of the great house were guards and servants ready to help us. I could only imagine what my mother would have said. "A cart? My word. I told you to rent a coach! You only have one chance to make an impression."

"Master Shakespeare," a steward/footman said. I could tell he was such, but his outfit outdid Will's. Red doublet, black coat with gold brocade and puffy shoulders. Fancy black pants and sleek silk stockings. In keeping with the steward, the housekeeper's splendor outdid mine, though her black dress was more subdued, not as flashy, though of a supple quality.

"I'm the country mouse," I whispered to myself as I clutched my writing supplies.

Will glanced at me and then said to the steward, "Lady Mary is expecting us."

The man bowed about a millimeter, eyes steel mints, and ushered us through the wide mouth of the grand stone doorway. Behind us, two men closed the enormous wooden doors with a thunk. Darkness and then light as my eyes adjusted to the yellow glow cast by flickering torches and huge candles. With all the flame, it was a miracle this edifice had lasted this long, never mind hanging around till 1666. And how sad that it would burn. The walls were covered with tapestries as big as entire houses. Lots of kings with their minions of devoted angels. Copper, silver, and gold on tables and shelves and in corners. In every room we passed, sideboards, tallboys, and buffet tables that looked as though they could house small families. Tables big enough for cabinet meetings. Fireplaces gaping and deep enough for choir practice.

"Do giants live here?" I said to Will as we followed the very stiff steward fellow down the rug-covered stone hallway.

"These are but the public rooms," Will said, taking my arm again.

I relaxed, breathed, listened to the echoing noise of our walking. Clack of heel, swish of dress and stiff fabrics.

"The size displays House Pembroke's importance," Will said. "Trust me, we dare not make this family angry."

It was horrible knowing the future and how it played out. William Herbert, Lord Pembroke, would die at 50 with no legal heir, his two children with Lady Mary Wroth née Sidney deemed illegitimate. His brother would take over the lord role. All that would be left of the Lord's and Will's relationship was mystery, scholars fossicking through the sonnets for clues. *Who was the Fair Youth? I know, I know!*

But this was a story that wasn't going to end well, and now I was in the middle of it, headed toward a business relationship with Lady Mary that could prove dangerous. The Red Queen in *Alice in Wonderland* was no joke around England: *Off with her head.*

The steward—his name coming to me to the beat of our steps (Mr. Tight-Ass, Beady Eyes)—walked us into a more cozy hall. Light was pouring in from a large bank of windows, glowing on the painted walls. The furniture shone impossibly oaken bright. We headed up a large staircase, down another hall, leading to a room where light shone beneath the large painted door.

With a brisk knock, Mr. Tight-Ass, Beady-Eyes opened the door, walked in, announced, "Master William Shakespeare and... guest."

As we passed him, he gave us a slight bow, and then there we were, standing in front of Lord Pembroke and Lady Mary Sidney. Or at least I thought we were. I kept my eyes down. My heart was pounding so hard, I was sure it was visible in the dip of my throat.

Will was bowing, pulling me down to my own curtsey. I dipped as low as I could, wanting to announce my full subservience. But then Will stood as I did, though I kept my gaze on the rug.

"Many thanks," Will began, "for asking my cousin Jessica to act as scribe, Lady Mary."

"It is nothing," she said, her tiny voice light and reedy. "I have great need of help, and Lord Pembroke suggests she has some skill."

154

I looked up enough to see the peacock blue and gold embroidery of her gown.

"Indeed, my lady," Will said, bowing again. "As she's lately from the Orkney Isles and tutelage from the nuns, she's ready for solitary work. Pray, excuse her odd speech."

"But it won't be solitary, Master Shakespeare," Lord Pembroke said. "As we shall all be here to keenly guide her in the scribing."

Will stilled. I turned to him and then looked over at Lord Pembroke, who was smiling, though under that grin was mischief or maybe malevolence. Gently, I moved my gaze to Lady Mary. Lady Mary. Lady? Hardly a lady, at least in terms of age. Lady Mary! A girl! She might have been a lady title-wise, but she was a child. Maybe twelve? Thirteen at the outside. How could Will have called her a strumpet? A harpy? An oyster wench? How could she be the Dark Lady? I shook my head, staring. Of course. My math was off. She was still so young, and certainly not one of Lord Pembroke's entourage at the hanging or the theater.

"My thanks," I said, casting about in my mind for her facts and details. "I hope to be of use."

Lady Mary gave me a curt nod but with more of a dip than the nasty steward. Will took my writing supplies and brought them to a gleaming mahogany desk. I followed behind him, listening as he and Lord Pembroke discussed my duties. But I couldn't get my mind wrapped around the young girl in the room.

Slowly, I pulled forth her details. In this timeline, she was at least five years from marriage to Sir Robert Wroth, from all accounts a jealous philander and full-throttle jerk. The marriage would not be happy. The Wroths would have one son, James, who would be born a month after Lady Mary's husband died of gangrene and deeply in debt. The poor child would die at age two. As I watched Lady Mary watching her cousin, my eyes filled. So young. She knew none of this. How could she? Here, she was still a maid, the daughter of Robert Sidney, Earl of Leicester. Everything about her was, without question, lovely.

Her hair was light and loose and wavy, falling over and past her shoulders and down her back. Her skin was white and truly flawless, her cheeks flushed and pink. Her dark eyes bright with intelligence and desire. But desire for Lord Pembroke? Maybe in a my-older-brother-is-a-football-hero way. But no, it was more. This girl desired it all, even if her love was aimed at this flashy, sexy, older cousin who would destroy so much, even his own life.

"My lady," I asked. "What shall we work on today?"

Lady Mary turned her gaze to me, her eyes still wide from holding the grand visage of her cousin's form. In her innocence, Mary reminded me of Shelby. But Mary was a true English rose, and it was all I could do to keep myself from reaching over and cupping her pink cheeks.

"Your language is rather strange and hard to understand," she said. "You are from the Orkney Isles?"

"Aye, your ladyship," I said.

"I needs must write my lady mother. And—" she looked toward Lord Pembroke, but he was giving Will some kind of lecture in the corner of the room. Seeing them together, head-to-head, the elation that had filled my body since the night before continued its slow leak from my heart. But I had my eyes wide open. Will loved Lord Pembroke, and I'd been there instead. "My new play."

"You are a playwright like Master Shakespeare?"

Mary's face finally unhinged from her strange adult mask, a broad, slightly crooked-toothed smile filling her face with joy. "A play with a unicorn and a witch."

I leaned close to her. "We should begin immediately. Let no potion go unstirred."

Mary nodded and sat straight in her brocaded chair. "Cousin, Jessica and I will start our time together."

Lord Pembroke gave her a cursory glance, his gaze dismissive. Bored. Not a spark of interest. Without a doubt, I hated him. He was a vacuum cleaner person, sucking up whoever got in his way and spinning him or her around with the dirt. Will. Lady Mary. His poor little wife, wherever she was. His family's estate. Perhaps he was a repressed gay man in an era of intolerance. That I could sympathize with. But there was a callous disregard for anyone else in that calm, superior gaze.

For the first time since we'd arrived at Baynard's Castle, Will gave me a real look, one that contained last night and all our previous nights in his chambers. His eyes warm, his expression saying *Just let me know, and we'll blow this pop stand.*

But I only nodded, smiling, a flush simmering under my stiff clothing.

"I will return ere long," he said.

Behind him, Lord Pembroke glowered his nasty glower. "You may begin," he said with a dismissive wave and walked out of the room ahead of Will.

"I'll be fine," I mouthed. Will followed Lord Pembroke, and Mr. Tight-Ass, Beady-Eyes closed the door behind them.

I turned to Lady Mary. I hadn't worked with children since my undergraduate years when I took a position as a writer-in-the-schools for an afterschool program. We'd played word games and made up characters and acted out scenes of plays we wrote based on fairytales (*Jack and the Beanstalk, Little Red Riding Hood*), but I'd spent hours with Shelby, helping her with her English homework. All those terrible haiku. The autobiography assignment. The report about the jellybean factory.

"My lady," I began. "Tell me your story. Spare no details."

Lady Mary stood, a girl under all her adult finery, almost hop-skipping to the desk and pulling forth a manuscript bound in a thick leather folder.

"It is about a witch who rides upon a unicorn. The witch is very powerful and casts spells upon the kingdom. Only the knight can vanquish her and save one and all."

"The knight," I said. "Handy to have around."

Hard to believe this hero's adventure was coming from the woman who would later write *Urania*. That story was an adventure that starred two women, Urania and Pamphilia, whose friendship was the core of the tale. This little girl standing in front of me now was years away from penning that tale. But not far away from the misery she would endure. The loss of her child. Her love for Lord Pembroke. Her family disowning her and not acknowledging her children.

Life was too damn hard.

"What say you?" Lady Mary demanded.

"Why is it the knight gets the best role?" I asked.

She stared at me, blinking. "The idea seems strange?"

"Maybe it is a maid? One with a simple charm to dispatch the witch?"

Mary regarded me much as the cleaning women had my first morning at Will's. A loon. Pure and simple.

But Mary smiled. "A maid," she said. "A maid vanquishes all. She needs not a knight."

"Why don't you list your thoughts for me? I'll capture them," I said, opening my ink, readying my quill.

I glanced up at Lady Mary, a girl in the flush of a good idea. "Oh, aye, indeed!"

Lady Mary and I worked for an hour or so on her "brainstorming," though I didn't mention the name of the process. Her maid was strong indeed, magic even, and her mother, it turns out, was a fairy.

"A good witch," I suggested. "Very possible. Trust me."

Then I handed over the sheets of her ideas, and she set to writing her scenes. Meanwhile, she tasked me with some letters to copy (she liked having a record of everything she sent out. Smart lass), and there were many. From my studies, I remembered she had ten siblings, though I wasn't sure if they were all born yet, and she wrote to several of them about her time with their cousin in the city. Most seemed to be living at the family home at Penshurst in Kent. As I copied out the last of her letters (to her younger brother Phillip), I worried over this creepy arrangement at Baynard's Castle, even though Mary's letters contained only the fun evidence of pleasant activities. The meals. The weather. Her social engagements. But what was Lord Pembroke doing with her here, alone, away from her tribe?

I wanted to bundle her up and take her back with me to Will's. No, I actually wanted to take her back home and enroll her in an accelerated academic program that would accept a girl who could read Ancient Greek, Latin, and French. I'd bring Daisy too, taking her away from a life of drudgery and failed romance.

Just before three, the door opened, Mr. Tight-Ass, Beady Eyes (heretofore Mr. TABE), and Lord Pembroke appeared, and Mary put down her quill, eyes brilliant.

Icy Mr. TABE informed me my ride home was waiting, though he said, "Conveyance," dragging out each syllable. I made my deep-curtsied goodbyes to Lady Mary and Lord Pembroke and followed Mr. TABE out of the room, down the halls, through the cavernous public spaces, to the cart where Hugh slumped, his hands on the reins, and Will sat, wide-eyed and waiting.

Clambering into the cart—sitting in my farthingale was like trying to get comfortable while wearing the Liberty Bell—I found my seat, falling to the bench with a *whuff*.

Hugh flicked the reins, and we headed off, down the rocky drive to the road and east toward Bishopsgate. For a second, I tried to locate myself, my head everywhere and nowhere. His time, my time. In the future, in textbooks, essays, and plays, in the past, the now, in the real noises of the world all around me. All the history, what did happen and what might happen due to my interference.

Will reached out his hand, and I took it, our skin cool and dry despite the misty fog hugging us. In the morning, he'd told me he needed to spend the day at the theater and with Richard and their investors discussing plans for The Globe, but my heart was jealous. Stubborn, too, caught on the looks Lord Pembroke had cast Will's way and the melting, pained expressions on Will's face as they'd spoken before leaving Mary and me to our work.

Leaning toward him, I turned my lips to his ear. "Lady Mary is but a little girl. A child!"

Will shrugged. "Of course."

"So why did you call her a strumpet?

159

He pressed my hand between his two. "I was unkind. My thoughts seem not my own these days."

"Whose are they then?"

"Yours," he said, the word hard and flat in my ear. "Lord Pembroke's. My characters'. Who could know?"

"But she's—"

He pulled one hand away and waved in the air. "Tell me not. My own eyes informed me thus. Today with her hair undone and be-ribboned, she was like my own Susanna or Judith. Little girls only. A child who deserves my solicitude. A child."

I took in a breath as I felt him think of Hamnet. I leaned in close.

Will shook his head. "Madness."

"But why such hard words for a young girl? She can't have harmed you in any way." Not yet, I thought.

Will glanced at me and then looked down at our clasp hands. All around us, London rumbled by, Hugh a mountain of slump in front of us.

"I have not been completely honest with you," Will began. My whole body stilled as I remembered Phillip turning to me and saying, "I haven't told you this. But wait. Let me explain. I'm married."

Of course, Will was married. Married. I sighed and closed my eyes.

"What's true, then?" I asked. "Tell me."

Will brought arm behind my back, pulling me closer. "You were not the first Jessica to speak to me about my future life. Another caterwauled during her too-long visitation."

"Why didn't you tell me this before?" A heat rose in my throat. "Who was she?"

"I know not. But for you, that Jessica stayed the longest. Minutes. Maybe like yourself, she was part of my supposed industry. But she had much to say about Lady Mary Sidney. Though it was curious. Called her Lady Mary Wroth. Screamed she was a harlot. Made mention of a ménage à trois. Spoke of research, and the word 'movies' as do you."

160

"Did you believe her?" I asked.

"Believe or not, her words rang in my ear and caught me unawares. And the fact she appeared at all made believing easier. Her words pierced me to the core."

"What else did she say?"

Will paused, rubbed his forehead, and then looked at me with his dark, serious eyes. The cart rumbled, jumped, both of us grabbing tight to one another. "She told me I was naught but a fraud. That I'd not written my own works. That I was only the front for a true genius hiding my small shadow. She ran at me, her hair uplifted and seeming on fire, her hands grasping. And then gone, like smoke."

Hugh made a quick, sharp turn, and Will and I clung to the seat, letting go of each other.

"Hugh," Will yelled. "Pray, attempt to keep us in the cart."

Sunny Hugh nodded but did not provide a quick, happy quip.

"I shouldn't explain any of this," I whispered once the cart settled.

"The continuum of time once again?"

I nodded. "I don't know what to say or not say. But you need to tell me. What do you think is going on between Lord Pembroke and Lady Mary? Why is she here alone? Don't you find that the least bit strange?"

"Of all the things in my current life, their acquaintance concerns me least."

"But is it normal for a girl cousin of her age to come for a visit unattended?"

"Why ever would it not be normal, as you say?"

"She's eleven," I persisted. "What can they have in common but family?"

"Her family is but poor compared to William's. There is some debt, and if William asks for his cousin, all the family can do is abide. Same as you needing to show up for your employment."

"What about some of her brothers? She's at a vulnerable age. She's too young for anything with—him."

"Now, mayhap," he said. "But later, a marriage could come to pass."

"God!" I turned to look out at the street, hating this time I loved with a passion. Of course. I understood the past. Aristocrats were married off at young ages to solidify houses and form political bonds. A woman's primary purpose was to marry, even if that meant she was promised off and married away at a young age. She couldn't choose her own husband, and she couldn't divorce him, either. Often, she wouldn't even inherit her estate if he died, as would happen when Lord Wroth died, leaving Mary in debt. If the husband were horrible, abusive, or just boring, all the unhappy wife could do was wait for him to die. Or die herself, as women often did, in childbirth.

But here, poor Mary was in thrall to her older cousin but doomed to marry an abusive drunkard. Despite her talent, ambition, and prescient views of gender roles, she'd live out her life in sorrow, mostly unacknowledged for her true gifts.

"He's a bastard," I hissed.

"Do you think he's interfered with her?" Will asked, stricken, face pale, eyes horrified.

"Do you?"

Will shook his head. "Nay. Nay, I don't. Truly. But there is a way about him when he speaks of her. It is perhaps unnatural." He leaned closer. "Yet who am I to claim thus?"

"We have to get her away from him."

"We cannot snatch her away if that is what you suggest," Will said. "The castle is a family home. She stays with her cousin, reasonably. From all accounts, she prospers in his care, and now she has you to work with. He sought you thus. Ill-treatment is not apparent, sweetling."

My mouth filled with retorts, but I caught the *sweetling*. I relaxed, letting his arm and shoulder support me as we passed folks headed toward their suppers at home and taverns and inns. In the distance, church bells. The sky above pewter, the air cupping us cold. My heart half love, half fury.

I grabbed his hand, unable to stop myself from asking, "What happened with Lord Pembroke when you left us."

Will glanced at me, sighed. "He pulled me close with words and promises, closer still with reminders of his generosity. Your employment. The money. Always the money. For the plays. For The Globe. He knows I need it."

And him, I thought.

As I wrangled my hips from the cart upon arriving at Will's residence, I caught Daisy's face peeking through the one large front window. Hugh didn't turn to look at the house or us, mumbling, "'night," as Will handed him some coins.

Will headed up the stairs, I tapped on the large great room door and pushed in, finding Daisy staring out the window, watching Hugh's back as he joggled away.

"What has happened? How is it you and Hugh aren't speaking?"

She turned to me, her eyes wet and weepy. "I made a horrible mistake, Mistress."

"How could you have done that?"

Daisy looked down, shook her head.

"Tell me, Daisy."

When she lifted her head, her face was red, eyes wet but blazing. "I told him how I felt, as you instructed. I asked him of his passing fancy. Then he told me about his cousin Alice, from Kent. Promised, they are. Hugh is to return home at the end of the year, leaving London. His sole purpose here to earn the funds to buy a small plot of land. And a cow!"

Daisy put her face in her hands and wept. I reached out to touch her shoulder, but then someone called for her, and she stormed off, slamming the great door behind her.

I slumped in a chair, the outside darkness filling the room. From the kitchen, I smelled supper and heard the other servants chatter as they went about preparing the trays for the rooms.

Me and my big mouth. Me and my futuristic ideas and notions. Who was I to apparate here and tell anyone what to do? Now I'd ruined things for Daisy. She'd just about gotten over Hugh. Same for Hugh with Daisy. I had brought back their mutual attraction, and now they were both sad.

I stood, left the room, closing the door behind me. I'd forgotten my *Star Trek* rules once again. And now I was set on trying to change Mary Sidney's life. Just because I was from the future didn't mean I was wise. How could a few books, a quick skim of her major work, and a Wikipedia page inform me about how Lady Mary felt for Lord Pembroke as she grew up? Maybe he was her love of a lifetime. Who made me the expert? After all, look at my relationship pattern with men. Love them, and they leave. Love them more, and they leave faster. And upstairs, a man I had no business sleeping with, in any sense, but what was I doing? Sleeping with him in all senses.

As I headed slowly up the stairs, I vowed to stop my interfering. At this point, I was worse than Lord Pembroke. So far, he'd only brought Mary to London for cultural entertainment. I was the facilitator of broken hearts, my own endangered heart now front and center.

Will had lit the candles, the room aglow with yellows and golds. On the table, plates of meat, vegetables, and bread. Two mugs of beer. A tart on the side, steaming. Hearing me, he turned, smiled, and I vowed the only heart I'd take responsibility for was my own. Mine could break. I had to be careful with everyone else's.

Chapter Fourteen – Going to Church, Trapped in a Terrible Room, and The Wife Thing

My family and I never went to church. Or, rather, *a* church. After my father left, my mother developed one of a few strange habits. We went to local churches as if they were buffets. Or classes. Or parties. One month going to the Lutheran church, then a stint at the Episcopalian church down the street from our house. One Sunday morning at the Mormon church, never repeated. "All that talk of canned food," my mother complained.

The Baptist church, the Zen Center, Santa Theresa's Catholic Church, the nondenominational but clearly born-again congregation, the back row of the synagogue on a Saturday (a surprise bar mitzvah to witness). One adventurous service at the Fremont Hindu Temple. I don't remember much of that day except my extreme feeling of otherness, but we were smiled at and handed translations of the *bhajans* so we could join in with the singing.

Week after week, month after month, at lunch afterward, my sister and I were asked to recount what we learned and thought.

Mostly, I just asked for more fries and prayed to all the various gods that it would stop.

It did. One Sunday, our mother woke us late and made pancakes. We read the Sunday newspaper at the table, sun streaming in the window. Our life of devotion was over. More than anything, my mother was finished with her marriage.

In 1598, though, church was necessary. In fact, not going was punishable. Nonattendance could get one labeled an atheist or a witch. Her father's Anglican daughter, Queen Elizabeth, had passed her Religious Settlement in 1559, yet folks were still hiding Catholics and priests in secret rooms and passages. Meanwhile, Puritans were wreaking havoc (Oh, just go to the New World, would you!).

But despite the tumult, Will was not a religious man. He took me to church, introduced me to the Reverend, Mr. Beadle and made the proper motions. Oh, he knew his Bible and used it in his work, but at home? No praying and kneeling morning, noon, and night. We never said grace, though all his constant toasting could be construed as thanks.

Most Sundays, though, we found ourselves on our knees in St. Helen's, praying along with Mr. Beadle. Accustomed to homilies, liturgies, and masses, I managed the long slog of ritual by pretending I was back in college sitting in a very long lecture, but what an ordeal for the lapsed person I was, hiding my true agnostic center. I rose, kneeled, and prayed with the congregation. Every service involved hymns, prayers, absolutions, lessons, salutations and responses, more prayers, and a litany, petitioning the help of just about every saint I'd ever heard of and then some. Then more praying. More singing:

Glory to the Father, and to the Son, and to the Holy Spirit

As it was in the beginning, and now, and always, and to ages and ages of ages.

Amen.

For over two months of Sundays, I'd dream my way through, and then Will would wake me up, and we'd burst into the sunlight and go to the theater. I was a familiar presence backstage, anticipating the actors rushing onto and off stage, the plays more familiar to me than ever. While I didn't really want to go home, now I could teach the hell out of *Richard II*. Even the students asleep in the back row would wake up and get it.

I was one of the gang. The cast called me "Jess," invited me to the inn after each performance, and toasted me soundly for my help with costumes and lines, not to mention the improvement of my speech. Most everyone understood me now.

Richard Burbage sidled up to me one afternoon just before the start of the play, his voice deep and low. "If ever you need a new *cousin*," he began.

I attempted to look appalled. "My word!"

"Jess, if you and Will are cousins, your family is wondrous strange."

"You two," I said, shaking my head. "Really. It's not a race."

"Life is only but a race." He winked and donned his hat before striding toward the stage. "I enjoy it best when winning!"

In the evenings, Will and I would retreat to his chambers where he would write, and I would too, though I was just copying some of his old plays. We'd light the tapers, hunker down in silence. He wouldn't let me see his new work, what I imagined to be *Much Ado* or maybe *Henry V*. Without him noticing, I picked out words from the page, until he glanced up, "Back to your own scribing," he said.

"Let me read a tiny bit!"

"It's fit only for the floor, crushed and tossed in crumpled wads of the should-have-never-been-written."

"Please," I said, carving out an elaborate S in thick dark ink. "Stop with the modesty. Doesn't work on me."

He laughed and bent over his words. He often took the pages with him during the day, so I couldn't even sneak a glance. But I did have work to do. Lady Mary had chided me, "You do need to pay more mind to your Ss. And your Fs. Practice."

FsFsFs.

Later, in bed, Pirate at our feet, Will held me tight, his mouth telling me stories without words. "Love," I murmured.

"How long a time lies in one little word," Will whispered, his hands sliding off my clothing.

Sometimes, we would talk about the mystery of the Jessicas and the way for me to return home, the subject touchy, both of us treading gingerly as we spoke.

"Most like the theater is key," Will said. "You said that night you had a vision."

"But I had been at home for hours before I found myself crammed in your wardrobe," I said, kissing his ear.

"Pray, don't allow me to make a bad metaphor about crammed." Will pulled me to him. "Too easy to play loose with words."

"That's not what I want you to play loose with," I said or thought I said because all I was doing next was touching him.

Mostly, though, we tried to forget I was on loan. For seconds and minutes and sometimes days, everything seemed perfect. I could forget *when* I was and be *where* I was. No worries about my old life or the terrors of the Elizabethan era. No Lord Pembroke controlling my lover or my pupil. Or me. Everything was only Will and me in the bed, the moon cutting glances at us as it slid across the darkest sky ever.

"Your witch," I said to Lady Mary.

Mary looked up from her writing. At least *she* let me read her words. "A terrible hag." She smiled. "A crooked nose and noxious breath."

"Might she be a bit too witchy?" I asked. "From the moment she slides across the page, we know she's up to no good just by what your characters say about her. Here."

I scanned the sheet in front of me. "Like you said. The nose. The breath. But her hair. What about that one wild eye? I mean, I get it. And the writing is most splendid. But maybe we could modulate her appearance."

I rattled on and then looked up. Mary sat stone-faced, implacable. My students often gave me this "I will never change one word, you horrible she-beast" look during office hours as they clung to their ideas. But Mary was having some ideological issues with the character change.

"Are not all witches thus?"

"Do you want to write 'all' witches?" I asked.

But, of course, Mary was right. There were stock Elizabethan characters that could almost move from play to play, author to author. The Jew (like Shylock), for one. The shrew. The clever servant. The ghost. Vice. The malcontent. In my mind, I saw Will's witches stirring their terrible pot.

"A rounded, changing character," I said, suddenly back in my classroom, in front of the board, scribbling away so intently a student would usually ask me to decode my scrawl. "Is one that develops. Becomes more authentic. More real. Flat characters stand still doing the same thing over and over. We need them, of course. But they do not change. They do not grow."

Mary looked down at her page, and then, one tear splatted on a new line, the ink liquefying again, starting to smear.

"My lady." I was horrified I'd hurt her feelings. In an instant, I flashed back to the Tyburn Tree, me swinging in my green dress, a flash of my red kirtle. "My humblest apologies."

Her head still bent over her work, Mary shook her head, her hair slipping over her shoulders, falling to the table with her tears.

"Should I call Mister . . ." I almost said "TABE," which would have been confusing. "Someone?"

"Nay," she whispered, now wiping her eyes with a handkerchief. "You are correct. I only wished other people spoke to me so truly. My family reports my work is without error. But I see now they have been treating me as a child."

At that, I wanted to reach over and stroke her hair, treating her as a child. But she was not Shelby, crying about not being able to go out with her friends (and boys) wearing a midriff blouse and skinny jeans. Mary was an English aristocrat, raised in power, full of it, too, even as a child.

"My lady, your work is amazing. This play." I did reach out to touch the sheet in front of her. "Is far better than many I have read before. But all work needs time and space to come into its own. Do I make sense?"

Under the curtain of her hair, Mary sniffed. Then she wiped her eyes and sat up straight, expression back in line.

"Less witchy?"

I nodded. "Let us commence with the nose."

During the next two sessions, Mary and I reworked her witch scenes, and when I arrived Friday, I expected we would push forward with new work. But when Mr. TABE brought me into the drawing room, Lady Mary Sidney was nowhere to be found. Instead, Lord Pembroke sat at her small desk, reading the play-in-progress, his hands all over her sheets, his eyes scanning her words.

He glanced up, his gaze ironic and condescending.

"So, is this the work that has brought Lady Mary such enjoyment?"

I curtsied and nodded. "Yes, my lord."

"Childish, certainly, but with a strain of truth," he said. "Methinks your influence."

My eyes stayed on the tremendous rug, thickly piled, swirling with reds and blues that twisted into roses, hearts, crowns. "Lady Mary has a keen mind. She knows quite a lot for her young age."

Lord Pembroke was silent. I glanced up, watched as he shoved the manuscript aside and stood up, adjusting his doublet and ruff as he did. He strode close to me, the fabric of his fine clothes *whisk whisking* as he walked.

"For that reason, I sent her home to be with her fair mother for the day."

"My lord, I gather you will be wishing for my absence. I beg your forgiveness for my intrusion."

Curtseying and turning to go, I gasped as I felt his hand grip my upper arm, his strong fingers tight. "Nay, Jessica. I need you for my scribe. Lady Mary will return before long. For now, my letters shall be your concern."

Lord Pembroke was so close, I could smell him, and he smelled of soap, perfume, and something sharp, anger maybe. From his clothing wafted a sleek sheen of lavender. His hair, brushed and combed, gleamed in the morning light that streamed through the big windows. His breath, mint. His hand slid to mine, and his fingers were soft, but tense. I could imagine them prying off jar lids or hurling brand-new baseballs. Or grabbing other, softer flesh, squeezing and enjoying the pain he inflicted.

I stepped back, and he let go, slowly. "Shall I sit at the desk, my lord?"

"That might not be the only place I shall ask you to sit," he said.

Pretending to ignore his *double entendre*, I sat down, arranging my ink and quill. Gently, I tucked Lady Mary's play into a safe spot under a book, my anger barely contained.

And yet, as he strode across the thick rug, feigning thought, his hand on his soft, attractive chin, he was compelling. I thought of Will's written lines from *Othello*, "He hath a daily beauty/ That makes me ugly." Compared to the shine and lift and waft of Lord Pembroke, I was nothing but a toad. No wonder two of the smartest people in London had fallen in his thrall.

I wanted to slap him into next Sunday, but using *Star Trek* as my guide, I raised my force field, picked up my quill, ignored his sexiness, his smile, his flat-out good smell and wrote out his words.

After three horrible hours, I curtsied low and slow. Mr. TABE ushered me out, the big door closing behind me, and then Hugh rumbled me home in the cart. Glum and downcast, Hugh said not one word. This time when we pulled up in front of Will's chambers, no Daisy peeked out the window.

Slowly, I pulled myself up the stairs. My body ached from sitting straight, still, and stiff to withstand Lord Pembroke's verbal advances. An incipient migraine pulsed behind my forehead.

"Does this phrase prick your imagination?" he had asked.

"Shall we rub down that last utterance?" He'd cut me a glance, his lips cradling a smile.

Holding back twenty eye rolls was tiring, as well. Finally, after he squeezed my shoulder three times during one letter to a tenant, I almost screamed, "Sexual harassment!"

But I held that back along with "Jackass," "Dumb shit," and "Horn-beast."

At the landing in front of Will's room, I stopped, took in a breath, and smoothed my skirts. With all that was roiling in Will about Lord Pembroke, I didn't want to give him anything else to think about.

Daisy—as downcast as Hugh—walked toward me from the other end of the hall, linens in her arms. At the sight of me, her mouth opened to say something, but as I turned the knob and walked inside, she didn't have time to utter a word.

Will wasn't home. But a strange woman with two teenagers was, the girls sitting on the edge of the bed, the woman sitting at Will's desk. As the door swung wide—Daisy gasping behind me in the hall—we all stared at each other. The woman was thin and fair, her light brown hair curly, her face a tad pinched, fine pale eyebrows over her dark eyes. She wore a modest gray dress (no farthingale) with a black kirtle and a fine black robe. Her shoes were sturdy but new. The girls, thin in their flowered dresses, looked up at me with wide eyes. The girl with the dark, curly hair was older—small breasts under her grown-up dress—and taller. The blonde was a jangly girl, pointy elbows and chin. Her eyes were bright, and she almost smiled at me but then thought the better of it.

"Um," I said, stopping as the older girl raised her face to mine, her soft brown eyes resting gently on me. And I was struck, hit, pummeled by the resemblance. She had her father's face. Susanna, Will's older daughter.

I turned to Anne Shakespeare neé Hathaway. "Mistress Shakespeare?" I curtsied, my legs trembling.

Anne continued to gaze my way and then stood, adjusting her skirts. "Aye. I am. Mistress Shakespeare, though we wait and wait for the master of that same name. Know you where he is...?"

She gave me a look, calling for my introduction. "I am Jessica," I mumbled.

"Chambermaids, Mistress," Daisy said, stepping forward and pushing me back a little. "Pardon for the intrusion. Jessica and I have brought the linens for the room. Hither."

Daisy carried the linens into the room like treasure. "For the bed."

Anne ran her hand across a pillow. "The cleanliness of these chambers is wondrous strange. So unlike my husband's usual state."

"The landlady, Mistress," Daisy lied smoothly. "All the rooms are such."

"Keeps us fair engaged," I managed, trying to keep myself from staring at the three of them. "Shall we make up the bed?"

Anne shook her head. "Nay, the girls shall jump and tumble till their father arrives. But supper?"

I looked back at the girls, Susanna, with her father's eyes, Judith her mother's. And in between them as they sat, the missing child, Judith's twin. Hamnet, dead and buried these two years. I closed my eyes.

"Anon, mistress," Daisy said, nudging me. Anne rose and pressed in my hand something small and cold. A vail. Daisy and I backed out of the room, my hands shaking on the doorknob, tears in my throat, a void in my chest. Closing my eyes, I leaned against the wall.

Most days, I pushed Anne Hathaway—that mythical wife—right out of my mind, convincing myself the Shakespeares had a marriage grown old and bad. But here she was with her two children, concerned about her husband, eager to see him.

Worse, I had done exactly what I had with Phillip. Over the years, I'd crafted his wife, Emma into a deadened, lifeless husk. Invisible and worthless (sometimes, during spiteful moments, I thought of her as ugly, lumpy, and stringy-haired for good measure). Of course later, she and I were in thrall to the same man, sad, united, and forever paired sisters. But after my long relationship with Phillip, it was impossible to imagine making amends. Instead, I'd sworn I'd never, ever be in this position again. And yet, here I was. A cheater, a front-loaded, time-traveling cheater.

"Mistress," Daisy whispered, pulling me toward the stairwell and safety. "Come to my room."

And with that, I understood Daisy knew everything—or at least enough—about Will and me. No doubt, she divined I was no travelers from the Orkney Isles.

In her small, dark room, Daisy and I sat down on her tidy bed. Her warm, kind self at my side, I forced myself not to cry, taking in, instead, deep breaths.

"Oh, Mistress," she said, patting my hand. "Men are worth less than a farthing."

For a second, I felt the small coin in my palm. Were Will or Hugh worth less than that small heft?

"I'm so sorry about Hugh." I smoothed my kirtle with my palms. "I should have minded my own business."

"Had you not told me, I would still be in waiting and hope. It's best to know, Mistress."

"Jessica," I said, breaking social protocol. "Call me Jessica."

We sat for a minute more, the house groaning around us, timbers creaking, fires crackling, doors slamming. Was one of those doors Will's? Did he now know what I did? His wife was arrived from Stratford with their children, ready for him to act the part of family man and father. Maybe even husband.

Anne Shakespeare was a cipher, a literary mystery. Twenty-six when she married Will, she died at 67, seven years after Will. I'd seen their graves during my first tour of Stratford at the Church of the Holy Trinity. I couldn't remember the exact words on her grave, but it was clear her family had loved her. "O mother, milk and life thou didst give me" read part of the inscription.

But her life? Her desires? Unclear. In sonnet 145 (the poem the critical world hated most for its odd use of rhyme), Will wrote: "But when she saw my woeful state,/ Straight in her heart did mercy come." There was love and affection between them as well as the shared grief of a lost child. But the future knew not much more than the location of her family home and the line in a will, Anne the remarkable recipient of Will's second-best bed. Maybe Anne had been married off to Will in a shotgun wedding, pregnant already with Susanna. Maybe she was an accepting partner in a loveless relationship. Maybe she pined for her husband all the while he lived in town. Or maybe she was thrilled to be left alone to raise her children and tend to her garden.

Who was I kidding? Like most people, Anne likely desired love and companionship.

"This situation with Master Shakespeare," I began, but then I stopped. It was wrong for me to make Daisy carry any part of this burden.

But Daisy was Daisy. She squeezed my hand in a moment of feeling and then stood, arranging her apron and smoothing her sleeves. "You need not explain. But I must tend to the kitchen."

"I'll come with you," I said. I'd had a reprieve from the real work of this labor-intensive time. Maybe now, with Anne back in the picture, Will would step away. As Will was the only reason Lord Pembroke was interested in my employ, I needed to learn to do more than scribe.

"Come on, then," Daisy said. "The pies won't bake themselves."

In 2018, pies didn't bake themselves either, but at least I could buy a Mrs. Hempell's Spring Cherry pie in the frozen foods section, thaw it out, and bake it in a 350-degree oven that turned on with a dial. Later, I could eat it from its aluminum pan with a fork over the kitchen sink.

Also, in 2018, meat arrived conveniently in small packages wrapped in cellophane. Milk in cartons. Butter in stick families in rectangle boxes. Vegetables in piles or bags, often "Washed three times!"

As a harried woman trying to get meals on the table, my mother had been a fan of squares of frozen peas and spinach, bags of red tamales from Costco, chips and tubs of salsa from Trader Joe's. Cakes from a box, cookies from a bag, bread ready-sliced and nutrient-free. After she made it through my father's departure and her subsequent depression, she burst with energy, none of it going into the kitchen. Suffice it to say, I gleaned all my cooking abilities from her, and then some, my dinners often frozen yogurt and baby carrot nubs for good measure.

I'd only seen glimpses of Mistress Gumble's kitchen before, but after that night's supper was cooked, delivered, and cleaned up, I never wanted to see that fiery hell again. I should have listened to the housekeeper, Mrs. Bunting, when she said, "Don't dare to learn the kitchen! What will Master Shakespeare say?"

I'd made up a story about needing to know what a kitchen was like for a play he was writing, though Mrs. Bunting only folded her arms over her wide bosom and shook her head.

The spit jack had stolen off back to Yorkshire, and for one-and-a-half hours, I turned the spit with my bare (and later rubbed raw and almost bleeding) hands. Once the rabbits were roasted, I helped poach eels in ale, a god-awful smell that enveloped the kitchen. I felt as though I were flat on the sand under the Santa Cruz Boardwalk with a raging Guinness hangover.

Under Mrs. Bunting's watchful eye, Daisy, Nan, and I made up the trays for every room. Off we went, bread, fish, and meat and a slap of boiled carrots. Pints of ale. I tottered down the first floor to deliver the trays to a Master Dorchester and a Mistress Plum. Daisy took Will's floor, and Nan took the rest. A half-hour later, we sat at the cleared and scrubbed with salt (my idea) kitchen table eating bread and butter until it was time to clear the trays.

"From the chamber, they must have fled, Mistress," Daisy whispered. "Neither the family nor the Master were there. Nan said they left all at once, with baggage."

Nan slogged back a full mug of ale, froth on her slightly crone-haired upper lip. "Off to an inn, I venture." Drinking didn't diminish her hearing. "Not enough space with the bairns. And you lot."

She gave me a look I couldn't ignore.

Scooting back from the table, I walked out into the hall, up the stairs, and pushed carefully into Will's room. It was empty, save for the tray on the table, uneaten. There were no satchels or clothes in the wardrobe. No ribbons or bonnets or stockings. Not even Will's coat or hat.

I sunk onto the mattress, breathing in the lavender Daisy and I had stuffed into the corners. Pirate crawled out from under the bed and meowed so loudly, I gave him the uneaten eels. Within minutes, he was finished and curled up at the bottom of the bed, licking his left paw and cleaning his chops.

My headache bloomed, pulsing at my temples and the base of my skull. It had been a long day: torture at the hands of Lord Pembroke, pain in the kitchen, surprise, and then a swift reality check in this very room. For a few weeks, I'd thought this was where I belonged. Where I lived and breathed and loved. But seeing Anne sitting at Will's desk, his beautiful girls on the bed, and the way they fit into his chamber as if they belonged there—which they did—proved I didn't.

Pirate stood, stretched, and walked toward me, his paws leaving kitty prints in the blanket. His purr roared into the emptiness. I scratched his head, stroked his smooth back from head to tail. Reclining onto the pillow, I closed my eyes against the pain in my body. Outside, the night took over the sky, the room darkening into dream.

Daisy awoke me early, banging on the door. "Hugh's downstairs waiting on you," she yelled through the wood. "I'm not the one to tell him you are inconvenienced."

Confused and slightly dizzy, I turned to look for Will, but in an instant, I saw he'd not come home. Only Pirate was with me, purring in my ear.

In ten minutes, Daisy had brought in a tray. After Pirate and I ate, I opened the window to allow him to the tiny balcony where I'd made him his Elizabethan kitty litter box.

"Madness," Will had groused at my ingenuity. "Cat shitting outside the window with the birds."

"Better than in the corners of the room. Leave the window open!"

Dressed, washed, combed, and smoothed, I rushed down the stairs, tears just behind my eyes, my face flushed with nerves. Not since I'd arrived had I been this alone. Will had either been in the room or close by; we were out together watching people swing from a tree or tread the boards. Even if I went out by myself or with Daisy, I always knew where he was or would be.

At home, I was often alone. Somehow, while being here with Will, I'd forgotten how.

Chapter Fifteen – A Fight, A Fever

Something was wrong. Mr. TABE actually seemed concerned. As I had for weeks now, I stepped off the cart, heading inside, Mr. TABE leading me in his usual stiff fashion, but he looked back at me one or two times, his blank-faced disdain morphed into a furrow of worry.

I was afraid to say anything. If this guy was put off by something and let it show, things were worse than I could imagine. Was it Mary? Had she taken ill? Or worse? My heart raced, and the tears I'd been trying to hold back since the night before started falling down my cheeks. I brushed at them quickly with the back of a hand, sniffing a little, and taking deep breaths despite the pressure from my stomacher.

We reached the drawing room, and Mr. TABE opened it for me. As I walked past, I glanced up at him. His eyes were serious, but he gave me a flick of a smile, a sort of "hang in there" expression. I walked in and scanned the room for Mary, but once again, the only one in the room was Lord Pembroke. As I curtsied, I took in his ensemble. Today, he was in full peacock mode. His doublet and pants were the deepest, shiniest midnight blue. From five feet away, I could almost breathe in the expense. The gold strands and tiny red embroidered diamonds in his puffy sleeves glinted despite the gloom outside the windows. His ruff was well beyond the cervical collar realm. Stiff, blindingly white, and huge, his head should have looked disembodied, but I must have been getting used to the times because he seemed imposing, regal, and formidable.

"My lord," I said.

"Mistress Randall," he said, performing his usual stroll in front of me, passing by me as if on greased wheels.

Standing up straight, my eyes still on the floor, I asked, "Is Lady Mary at home today?"

"She will not be here," Lord Pembroke said. "We shall continue our work together."

Worry thrummed inside me, and I pressed a hand to my stomach, needing more than whalebone to keep everything together. My hands burned from last night's kitchen work, and my heart ached.

"Sit," he said, indicating Lady Mary's desk. I nodded, compliant, and walked toward the desk, readying my writing materials.

"Start with a letter, shall we?" Lord Pembroke moved closer to the desk, so near I breathed in the waft of brand-new leather shoes.

I dipped my quill in the inkpot, my hands trembling. Mr. TABE's stare and nod and Lord Pembroke's assertive clothing had rattled me.

"Dear Will," Lord Pembroke began.

I looked up, hand and quill frozen. "Lord, I might relay a message personally."

"No relaying this message *personally*. Will's and my messages are all going through you." He moved closer, reaching out a finger ringed with a large ruby set in gold. Quickly, he ran it up my neck to my ear and then fanned out his hand to run it in my hair. I jumped, ink splatting.

"My apologies, my lord." I dipped my quill again, scratching out *Dear Will*. Sweat ran in a line down the middle of my back, and I shivered.

"Dear Will," he repeated, pulling away. "It is my dearest hope this letter finds you well. Though I do want to present a difficult subject, one we spoke..." He paused, allowing me to catch up. But I didn't want to, fearing the difficult subject was me. "...of at length. I told you of my strong feelings for a certain relation..."

Lord Pembroke again waited for me. Elbows bent, forehead close to the paper, I focused on the crafting of each letter, praying for something to make

179

him stop. It was time for the California earthquake I'd spent my whole life trying to avoid. Tornado. Cyclone. Tsunami. But no such luck. My heart raced, and I thought I would faint. Not that I knew what that felt like, though since I'd been wearing the damn stomacher, I'd often found myself short of breath. But tiny blobs of crabby light scuttled at the periphery of my vision, and the dizziness I'd awakened with circled my head like a hula-hoop.

"Your *cousin* Jessica." He finished the sentence and walked toward the desk, leaning against the edge closest to my right hand. Again, the slip of his finger, this time on the first knuckle of my index finger. Then the whole finger. My hand. I stuttered the quill across the paper, words jumbling, and sat back, surprised. As I gaped, he lunged forward and grabbed me to standing, his strong fingers gripping me painfully under each arm.

I jerked my head up, gasping at his fury. "My Lord," I panted, unable to breathe. "I'm sorry. Please excuse. I did not intend to make such an error."

His eyes watered, his face reddened, and he squeezed me harder. In that instant, I was back at the Tyburn Tree, men swinging for crimes they'd pay a fine for in my time. Community service. Plea bargains. Lord Pembroke so pleased with himself that the stealers of hawks would die for their crimes. Imagine what a refuser of kisses would get.

Lord Pembroke yanked me close and hard, the closures on my garments straining. His face was at my neck, hands moving down my body, pressing as hard as he could against my belly, first with his hand and then with his body.

"Please," I whispered.

"Of course," he whispered back. "My pleasure."

"No," I said, louder. "No."

But no was not *no* in 1598. Not if you were a sad wretch from the Orkney Isles. Not when you were a woman without means or status. Or even if you were.

"Did you think you could have him?" Lord Pembroke spat as pushed me onto the desk. He held me down with one strong arm, and with another, he slowly lifted my skirts. Running so late, I'd not had time to deal with my farthingale or my bolster, so his job was made easier, all of me accessible. I felt the chill of the room on my ankles, calves, thighs, his hand moving from my foot and ankle. He grabbed one stocking and then another, pushing them down. As he touched my bare skin, I struggled against his grasp, but he had me pinned like a butterfly on a display board, my dress my crumpled wings, broken and spread out around me.

"So soft," he said, spreading my legs with one push, and then two. He positioned himself, both hands now yanking me to his body, which was ready. I saw and then felt him as he leaned over and laughed.

My whole body pounded, my head probably would have fallen off if Lord Pembroke hadn't gabbed my hair in one fist and started tugging at my dress, stomacher, and shift. I closed my eyes, listening to fabric rip, each tear bringing me closer to something I could not stop. I was alone in this. Will—the only person in this world who knew when I was from—had gone back to his family. Had I really believed William Shakespeare loved me?

"He's not yours," Lord Pembroke said, agreeing with my thoughts. "And you are not his."

His hand pushed aside my shift, grabbed one of my breasts, squeezing a nipple so hard I yelped.

"If you want him," I pleaded, my face wet, "why don't you tell him?"

"I cannot," he hissed against my cheek, pressing his body against mine, one hand reaching my inner thigh. "I cannot tell him, and I cannot have him. He cannot be mine."

His breath was hot and horrible, his smell nothing now but anger and need. Knowing I might regret everything I did next—but not wanting to live through what he was going to do—I kicked, battering his calves with my heels, pushed at him with the heels of my hands. I tried to wedge my arms between us, my flails not hits but defensive moves.

"A cat," he laughed, taking my blows as if they were nothing. More fabric ripped, my new clothes shredding as we tussled. The scene was likely ridiculous, me prostrate on the desk, legs kicking. But I was going to be raped. And I had to fight as best I could. There was no pepper spray, no keys situated between my fingers to scratch a would-be attacker, no whistle, and no 911 on speed dial. I'd come to this world unprepared for a man like this.

"Come now, open your eyes," he hissed as he seemed to fumble with his own clothing. "Look at me. See what I'm going to do to you and with what."

Nausea swirled in my stomach and throat, acid burning into my mouth. My face flamed, and I lunged forward, knocking him off balance a bit. He pushed me back, inkpot and papers flying. Then I opened my eyes, staring into his. His gaze was intense, half-crazy, matching the diamond snake eyes in the fabric of his clothing. In his look: anger and hurt. Rage and pain.

"No," I begged, but he wasn't hearing anything, pushing nearer, his skin against my skin. His breath hot and dry on my face.

This thing was going to happen. No more fairytale time travel story. This was about real life and jealousy and anger. Hatred, too.

"Oh, yes," Lord Pembroke said, almost laughing. But then there was a yell, a noise, and I toppled off the desk, falling onto the rug, my hands clutching the thick red fabric. My head felt so heavy, but as I sprawled, I looked up and saw Will grabbing Lord Pembroke by the throat, both grunting with exertion. Will's face was red, his hair wild. He spat as he yelled.

"Lout!" he cried, shaking the lord. "Varlot."

Pembroke—pale-faced, shocked silent, choked by Will and his ruff— fought back, grabbing Will and pulling him forward. Turning on my side, I watched them be as physical as they probably ever had. Will shaking Lord Pembroke, Lord Pembroke yanking him close, closer.

In the corner, Mr. TABE watched them both, holding a heavy porcelain vase in his hands. Who was he intending to use it on?

"How dare you!" Will cried. At that, Lord Pembroke took the advantage, spinning Will and pushing him up against the pianoforte, their bodies churning together.

"Your sweet cousin," the lord said, leaning closer. If I weren't so tired, so exhausted, I was sure I'd see that look in Lord Pembroke's eyes, true love for Will even as they battled. But I could see Will's face. And there was no love there. No tenderness. Not anymore. As he strained against Lord Pembroke, he was looking right at me.

"Yes," Will yelled, pushing him off, backing away. "Mine!"

Lord Pembroke fell back, gave up, sank back on his elbows, and moved away. Mr. TABE put the vase on a nearby table. Will rushed toward me, helped me to my feet, holding me close.

"Are you?" he began.

I wanted to tell him I was okay, but I couldn't seem to talk. Without another word, Will picked me up in his arms and carried me out of the room. My eyes closed, the room seemed to tilt; my body grew weightless, empty, gone.

I woke to the sweat and heat of my own body, a cool cloth on my head, and a slice of sharp pain on my arm.

"No," I whispered, understanding immediately what that sharp pain meant, feeling the razor that had caused it with every throb. I was being bled. Some hack was trying to rid me of ill humors. I tried to move my arm from the source of discomfort, but my body was too heavy.

"Jessica," Will said. "Rest."

There were mumbles around me, sounds of the door opening and closing, and then warmth against my side. The cool cloth on my forehead again.

Despite my efforts, I could not keep my eyes open or move. I wanted to fling off the blankets. I wanted to sit up and cry out for antibiotics and Nyquil. Tamiflu and green tea with honey and lemon. Tylenol, codeine, and Sudafed. What about Vicks Vapor Rub? But all I could do was moan and fall back asleep.

In my dream, I searched for Mistress Meade, running up and down the cobblestone streets, knocking on every door, all of which were red. But the only person who showed up was my mother, shaking her finger, *tsking* me. I hovered and flew over all my mistakes, circling my years with Phillip like a buzzard. Off I was to my work, watching myself in a class alive and happy, my students understanding the flow of the play we were reading but then it was over, and I was in my office alone, the door closed, all my colleagues in the hallway passing me by, not even Dan Gordon stopping to chat because he was too busy.

See, I thought. Look at me screw up.

"Stop," the voice came. "Hush."

Hush? How to hush when I'd come to the place of no return? Literally, I couldn't return to try to fix things. And wouldn't you know, I'd messed up here, too.

"Hush," said the voice, smoothing my hair. "Hush, now. Sleep."

When I finally woke up and opened my eyes, it was dark outside, the room lit up with candles. The air around me was closed in and hot, the fire flickering in the grate. Will sat at his desk, writing. Pirate was at my feet, purring. Feeling me stir, he stretched and began to knead the blanket, his motor revving enough that Will looked over.

He pushed back from the desk and came to the bed, sitting down and putting a hand on my forehead.

"The fever has broken," he said, pouring some water and bringing the mug to my lips. I slurped and sputtered, taking in as much as I could, feeling parched and desiccated, a desert of a person. "Go slowly. There."

Sighing, I lay my head back on the pillow and breathed in. My lungs ached, but not as they had during my restless sleep.

"Don't bleed me," I said.

"The doctor will be in later."

"No more bleeding," I said. "Please."

Will raised his eyebrows. "Bleeding has been found to be of little to no use? Of harm? Vile mayhap?"

I nodded, endeavoring to keep my eyes open so I could take him in, this man who had saved me. Again and again.

"Agreed then," Will said as he stroked my hair, my shoulder.

For a moment, I calmed, but then panic sliced through me. "Not the plague?"

Will smiled. "Nay. Naught but a pallid contagion."

"The influenza?"

Will stared at me, nodded, and put the mug on the chair. "You have been asleep for three days. One in the hard grip of the fever. I did not know—I was greatly afraid. For so many reasons." He pushed his hair back with both hands. "I wasn't too late, was I?"

I turned my head to look at him more clearly, the effort Herculean. "For what?"

"To save you from Lord Pembroke. From..." He stopped. "His attack."

I shook my head against the bedding. "Not too late. But how did you know to come to the castle?"

Will took my hand. "He was the very scoundrel who sent for Anne from Stratford. Bade her come to town with the girls."

"You didn't know?"

"She and I—we have not that relationship. Not for these many years, though she is my good, dear friend. I would not have made either of you suffer from such a surprise introduction, though Daisy tells me you played quite the role as housekeeper."

"Where is she?" I said.

"She left not your side for hours, but she grew fatigued, and I sent her to her chamber. But then with the doctor and Hugh and his cart? Zounds, the situation has changed between our erstwhile lovers. Your emergency has had a tremendous good effect on love."

All but ours, I thought. Mistress Meade had been right about those two. An emergency had done the trick. But what would that wise woman think about me following in my own footsteps, here with a married man, one with two children?

Will put a hand to the side of my face. "When I returned from rehearsal, Anne and I realized the confusion. Though it was boon to see the girls." He paused, smiled. "By the time we found more commodious lodgings, we determined the cause of the mistake. But by that time, it was very late, and the streets were deserted, so I stayed with them and visited. In the morning, I returned here, but the chamber was empty."

I wanted to ask him why he didn't let me know where he was. But it wasn't as though he could have texted me.

"Once Daisy informed me of your location, I knew Lord Pembroke could be up to only ill. Hugh brought me to Baynard's Castle, and that is where I found..."

Will kissed my forehead, grasped my hand. "Oh, that most pernicious villain. I would like to have murdered him. I freed you from Lord Pembroke's grasp, but then you swooned from this great illness. To bed I brought you, and it is where you have been since that terrible altercation."

When I closed my eyes, I saw the hate in Lord Pembroke's eyes. Not for me but for what he wanted. He'd not been used to refusal of any kind. And it wasn't me who had refused him. Will had.

"I saw you fight," I said.

Will nodded. "It is over. I have not had notice from him since. Not from the Castle. Not from Wilton."

Over, I thought. In so many ways.

"We can't keep doing this. Not with Anne—"

"Sweetling, I told her all about you. Not the part about time, of course. But our conversation is the reason the night went so long. She understands my feelings."

"But still, you're married."

"Anne and I have a longstanding relationship. We expect little now of our long-ago love." Will looked down at our clasped hands.

For a moment, I paused, let my eyes close. My body was drained, literally, and light. The phrase *long-ago love* floated in my mind. Maybe I'd not actually had love long ago at all. I'd been clinging to Phillip like a bad raft, one that kept me from drowning but also from shore.

I opened my eyes and looked into Will's dear face, wishing I could move my arm put my palm on his cheek. How I could spend my life with that simple want.

"I've been in the middle of a marriage before. With a man I thought loved me. I believed he would leave his wife and stay with me for the rest of our lives."

"But this is not our case."

"It is," I said. "You are married, but not to me."

"Anne and I need not each other in this way."

I shrugged, settling back on the bed. "Maybe."

"No *may* about it."

"You have two lovely girls and a wife trusted and true. You have a home. A town. A place where you belong. It may not seem like enough. But so much better than a woman who might disappear."

He grasped my hands. "But you are here now, Jessica. At this moment. In my bed."

"But for how long? And isn't it still wrong, even if I'm going to leave?"

"Again, I say it one more time. You are here. No one else. Only you. You who understands all. You who inspires me to write the plays. You have seen me write every evening till the candle burns down! It is you, my muse."

Will stared at me, waiting. I wanted to say more. True, I may have saved him from a string of Jessica hauntings, but I hadn't solved the mystery. Also, I'd made things worse with Lord Pembroke. Who knew if the raping bastard might press assault charges?

Worse, I probably ruined things with Anne. In a few years, when the plague closed down the theaters again, Will was slated to go back to Stratford to live out his days with her. From all accounts, they managed to find comfort with each other those final years. My very presence might have destroyed that option. Instead, he'd be here in London, surrounded by heat, fleas, and festering bodies. Because of me, he would die even earlier than he had.

Despite my early resolve to protect the continuum, I had broken it.

More than anything, I needed to find a way to help him. But the sad fact was if I were to live in this place I didn't belong, I needed to find my own way. A way right and real. By temporal accident or curse, I had been plunked down here, but this life was far from ideal, for either of us. So I had no choice. Divorce was out of the question. And Lord Pembroke's anger so violent, immediate, and spiteful, I needed to back away. Get a job. Scribe, charwoman, or spit jack. Governess, barkeep, or hawker. No matter how much I loved William Shakespeare—and I did—I had to find my own path, no matter how new age that seemed.

I took in his face, his concern, and forced myself to breathe. To pull back. Away.

But there was one thing I could do for certain. After I slept for a very long time, I needed to save Mary Sidney. Save her here and now, and save her later.

Chapter Sixteen—Fixing the Curse, Time-Travel Rule Breaking, and Other Space-Time Considerations

Two weeks later, during my last days of recuperation, finally able to swing my legs over the edge of the bed and stand, I received a note from Lady Mary Sidney, asking me to resume our work together.

My Dear Jessica,

I am returned to Baynard's Castle, my cousin William off to Wilton for an extended time. My play needs the help only you can supply. Pray, do come tomorrow. I will send the coach.

Your pupil,

Lady Mary Sidney

After reading the letter, I turned to Will to ask his opinion. But he was bent over his desk, scratching away, immersed in his own work, which had taken up more and more of his time since my fever broke.

And we weren't talking much, though things had leveled out after our fight two nights ago. Will had staggered home from The Bull after a meeting with his business partners, smelling of rum and full of desire.

He'd crept on the bed, kissing my temple, and I'd shifted away from his embrace, despite wanting nothing more than to lean into it. Upset, he then commenced with the throwing of plates and mugs and general all-around yelling (his), enough that the downstairs neighbor had begun his ritual ceiling thumping.

"This makes no sense but nonsense," Will cried.

But before and since that fight, he'd been tender and a good nurse, spoon-feeding me and then sitting on the edge of the bed as my appetite increased, and I tore into the pasties Daisy brought from the market.

"Sweetling?" he'd ask as I lay back on the pillows.

Despite my urge to reach out to him, the continuum I'd disregarded, stomped on, and broken caught me up short. All I could see was Will in London, staying too long, leaving too late, his life diminished because of me. I saw the heaps of dead, Will sick with the plague.

But sometimes I forgot, too. One night I'd turned to him, holding him as I had before my illness. He felt wonderful, his soft breath lovely near my cheek.

He asked, "Jess, have you changed your mind?"

"If only I could," I said into the space between us that only grew. From that night onward, we'd pulled back from each other, wrapped our hearts up in protective gauze, and moved on. At night, Pirate purred and kneaded my back, his kitty warmth a true but poor substitute. I'd asked for this separation. But it felt like a mistake in my heart, head, and body.

At least Will had his vocation. I needed to get back to mine. So, I needed to get out of bed and into the bath. When next Daisy came in, I bade her bring hot water, Will nodding at me from the desk.

"It will do you good to get out-of-doors," he said.

Backlit, the sun shining through the window, his hair gleamed.

I pushed off the blankets, my feet on the clean straw, Pirate at my side purring. My legs were pale and thin, but stronger. When the fever broke, I had asked Daisy to bring me beefsteaks, spinach, and dried fruit, all rich in iron. I ate like a bear. Now I was finally ready to stop hibernating.

The next day as the coach pulled up in front of the castle and I stepped out onto the drive, I waited for a wave of fear to knock me down. But all I felt was thankful. My noisy rescue from the castle had lit a tiny flame of scandal, and

Lord Pembroke had removed himself most elegantly to Wilton in Salisbury. In his absence, Lady Mary had returned with an elder brother from her family home, Penshurst, and was ready to finish her play. And when Mr. TABE gave me a full smile and a true bow, I curtsied in return and followed him down the familiar hallway. When he opened the door, Mary ran toward me, and I thought it was possible she would throw her arms around my neck, just as Shelby would have, jumping up and down as she did, eager to fill me in about her day. But in the nick of time, Mary's rank and position took over, and she stopped, smoothed her skirt, though nothing could take away her bright, broad smile.

"To your play?" I said in my professor voice. "Much for both of us to do."

After an hour of catching up on the events of her trip home and her characters' escapades, Mary and I began writing, the story spreading down the page in my getting-better scrawl, the last scene in our sites. While recuperating in bed, I had spent most of my free time practicing my handwriting, enough so that after perusing my work, Will said, "Now for certain you can find a true vocation."

We had stared at each other, and in our sadness, I saw my own little rooms, my drab clothing, my rickety furniture, my empty bed.

"Jessica," Mary asked, once the last word was placed in the last bit of dialogue.

I blew on the last page of her play and sprinkled the words with pounce, the ink drying as I watched. "Yes?"

"Tell me true. You are not from the Orkney Isles."

I put the perfect, crackly page into the folder, blew one more time on the final word, and closed the cover. In less than three months, she'd completed a final draft of a play that had started with a witch and a unicorn, and that had become a treatise on the lot of girls, even wealthy, rich, pampered ones. There was a tribe of girls in the forest, refusing to return to civilization. Mary's characters stayed in the fairytale rather than return home. The witch was now their teacher. The unicorn their passage home, should they need it. But none of them ever would. A reverse *Peter Pan* and not as creepy. One day, I hoped, should I ever return to my life, I would find Lady Mary Sidney's juvenilia.

She would have saved herself.

"No, I'm not from the Orkney Isles," I said, using my unadulterated 2018 voice. "Not at all."

She stared at me, her eyes wide and waiting.

"You won't believe where if I told you."

Mary crossed her arms and sat back in her chair. I could hear her shoe click against the chair rail. "You are different from most women of my acquaintance. At first, I imagined it was simply birth. You have a certain lightness about things as if I should have no worry about my stories. My desired occupation. And your language. Many strange pronouncements," she said. "There have been English words unknown to me. Or to anyone, save Master Shakespeare who understands you well."

"He does," I said. "We understand each other very well."

"Why is that?" she asked.

"I'm not really certain," I said. "But from the moment of my arrival, he understood most of what I said."

I pictured him as he'd been the night before, clinging to the far corner of the bed, lest he touch me. Soon, once I found my bearings, he'd make for Stratford and Anne and his daughters. I was going to find my own lodgings and ask Lady Mary for a referral.

We were on opposite shores of the River Trust. No unicorn to save us.

"To me, he is a genius. My cousin has no idea of Master Shakespeare's skill, I think, though he does ply the theater with money."

"To be fair, "I said, though I wasn't sure why I needed to say this. "He did appreciate Will's plays. Defended them, actually. There are parts of Will's work I don't like much. But their relationship is not just the money."

Mary nodded. "Lord Pembroke plays with Master Shakespeare's affections."

Shocked, I looked up. This eleven-year-old girl was spot on about so much. Her eyes were full of the truth about her cousin and Will. Her cousin and his flirtation with me. With me and my otherworldly diction and syntax.

"I chanced upon Will during a hard time in his life. His son's death, which he doesn't talk about much. His work for your aunt—"

"Pray, what work was that?" Mary asked.

I swallowed, wishing I'd not opened that dark drawer, but Mary's eyes were on me. And wasn't this information that might help her move past him? "Your aunt wished Lord Pembroke to marry a particular lady and hoped Will could write a few poems to convince him to do so. The plan didn't go as she'd hoped."

Mary stared at me and then seemed to understand. "When I arrived," I went on, "Will was busy writing the sonnets but also with the big plan to move from The Theater to The Globe. He was a wreck, and—"

She nodded, expectant, patient, hands folded on her lap, waiting. Of all the people other than Will that I'd met since turning up here—Daisy, Hugh, Will's theater friends, parish locals, the Baynard's Castle folk—this little girl seemed the right person to tell the truth.

"I've been here for three months, going on four. I showed up one evening in William Shakespeare's chambers. Unannounced." I looked up toward the door, expecting to see it crack open, maidservant, Mr. TABE, or Lord Pembroke there eavesdropping. But we were alone. "I came from the future. Poof! Like magic."

As I said the words, I half expected her to call out for Mr. TABE, who—a vase at the ready—would be instructed to cart me away to Bedlam, a fine and deranged place, where the mentally ill of this century lived in squalor and hopelessness. Once there, I assumed my shot at transporting out of 1598 would be doomed, all the clues and hints and hopes outside the locked cell, doors, walls.

My insides gripped themselves. My hands white as I held onto the desk as if I were sinking. It was possible, too, my heart had stopped beating.

"You were always something forward," Mary said finally. "But how much in the future? Pray, what year came you from?"

One tense fiber at a time, tiny muscles in my stomach relaxed. "2018."

At that, Mary jumped a little, blinking, her mouth open slightly. "Over four hundred years! And do you live in England? Or mayhap France? You oft seem a little French."

In this, I did not sense a compliment.

"Farther than you can imagine, my lady. The world in 2018 is a bigger place."

"The Indies," she whispered.

"Of sorts."

"So many years from now," Mary said, her words filled with wonder.

"In a certain light, I am a very old woman." The burden of time was draped on my shoulders, heavy as I learned the new old ways.

Mary seemed unable to conjure another question. She watched me, pulling unconsciously on a long lock of hair, twirling it around two fingers. Then she tucked it behind her ear and blinked at me, her mouth open.

"Zounds," she said finally. "Never in all my imaginings could I have dreamt such."

"Pardon me, my lady, but you've been writing about a witch and all her magic. Not to mention the unicorn. Time travel isn't far removed."

She giggled suddenly, her face turning, as it sometimes did, back into pure child. "But such magic never happens!"

"As far as we know," I said. "Though enough women will be hanged for such."

Her giggling stopped, and she contemplated me further.

"You are not mad." She paused. "Also, you are not a witch."

"Thank you, my lady."

"So how do you believe you shall return home?"

Outside the window, two crows cawed from their turret perch. The sky was blustery with cloud and wind, their black wings moving. I shook my head. "I don't know. I've been trying to figure it out."

"Do you love your time more than this one?"

A sigh as big as an air balloon filled my chest. Parts of this time were the best of all my life. But I did not belong, and I had so many things to finish where I started.

"I've known such joy here. Much of that joy has been here, working with you."

Mary looked down, not able to hide her smile.

"But my time is where I live. It's *when* I live," I said simply. "I have pupils there, too. A vocation I've not really figured out but one I love. Family. Friends." For a second, Dan Gordon flickered in my mind. "I cannot fully fit in here."

"You know not how you arrived?"

I shook my head. "There is one clue."

"Pray, tell!"

"I am not the first to haunt Master Shakespeare. Every night for months before I arrived, various Jessicas from all around the world and all through time haunted him. Specters, nightly, two, three. All named Jessica. Then I showed up. And stayed. Then no more Jessicas."

Mary brought a finger to her lips. "Your name Jessica. It's from *The Merchant of Venice*? My cousin brought me to that entertainment. Jessica is the Jew's daughter."

I cringed, despite myself.

"Say I something ill?"

"In my time, Mary, we don't call people Jews. I mean, they are Jews. But we say Jewish. And in my time, Will's depiction of Shylock isn't seen as funny. But negative. Cause for riot and protest. When the play is performed in my time, one must always explain Will's treatment of Shylock."

Mary shook her head, smiling. "Performed still? Hundreds of years hence?"

"You wouldn't believe it. He's a rock star—well, Will is truly famous."

"Despite this ill-treatment of the Jewish people?"

I nodded, not really wanting to get into *Othello* or *Titus Andronicus* and Will's "black" characters. It might be too much for Mary, but she was treating the subject of my time travel with no more fanfare than she might a trip to Cheapside.

"What if you but changed the play? All the untoward and unsavory parts?"

I flashed to the scene I'd practiced my writing with so many weeks ago, turning Portia's sentence of Shylock toward kindness and redemption. "I've wanted to do just that. Some revision would make it more performable in my time—"

"Nay," she said, leaning forward, her eyes alight. "Not for performance's sake. Not for entertainment. Not for the Jewish people. But to undo the spell, reverse the curse, and return you home. As in my play. You remember the scene. When the girls rip up the list of their names? They become Tree, Earth, Sky instead. Their true selves in the place they belong. Where they should live."

I lessened my grip on the desk, leaned back against my chair, stared at my pupil's earnest face. I'd taken to reworking *Merchant* during my practice with the quill, but what with Will and Lord Pembroke and his detonations in my life, I'd forgotten that work of so many weeks ago. There were many more spots to focus on, but I could rewrite them all.

"You think I might reverse the curse and return to my life?" I asked, mostly to the air.

"Mayhap," Mary said. "Master Shakespeare created the name. Jessica is the creature most important to Shylock. Her repeated visitations to Master Shakespeare is the punishment. Rework the sections most appalling, and your life may belong to you once again."

"Couldn't hurt to fix the play, even if I do stay here," I said. "For posterity."

Mary watched me evenly, though her lower lip trembled a little. "I would be loath to see you away, Jessica Randall. You have been my best friend and true confidant. You have shown me ways to write I could not have pulled from the air or my own thoughts. And if it does not work—if it is here and now you are to remain—you will stay my friend, and we shall write anon and anon."

She stood and walked to the bookcase behind her desk and pulled out another leather folder, this one fat with pages.

"Here I have several plays by Master Shakespeare," she said. "Let us find what needs alteration. And Jessica?"

I gazed as this girl, so big in hopes and enormous in passion. "Yes?"

"More than any other," she said, looking up at me with those intelligent eyes, "you have been most important to my heart."

I nodded because I couldn't do more. Inside me, water and feeling. Relief and sadness. Hope, even, though none of my thoughts or ill-formed prayers had worked up to this point. The prayers to leave, the prayers to stay. Maybe this would work.

Later, on my way out, I followed behind Mr. TABE as usual. But this time at the door, he turned to me, looking me in the eye, and smiled. "Many thanks for giving your gifts to wee Lady Mary," he said, his voice with a sudden Highland lilt. I startled.

"You are most welcome," I said. "She is extraordinary."

I paused, remembering his look—his warning—to me the day of Lord Pembroke's attack as well Will's account of how the steward raced him to the drawing room.

"I don't know your real name," I said.

He nodded, bowed a little. "Donald McDonald," Donald said. "The family calls me things other."

So did I, I thought, reaching out for his hand and squeezing. "Thank you for everything, Mr. McDonald."

On the way back to Will's, the sun still hanging full in the sky, I suddenly called up to Lord Pembroke's coach driver.

"I need to stop!" I cried.

"Huh?" He held onto the reins and his hat.

"Stop!" I cried.

So instead of dropping me off in front of Will's, he left me in front of the milk and fish stalls at Cheapside. The market was mostly closed, the best of the fresh long gone, the air a waft of old fish, stale bread, and sour milk. Even the perfume and soap shoppers had gone home to fill up their drawing rooms with the scent of lavender, rose, and clove.

I waved to the driver, who nodded, and then I tried to retrace Daisy's and my steps of months ago. Where had we gone? What had we purchased? Pulling my shawl around my shoulders, I walked between the stalls, noting where we had bought the pasties. There, the barrel we sat on as she griped about Hugh and his lack of attention. There, the actual Charing Cross. I walked on, turned right. Another turn, and there! The path leading to the tunnel that opened up into the small neat courtyard. Walking on through the second passage, I tottered on cobblestones till I found Mistress Meade's small reddish door.

Standing in front of it, my hand raised and in a fist, I wondered what I would ask her. Did she know the answer to the question I couldn't even formulate? Closing my eyes, my shoulders slumping, I lowered my fist. When I first got here, I believed I was living in a dream, a confusing one. Then the dream turned happy. And then, my life here became my life. I lived it. Living, working, loving, waking up in the morning knowing what I needed to do, and doing it. Loving the day and the man I came home to.

Hadn't I figured out how to live fully? And if I'd done that, couldn't I live everywhere? Anywhere? Regardless of my relationship to Will, no matter what would happen next time wise, hadn't I fixed my broken part in both timelines? Hadn't I been taught and taught better myself? Wasn't I now a person who could love, despite all, and be loved in return? Didn't my relationship with Phillip seem like an old postcard, words faded, thoughts barely legible?

But what or Will and me? I wasn't sure what to think about us, here or in 2018. What had happened between us wouldn't stand between me and happiness, with him or without him. No matter what, I would never, ever be without him.

All around me, the air had started to cool, the alley a whisk of cold air, rooftops casting shadows, the sun soon to set. I had to set off walking, or I'd end up hiring a cart.

I straightened my hat, adjusted my shawl, and took in a breath. Whatever would happen next, I could take it.

The door opened with a whoosh. I stepped back, gasped. There was Mistress Meade, smooth-headed, clear-eyed, white-toothed.

"Soup?" she asked.

I would swear she winked.

Later, at her table, she placed before me a steaming bowl of the same soup she'd served Daisy and me. But if it were possible, this batch tasted even better, the taste perfect on my tongue. Perfect temperature, perfect seasonings.

"What did you mean about taking it home?" I asked her as I blew on my second spoonful. "How can I take anything home from here? Aren't there rules and regulations?"

Mistress Meade leaned a bony elbow on her table, put her face in her hand. "There is part of this life you need at home, most like. Something you want to save?"

I sipped the soup, the taste loosening me, lightening me. "Maybe."

"Perhaps, then, you can find a way to tuck it into safety."

I ate another spoonful, the room warm and safe. "Maybe," I said, wondering what from this time I could hide away. But then as I took spoonful after spoonful, I forgot the most important questions. The ones about her, such as how the hell did she get here and back? Or stay here and not go back? More importantly, I needed to know if the crafty plan Lady Mary and I concocted had a chance of working.

But instead and without volition, I drifted into the food coma Daisy fell into. I tried to find my thoughts, but all I thought was carrot, celery, chicken, garlic, salt.

One thing I remembered, mostly later. A lot later. At some point between finishing the soup and standing outside her door alone, getting my bearings, Mistress Meade had said, "You have it all now."

Whatever that meant.

At least, that's what I thought then.

An hour later, a cart diver dropped me off in front of Will's. Pleasantly full of Mistress Meade's wonderful soup, I strolled up the stairs, opened Will's chamber door, and found Daisy bent near the fireplace, a pile of papers in front of her. Burning on the grate were well and oft written upon papers, used for drafting and scrap. And in her hand, the folder of sonnets more familiar than I cared to admit.

"No!" I said, rushing in and grabbing them from her. "What are you doing?"

Taken aback and distressed, Daisy stood, her face down. Suddenly, I was no longer her pal upstairs but Mistress Randall. Mistress, at least.

"Master bade me burn the paper. He said toss it all in."

I clutched the folder hard. Of course, he could ask Daisy to do so. She couldn't read, and she would hardly glance at the sensual words he'd written about Lord Pembroke.

"Did he tell you why?"

"To but clean the room," she said. "Told me you had an unearthly need for order."

"Burn away," I said. "But Daisy, do not tell Master Shakespeare about this folder. I will get rid of it myself." I paused. "I'm sorry I was rushed and harsh. You simply surprised me."

She shrugged a little, uncomfortable, our boundaries all crossed up, and I backed out of the room and headed down the steps. Out on the street, I turned toward the church and hurried onward, hoping to get there before dark.

Will wanted the poems gone now that his "madness" had disappeared. But if Mary's plan worked, the spell that held me in place would be broken. Of course, the plan could be as much fiction as Mary's play, but it seemed more purposeful than jumping into a closet and hoping to disappear. In any case, these poems could not be destroyed. Someone had to care-take Will's legacy.

The sun had gone down by the time I got to the church and pushed through the large front doors. Huge yellow tapers were lit in the nave and what used to be the nun's choir, the ceiling illumined and brilliant. I slipped along a side wall, toward the chancel, searching as I went. Where to hide the poems? In all my past touristy moments in London, I'd spent hours in old churches, creeping around and about, from bell towers to sub-basements. It was in the very bottom levels most archeological excavation occurred, all those crypts and hidden burials. Also, when there were storms and floods, those floors were most at risk. So where?

Mr. Beadle was nowhere to be seen, so I slipped through and beyond the chancel, and crept down the small staircase at the back, feeling for a loose stone as I carefully headed down, step by step. What about a surprise and unused cubby, a dark, dusty corner, a window never used, the casement a perfect place to tuck a folder? Nothing. I headed down a hall, discovering a small room with a bench and a candle. I ran my hands along the walls. No loose stones. Too easy. I slid my feet over the pavers, all firm and sure. But then, in the corner, a gap above the floor. I put down the folder, lay on my stomach, and pulled, yanking on a stone, starting to sweat, and it slid out. Pressing myself as flat and long as possible, I stretched my arm as far as I could reach. If I rolled up the folder, there was space enough.

As I had told Will on our first walk the night we went to The Bull, the church would survive the fire of 1666. All the wars. The bombings. The transformation from stone to sweeping metal and glass architecture. This room was directly under the Lady Chapel, so it wasn't going anywhere. At least, I hoped it wasn't. I took my arm out of the hole and picked up the folder. Here I was, hiding Shakespeare's erotic love poems in a church. Tucking them away on the off chance magic would strike twice, and they would survive time and time travel. Maybe this is what Mistress Meade meant. By hiding the poems here in the past, I was taking them home to the future. Maybe this was the *it* that I had *now*.

Above me, there was a footstep, something clunking on the ceiling above. My mouth dry with dust and fear, I sat up and rolled the folder as tight as I could. Almost panting, I reached down and shoved hard with all my might until I felt the dense manuscript hit the back of the wall. With as much precision as the darkness allowed, I placed the stone into its original spot, sweeping the loosened mortar into the corners with my hands.

The noise above louder, I stood, brushed my dress, smoothed my hair, and prepared yet another story for when I ran into Mr. Beadle. I needed forgiveness, information, directions.

But the poems were safe.

Chapter Seventeen – The Portia Thing and That Pound of Flesh

Will slipped into the room long after Daisy cleared away the supper tray, though she'd left a pasty for him wrapped in a cloth. Since Hugh had gone to Kent to break it off with poor Alice, Daisy was in a baking frenzy, pastries and pies at every meal, her smiles as sweet as her confections.

I was wearing my shift, a blanket wrapped around my shoulders, writing by the light of a candle on the desk and the small fire blazing in the fireplace. Pirate was curled in my lap, rats in the corners laughing. I'd pulled out the work I'd done on *Merchant* weeks earlier and was studying the rest of the play. Mary's words burned in my chest. And they had been my words, really, the very ones I'd given to her about her own play. Maybe all along, I'd known this was the way out, the path I'd wanted to find and avoid in equal measure. But like the Robert Frost line I'd quoted Will before, the best way out is always through.

I pushed back from the desk and walked toward him. He avoided my gaze and didn't respond to my "Hello." Throwing his hat and coat on the bed, he moved toward the table, picking up an empty mug and then putting it down.

"Will," I said, my voice loud, a tread of urgency even I noted. I took a breath. "I'm sorry."

He turned to me, his eyes shiny and flickering in the candlelight. "There is nothing for you to be sorry for. We are too much a torment for one another."

"That's not true," I said. "When I was sick, I realized my being here could do much more harm than good. There was Anne and your girls to think of. But the timeline I know about—I can't ignore it. I can't tell you too much, but I know things that make it very important for me to go home."

"But you declared you were not the judge of the continuum nor the mistress of the fathomless rules."

"I'm neither. It's just something I know. I wish I didn't."

With one quick, familiar move, Will pulled me onto his lap, kissing my temple, my hair, my cheek, his arms tight around me.

"So, what are we to do with all of this?"

This was us. The time. The wrongness despite all the rightness.

"I know what to do," I whispered as I turned my face to kiss him once, twice. He smelled like beer and smoke and his own wonderful good self. "We have no choice. We have to write our way out."

Hours later, the candle burned to a stub, another in its place, we'd gone through my earlier attempts, and now we were back at the trial, Shylock imagining he was winning. In his mind, he was about to be given permission to cut out Antonio's beating heart.

"So harsh," I said.

"It's the law," Will said, his voice monotone as he scratched out the new beginnings of the scene. "And pray, the man had his chance. The Duke gives him the answer to all his troubles. He could have made the right choice."

Will took the page from me, reading:

"Shylock, the world thinks, and I think so too,

That thou but leadest this fashion of thy malice

To the last hour of act, and then '''tis thought

Thou'lt show thy mercy...

We all expect a gentle answer, Jew!—"

"Right choice? Gentle answer? What are they expecting?" I interrupted. "He lent money no one repaid. His daughter's gone, aided and abetted by those known to Bassanio and Antonio. At that moment, Shylock is in the right, emotionally and legally. Why would he listen? He wants what they all would."

Will shot me a glance and then scanned the page. "Mayhap Shylock's answer is too elaborate. He needs not all the reasons to simply say he wants repayment of his bond."

"This is a little more than *elaborate*. Offensive, more like. What about the gaping pig part? Twice?"

Will ran a hand through his hair, which was almost standing upright at this point. "I see your point."

On the fresh sheet of paper, Will began to rework the passages. I scanned Act IV, scene i once again. Though Sherry Maita had cast a shy Shylock, a man barely able to project his lines, in some productions I'd attended, Shylock was a pacing, slavering madman. Or a whiny, fretful annoyance. Often, part of the audience stood up and walked out, some even slamming theater doors. Sometimes, before the performance, protests, outcry, interviews on local stations about anti-Semitism and plain bad taste. But no matter the label, how horrible to watch Shylock's desire at any cost to make Antonio pay—not just for the forfeited bond but Antonio's Christian privilege—and then Shylock's complete undoing by the very privilege he sought to shatter.

As Will wrote on, I smoothed his hair, letting my fingers linger on the long strands, his fine high forehead. Maybe all this would soon be over. Despite being in the past, the weeks had been outside time, far-flung from real life. In some of his plays, Will pulled the entire cast into the wild forest and let them frolic and play. Perhaps these months had been my wild rumpus. But maybe my revels now had ended.

Will threw down his quill, the end spitting out a fan of black. "How to change what cannot be rearranged?"

"Portia," I said, sitting up straight.

"She's my judge."

"She's a woman pretending to be a man pretending to be a judge. She's faking everything."

"Mayhap she's angry at her long-absent father."

"Who isn't! She's hurting everyone because of him. But is she really so shallow she can't see past that? She has not one shred of mercy for Shylock, even though she is the one who says, 'The quality of mercy is not strain'd.' She's too smart. Too cruel. She taunts him, knowing full well why he can't kill Antonio. 'Why doth the Jew pause? Take thy forfeiture.' And then once he's lost his entire estate, Antonio swoops in and says not only will Shylock lose everything, he will 'presently become a Christian.' Wow. Shylock has lost his daughter Jessica, his money, his reputation, and his religion. And all he did, Will—all he really did—was agree to loan money to a man who was rude to him. Who spat on him. On his gabardine."

Will slumped at the desk, his head in his hands. "I cannot write more."

He put his head down on the desk, and in a moment, I saw his sleeping breath, clear and even. I picked up the pages, reading Shylock fall for Portia's perfect plan, her agile mind twisting Shylock up and then capturing him. Where was the comic "Jew" that Will spoke of? The clown with his hooked nose and red wig?

But it wasn't just Shylock who suffered. There was Antonio, in love with Bassanio, ready to give his life for the wedded bliss of his beloved.

At that thought, air punched out of my body as if I'd been hit by a flung fist. *Giving his life for the wedded bliss of his beloved.*

As Shylock was ready to cut his heart from his chest, Antonio gave in and up. All for Bassanio. He may have been close to death, but he wanted his love carried on.

"...Commend me to your honorable wife,
Tell her the process of Antonio's end,
Say how I lov'd you, speak me fair in death;
And when the tale is told, bid her be judge
Whether Bassanio had not once a love.
Repent but you that you shall lose your friend,
And he repents not that he pays your debt;

206

For if the Jew do cut but deep enough,

I'll pay it instantly with all my heart."

These lines were written when Lord Pembroke's family was pushing the lord to marry and marry well. Ironically, Lord Pembroke had talked up the talented playwright, his mother grasping at straws and paying Will to convince her son with witty, soulful poems that extolled the virtues of love, connection, family. Will, grief-stricken and desolate, had fallen into the job and fallen in love. A few sonnets that bloomed into a love never fully reciprocated. Will may as well have had his heart cut out of his body, that aching terrible pound of flesh.

Shylock wasn't who Will was trying to flay with his words. The court scene had nothing to do with being Jewish. It was the marriage, and not Bassanio and Portia's, but Lord Pembroke's. After trying to convince Lord Pembroke to marry and falling in love with him instead, Will, like Antonio, looked out at the deadened world to say, "In sooth, I know not why I am so sad;/ It wearies me."

My poor Will. As he wrote these words, he was thinking of Lord Pembroke and trying so hard not to think of Hamnet. Like Antonio, Will let go, gave Lord Pembroke up. But unlike Antonio, Will had his heart ripped out, blood and all.

"Will," I whispered.

"Yes?" he mumbled.

"We change but Portia's treatment of Shylock now, and all is well. She shows mercy more than kind."

He sat up, pulled me onto his lap, held me tight. "That's all?"

"That's all."

"But then you will leave me."

"Who knows if it will work," I said.

"But should it, I will be here bereft," he said. "Without you. Alone."

"Never alone. With your friends and family and work. Your writing. The Globe."

"But not you," he said. "Your true life is elsewhere. And not with me."

"Not in this way," I said, knowing that who awaited me at home was Will. But only in books.

"Shall you remember me in the flesh and blood?" He held my face between his hands, kissed my chin, my jaw, my ear. "Oh, pray, tell me our time will be a dream but more like life than life! Let this time be the center and not the ending, my sweet."

I stared into his eyes, the gaze from countless portraits. On hundreds of textbooks, playbills, and handouts. His was the face that held all the imagination in the world. But this candlelit and particular gaze was mine. His heat, his strong grip, his lips. Not for Lord Pembroke or Anne Hathaway or his children. Not his audience, fans, or friends. Me. How could I ever forget?

This magic had to work. We would end the curse, and I would go back to my time. He would go home to live with Anne and be safe. This one last night but a memory for us both. Wrong, maybe. Immoral, perhaps. Thoughtless at the very least. But I wanted this one last time with my dear Will.

"Remember you?" I said as he stood, paper and quill tipping off the desk and spilling to the floor. He cradled me in his arms and carried me to the bed. "I will remember you. I will remember everything."

What we forgot in the morning was to wake up. The sun streaming in, the still unfinished revision scattered on the desk and floor, Will and I came to consciousness in time to eat, feed Pirate, scribble out the last of Portia's new language, and then rush off to The Theater. There was no time to even think of the magic we hoped to conjure. The play was the thing, the company in the last days of the *Richard II* production, and I'd promised to help sew together the tatters of their costumes. Richard Burbage's Richard was threadbare and torn, and even triumphant Henry Bullingbrook was looking less kingly with every performance.

"Mayhap you can sew a kiss into the rear of my fabric," Richard whispered in my ear. "And then more?"

"Fie on you, sir," I said, swatting his shoulder with a handy crown. "If you don't cease, I'll sew a kick in the pants into your every article of clothing."

Richard snorted and feigned irritation, and Will laughed, giving me a look so dear I almost dropped my mending. His eyes, warm and dark, took me in, reflecting back our night of love. But then the actor who played Sir Pierce Exton, the man who kills King Richard, came in to ask a question. Will turned from me, his focus on the play and the conundrum of swordplay. Neck or chest? Chest this time. A quick decisive stab. Much neater.

Oh, the theater. I made two additional stitches and handed Richard his mended costume. Then I helped with others, passing out cloaks and hats and capes. Next with props, swords, candles, and chains. I ran back and forth backstage, not seeing Will but hearing his direction through every scene.

Near the end of the play, I was barely able to stay awake. We'd worked through lunch, not taking any breaks, so during Act V, scene vi, I sat on a pile of burlap sacks, listening to the bloody end. As at the start of my visit, I was back to executions. Not even kings, earls, or dukes were safe, Northumberland telling the new King Henry, "I have to London sent the heads of Salisbury, Spencer, Blunt, and Kent."

Ouch.

The story's end crashed over me, King Henry mourning his cousin Richard even as he takes the crown as his own. Hypocrite. How could he possibly be half the king Richard was? How could he be replaced? Ridiculous, I laughed to myself, snuggling into the burlap. The backstage grew warm, and the voices of the players wrapped around me. I felt the heat of Will's bed, the comfort of his arms, Pirate's roaring purr between us. I rocked between sleep and consciousness, floating above the action but in it. I heard Will's question from the night before: "Will you remember me in the flesh and blood?"

I floated higher and higher, the sounds of the play far away.

Chapter Eighteen – Parting is Such Sweet Sorrow

"What took you so long to answer?" Kate said.

"I did answer," I mumbled. Something wet slopped across my face. Horatio. Horatio! I grabbed him toward me, smelling his just-groomed fur. He licked my face in his special "time-to-eat-now-or-die" way. I closed my eyes against his rough tongue, breathing in the distinctive smell of his groomer's green tea doggie shampoo.

"Why didn't the voicemail pick up? Why didn't you answer any of my texts?"

I turned on my back and blinked into the brilliant white of my room. My room. My bed. Home. Home!

Bolting upright, eyes wide, breath gone, I looked around. I was here in my bedroom, with my dog, without my lover or my cat.

"When are we?" I almost shouted into the phone.

"Jess, you need to stop drinking while you grade papers."

"I'm serious!" I jumped out of bed and ran around in ridiculous circles as if searching for a spot in the room that made sense. But none did. How could I suddenly be back as if I'd never left at all? I pressed the phone against my ear and slumped into the chair at my desk. Horatio rubbed his head against my thigh, licking my knee to remind me once again about breakfast.

"It's today. October 19th. Friday. You know, Fri-day. The day we usually have breakfast together."

My computer whirred on from hibernation, the email alert dinging. The date (yes, October 19th), the weather (sunny but cool), the exact time (10:15 am). This was the day I should have awakened months ago. No time had passed in 2018 but a normal night's sleep. Nothing. There were my students' essays. I'd graded some of them, but at this point, I didn't even remember what I'd asked them to write about.

"Jess!" Kate called into my ear. "Are you there?"

"I'm here," I said. "I'm totally here. Back here."

Kate sighed loudly enough for me to hear through the phone. "Do I need to come over there or anything? Don't make me call Mom."

"Sorry. I overslept."

By three months.

"I'll say. You missed breakfast with Shelby and me. We gave up. She was worried sick. I dropped her off at school and then went to work."

A plan I'd made months ago flashed through my mind. My sister, my niece, coffee, early, at Big Stack. But I'd been with Will. And now I was in a century he'd never seen, in a world where he was no longer alive.

I sat back in my chair, pressing the phone against my ear, my eyes closed. Horatio put his warm snout on my leg, and I put a hand on his head, stroking his fur. Waves of sadness I'd known to expect washed through me like high, relentless tides. I'd loved Will my whole life, and he'd been gone then, too. But I hadn't known him in the true and honest flesh. Loved him. Learned his secrets. Told him mine.

"Are you still there?" Kate asked.

"Go on."

My sister began her updates, first about my niece: Shelby's new, very hot soccer coach, her project on the Revolutionary War, and the pink-and-green streaks in her long golden hair (a surprise to Kate). Then Kate talked about work and the little black dress she'd bought for half price online. Free shipping. After some more chitchat, I heard myself making breakfast plans for the next week. Finally, we hung up, and I bent over, crying onto my knees. Maybe all of that had been a dream, I thought, sobbing, Horatio on high lick alert at my distress. Maybe the months of learning to live in 1598 had been a confabulation, just as Will and I had both believed when I first apparated into his world.

But as I wiped my eyes, sniffling, I remembered, as I promised him I would. How he called me sweetling.

How he looked at me when he rolled over in bed, his dark-brown eyes on mine.

Rumbling in the cart everywhere, Will at my side, Hugh's smile beaming on us.

Will's yell as he burst into the room at Baynard's Castle to save me.

Will holding Pirate up at the doorway.

The countless baths, soap on his back.

Combing out his hair.

His teasing Daisy about her baking frenzy.

The theater, *Richard II* in full swing, Will at my side.

Will's words, all of them, even the unfinished poems.

Eating at the table, talking about stories.

His heart-wrenching admission about Lord Pembroke.

The night he told me about Hamnet, his grief so deep.

His laugh. His smile. His sorrow.

His body. His body. His body.

Taking in a deep breath, I opened a new document and wrote everything I could. Fast. No commas. No periods. Just stream of consciousness one hundred percent Will, until Horatio couldn't take it one more second, and I had two pages of what had happened to me. Perhaps that will be all that remains, I thought, as I put on my robe, opened the door to my small patio and lawn, Horatio racing out to do his business. As I waited at the doorjamb, I realized nothing had changed. Not even after all those weeks in the dead center of what I'd studied my entire adult life. As usual, words would be all I had left.

But seconds into my misery, I had a redemptive moment of glory hallelujah when I went into the bathroom. My toilet! That flushed! With water! The porcelain sink with hot and cold! My shower. Oh, my! The heavens sang. My God, how I'd missed it all. The shampoo, toothpaste, toothbrush, soaps, deodorant, toenail clippers, hairbrush, tweezers, and razors. Piles of towels, jars of cotton balls and swabs, bottles of cream and lotions. Mud masks, hot oil treatments, clear fingernail polish. I sank to my knees on the pile of my fuzzy green bath mat. Will's words and the bathroom.

Both would have to be enough.

Two cups of strong, dark coffee, a dog walk, and a slice of toast with jam later, I sat at my computer, checking the calendar I hadn't seen in so long. There it was. My life. No classes on Fridays, I didn't have to go to campus until later for the mandatory faculty meeting, Susan Franklin wanting to organize the literary festival for the spring.

"How about a time travel event?" I could venture. "I'll take Shakespeare. Susan, what about Chaucer for you? Perhaps you could explore medieval torture practices? See you later!"

She'd vanish like hot air.

"How about a trip to a psychiatric facility," Susan would retort. "I'll drive the little white bus. All aboard!"

My cursor hovered over the link to my school email account. Once I clicked on again and started reading the essays, I was back in my world. I was a Professor of English. *Shakespeare and His World,* my class. This was what I did. Whatever had happened to me in the past couldn't or shouldn't be explained but tucked away in a tiny memory brain fold. This life is what I wanted, at least mostly. The rest? Who should ask for everything?

But the email could wait.

In the shower, I checked my body for clues, running a palm up my left forearm, searching for the cuts from my bloodletting. Maybe there was the faintest trace, a tiny red line just below the crook of my elbow. But I couldn't be sure if I were imagining the ridge or not. My bedbug bites had long ago healed, and the only other time I'd been penetrated had been, well, the times

Will and I had sex. I brought a hand down to touch myself, but I felt normal. I wasn't sure what I was expecting (a *Will Was Here* sign?), but nothing down there seemed changed.

So I gave myself up to the epic shower. Two shampoos, a half a bottle of conditioner I let sit on my head as I focused on my body, a thorough shaving, though my legs seemed very recently shaved. Like yesterday shaved, merely tiny prickles on my shins. My underarms, too. In fact, my body was as well-tended as ever. Only in my imagination, it appeared, had anything altered from my daily routine.

But I had been altered. I had. I must have. And as I rinsed myself, I wished I could bring Will in here with me, showering him with the warm water, watching his eyes light with joy and then maybe more, as I pressed my sudsy body to his.

Later, my hair slightly over-conditioned, I marched down Coventry Hall toward my office, waving to people I felt I hadn't seen forever. My colleagues waved back with tentative hands. In my office, I dumped my bag on my desk and started to dig through the pile of mail and notes. But my attention was drawn to the wall behind my chair, a poster I'd never seen before:

Shakespeare's The Face of Heaven *The Globe Spring 2013*

I walked around my desk. Who had put that up? Was it a joke? I leaned closer reading the cast: Judy Dench, Sean Bean, Rebecca Hall, Orlando Bloom, all famous amazing British actors. Was *The Face of Heaven* a new work? By why the Shakespeare part? In spring 2013, I was in London and had gone to many plays at The Globe. This one had not been an option.

Blinking into the shiny red of the poster, noting the swirls of costume and frolic of the cast, I was clearly reading an ad for a comedy, but not one that had been in existence before I'd left the night before.

My head started to hum, lights flickering at the edges of my vision, so I turned back to my piles of paper, taking deep breaths as I did the ordinary and expected. I collected my mail—catalogs for conferences, ads for new textbooks, and requests from students for recommendations—and picked up a notepad to jot down meeting notes. At the last moment, I grabbed my laptop from my desk, imagining I could read a few student papers online while waiting for everyone to discuss, amend, and approve the long minutes from the last meeting.

I closed the door, ignoring the poster. I would figure that out later.

Slipping into the dark corner of the room at the edge of the square of tables, I turned on my computer and sat back in my chair. For a second, I was disembodied, off-kilter, as if I needed to right myself in my chair. Things were weird, and not in the I-just-returned-from-1598 weird. There were four people sitting at the table I didn't recognize. And there were different posters on the announcement wall, advertising Shakespeare conferences and festivals I didn't know about. I'd have to read them after the meeting dispersed. But at the moment, I was contending with all the sounds. The whirring electric heaters, the dings, pings, and rings from people's phones. The clackity clanks of the department printer. Outside, amplified music from the quad.

How was I going to get used to the 21C again? If only there were clear rules for returning from a time travel vacation.

What to Expect When You've Been Gone for Four Hundred Years.

How to Unpack History and Whatever Else You've Brought Back (Bug Check).

To Tell or Not to Tell: Space-Time Continuum Etiquette.

Should I Stay or Should I Go: How to Figure Out Your New Life Back Home—or Not.

Just before the meeting started, Dan came in, smiled at me, and sat down in the chair to my left.

"You beat me," he said.

I didn't tell him I'd had three months to prepare. "Pretty amazing, huh?"

"Have you recovered from last night's Shakespeare extravaganza?"

Not hardly, I thought, almost laughing. "I think so. I suppose we're on call this weekend."

"Maybe we can have dinner? Saturday? Tomorrow? I know a great Thai place."

Just then, Susan cleared her throat and called the meeting to order. I smiled back at Dan, and though it made no sense, I felt as though I were cheating on Will.

215

I shifted in my uncomfortable plastic chair, time-bound and chained. I was really back. And at a faculty meeting, more proof I'd simply had the longest most intense dream in history. It was possible I needed to dig up the therapist recommendation Kate had given me during my last fit of despair over my love life.

"Jessica Randall?" Susan called.

"Present," I said, raising my hand. Indeed. Dead set and exhausted in the middle of the present. I had a jetlag I'd never be able to explain.

As my colleagues argued about the order of the past discussion about curriculum development, I started to quietly open my snail mail. A new edition of Phillip Sidney's *Arcadia*. An anthology of lesser-known Elizabethans, a composition text using only poetry. A creative nonfiction conference. The yearly Associated Writers and Writing Program conference. *Sign up now for the early-bird discount.* I put the flyer aside, opening up the Modern Language Association conference envelope. Same early-bird special. As Susan moved onto a discrepancy in the Student Learning Outcomes discussion, I turned off the volume on my laptop and clicked on the MLA site. Maybe it would be good to get away in January when the Central California Valley was socked in with fog truly sock-like. Instead of staring out my window with dismay, I could sleep on a "best-ever" bed and then attend panel after panel about Will. Maybe I could pretend he was sitting next to me, holding my hand, and whispering caustic asides into my ear.

"Who is this onion-eyed Freud? How he knows my Hamlet?"

I raised my hand to approve the minutes, and Susan started a very long list of announcements. Then I clicked on the MLA panel schedule, searching for Shakespeare and found:

From Stereotype to Compassion: The 1598 version of The Merchant of Venice.

And:

The Bard Electric: Modern Inventions in Shakespeare's Later Work

I leaned forward, blinking, breath leaving my body. I read on:

The Vision of the Dark Lady: Love in Shakespeare's Later Plays, 1635-1652

Sitting back with a slight plastic click, I counted in my swirling brain. Will died in 1616 from typhus, surrounded by Anne, his two daughters, and their families in Stratford. His jittery handwriting on his last will depicted an illness of some kind. Scholars had long surmised either fever or end-stage syphilis. But here? His last plays? 1635-1652.

"Jessica," Dan asked, leaning close. "Are you okay?"

I looked up at him. "Huh?"

"You look a little green." He pushed his glasses back against his forehead and stared at me. He reached out a hand, lightly touching my wrist as if to feel for an erratic pulse.

"Yes, um," I muttered, pulling my arm away. "Thanks."

Clicking out of the MLA site and then back didn't change the panel titles. Hands shaking, I opened another browser screen, going to Wikipedia.

"William Shakespeare (/ˈʃeɪkspɪər/; 26 April 1564 (baptized) – 16 October 1652) was an English poet, playwright, and actor, widely regarded as the greatest writer in the English language and the world's preeminent dramatist. He is often called England's national poet and the "Bard of Avon." His extant works, including some collaborations, consist of about 55 plays, 250 sonnets, six long narrative poems, and many other verses. His later work is considered revelatory and revolutionary, focusing a harsh Jacobean light on racism, genocide, religion, and the monarchy. His plays have been translated into every major living language and are performed more often than those of any other playwright."

"No way," I breathed out, sitting back in my chair and looking around the room. How could my colleagues be so calm? How could anyone be sitting still? "William Shakespeare lived until he was 88!"

Susan took off her tortoiseshell glasses and stared at me, her dark bangs a flash against her disapproving forehead. "Jessica, we are in the middle of our announcements."

Dan shifted next to me. I waved Susan off, typing in Lady Mary Wroth.

No one found. A flush of giddiness filled me. I clicked, Lady Mary Sidney, and read:

Lady Mary Sidney (18 October 1587—November 1677) was an English poet of the Renaissance. A member of a distinguished literary family, she was among the first female writers to have achieved an enduring reputation.

And here is where the bio began to change:

Though King James sought to marry her to a worthy aristocrat, she refused all marriage proposals and, at one time, faced time in the Tower. Her family managed to keep her free, and she retired to Penshurst, where she lived the rest of her life writing poems, prose, and plays, many of which were produced. Upon the Earl of Pembroke's death—her first cousin—death, she was awarded a yearly annuity, which allowed her writing to flourish.

"Can you believe it?" I whispered, grabbing Dan's wrist. "She left that bastard! Both of them! Both bastards. Good god!"

"Professor Randall!" Susan called out, her voice a sharp sword through the dense meeting air.

Dan turned to me, his hand now on top of mine. I swallowed, nodding. "I'd better leave," I said.

"A good idea," he whispered. "Should I come with you?"

I shook my head, gathered my belongings, and rushed out of the room and down the hall back to my office. Closing the door, I flung myself into my desk chair, reopened my laptop, and read both Will's and Mary's bios, over and over again. Will did go back to Stratford shortly after opening The Globe, but there, with his family, he lived a very long time, making trips into London to oversee his plays, one of which was *The Face of Heaven*. In some other timeline, I'd seen it and bought the poster.

While there were breaks in production due to plagues and the Reformation and other religious and political atrocities, all his plays lived on, and the Shakespeare family thrived. He didn't die of typhus or syphilis, but old age in his first-best bed, with his family (the two girls I'd met, Susana and Judith and a boy, Charles, born 1600, and several grand-and great-grandchildren) around him. He was no longer a mystery. His plays were all dated and authenticated. Now, William Shakespeare was one hundred percent William Shakespeare.

My heart did a little *pang* in my chest. He'd gone back to the very good Anne, who'd convinced me with her sensible gaze. Perhaps he'd listened when I talked about the value of friendship. Maybe in old age, true love had blossomed. Perhaps, his love for Lord Pembroke and me had likely been unresolved. But Will had used all that feeling to write and live on and well.

Although, Lady Mary Sidney never married, though she apparently had two long-lasting love relationships, the identities of both men a mystery. The portraits of her were of a happy woman, with bright eyes, and lovely gowns. In the portraits of her as a grown woman, I saw her as she'd been as a girl. Bright, wicked smart, and desperate to have her ideas on the page and in the world. The list of her seminal feminist poems and plays was long, the most important a pastoral involving a witch and a unicorn, symbols of a political landscape gone wrong as well as gender inequities.

"Oh, Mary!" My entire body tingled, and I actually clapped my hands. "You did it."

There wasn't much about Lord Pembroke. His Wikipedia page had suffered a purge since I'd last visited a few years earlier. Where once there had been an entire section, "William Herbert and Shakespeare's Sonnets," now there was only a quick mention of a brief patronage. He'd scurried back to Wilton and stayed there, apparently not marrying Lady Mary Talbot out of revenge. And Lady Mary Wroth née Sidney wasn't a link on his page at all. As he had in his earlier timeline, Lord Pembroke died at 50, his title and property passing to his brother Phillip. That was it. Not even a mention of the sonnets.

Sitting back, I made a little whoop, glad to be hidden in my office. I whirled around in my chair once, twice, three times, the red of the poster flashing in my eyes. Everything inside me trembled and jittered. What else had changed? I scrolled to the bottom of Lord Pembroke's page and then Googled "Shakespeare's sonnets," finding a page that purported to have all of the 250 written during his lifetime. I clicked down through the first 17, and—and the poems about the Fair Youth were gone.

Everything in me stilled. I clicked and linked and scrolled, jumping from page to page to page. They were gone. 154 poems vanished.

Not one survived my visit. All those lovely, lovely lines that had influenced countless generations:

"Shall I compare thee to a summer's day..."

"Let me not to the marriage of true minds admit impediments..."

"Where art thou, Muse, that though forget'st so long..."

"To me, fair friend, you never can be old..."

"Never say that I was false of heart..."

I blinked into the computer screen. There were other sonnets, of course. The internet said so. As the Wikipedia page stated, he'd published 250 during his life. But now I remembered how upset he'd been when I'd told him the future knew about Lord Pembroke and Will's love for him.

"What must they think of me?" Will had whispered about his future audience, they who knew of his passion for the lord.

No matter how often I'd reassured him, told him his poemsmeant so much to so many, he'd simply shaken his head. One important piece of information (along with his death) that I'd kept from him was the publication history of the sonnets. I'd not told him the unsavory Thomas Thorpe had published his poems without consent in 1609. But maybe Will had taken matters into his own hands and removed all evidence of the Fair Youth and WH.

I started to Google Thomas Thorpe, needing to see if his 1609 edition had vanished, but someone knocked on my door. Dan stuck his head into my office.

"Hey there," he began. "You okay?"

"Not really," I said. "But—well..."

"Do you need me to call anyone?" Dan pushed his glasses back against his forehead, his big blue eyes magnified and worried. He clutched his agenda, the long list of items going down the entire page.

"Is the meeting over?" I asked, distracted, my heart beating to ideas I couldn't name. I recycled the flyers, stared at the screen, looked at Dan. If I didn't chill out, he would have to 5150 me. Nothing like an involuntary psychiatric hold to get one focused. Perhaps, I thought, I should just do it myself. Beat everyone to the punch.

"I was concerned," he said. "You seem a bit—frazzled. Did something happen since last night?"

"Not really. I probably just need a little break." I stood up and then sat down again. He stared at me, clearly concerned.

"Can you tell me what's going on?" Dan shrugged, a smooth hitch in his stance.

"Not really," I said. "Thanks for asking. It's nice to have a friend."

Whatever I was saying wasn't making much sense, to me or Dan.

"I wasn't sure you really wanted one," Dan said.

As he watched me, calm and waiting, I let my heart beat its strange rhythm in my chest. Breathing in, one, two, I wondered why it had taken us so long to sit down in a theater together.

"Do you like teaching here?" Dan asked.

"Probably not as much as I should," I said. "I'm having a hard time this semester."

Again, that hitch. "Sorry. I didn't mean to hurt your feelings."

I could feel my former reserve try to rear, but I pushed it back. "You didn't. It's true. Can't fault an honest man."

Dan laughed, pushed his glasses back again. For a second, I stared at him and then bent over my purse and pulled out a small glasses kit. "Let me see those." I held out my hand.

He started, almost grimaced, but then he sat at the student "chair of shame" on the other side of my desk, the one students complained and cried in. Taking my tiny screwdriver in hand, I tightened the screws in the corners of his glasses.

"Here," I said, handing them back.

Dan put them on, adjusted them a bit, and then smiled. "Thanks."

I nodded, slamming shut my laptop and packing up my belongings. "I've got to get home."

"Really, what's going on?" He grabbed my hand as I swept stuff off my desk into my bag. "What did you mean about Shakespeare living until he was 88? You knew that. He is your area."

My industry. Almost what Will would have said. For about three seconds, I wanted to tell him everything. Dan's expression behind the slip-sliding rims had always been kind.

My mouth opened, the entire wild, weird, time-travel story gift-wrapped in gilt on my tongue. Who better to understand my story than a lover of literature? Someone who would mourn for the missing sonnets. A man who would get how I fell in love with someone and his words. Maybe he'd 5150 me afterward, but while I was telling him how I'd shown up in 1598, Dan would understand.

But then, no. Something stopped me. Though we'd been working on *Merchant* together, it wasn't time. Self-preservation kicked in. I couldn't tell anyone about this. Not yet. There was something I had to do.

There was someplace I had to go.

Chapter Nineteen — Test Pattern

At a cruising altitude of 36,000 miles, after thinking about Will, Will, Will, Daisy, Mary, Lord Pembroke, sonnets, pasties, and soup, it suddenly struck me I'd never used the linen cloths Daisy had handed me that first week at Will's. The random thought struck as I stared out at the clouds over the Arctic. I really should have been thinking about my big lie, calling in sick and handing over my classes to a helpful but perplexed Dan. Or bringing Horatio over to Kate's without much of an explanation. Shelby's dog-sitter excitement made it possible for me to slip away without giving my sister more than just my flight itinerary and hotel information. My main concerns should be my students still waiting for me to return their papers, Susan Franklin ready to write up a teaching performance plan, and my sister, amazed and confused I'd canceled yet another breakfast date. Maybe I should have focused on the fact those four new people at the department meeting had been the "other" Shakespeareans, all apparently hired before I'd arrived on campus. In fact, there was an opening for another assistant professor, every section in the "Shakespeare Studies" program full, thriving, and packed-to-the-gills.

But who had time for those worries? Crammed into my coach seat headed to Heathrow, the only thing I could think about was my period.

The plane zoomed through the thin air, nothing but white outside the small windows. The men next to me snored in a strange syncopated rhythm, snorting and shuddering. The flight attendants came by with water, and I took a large cool plastic cupful, glad to have something to do with my nervousness. But that led me to have to pee, which led to crawling over the two sleeping giants. And then, there I was, stuck with my naked bottom half in the small smelly bathroom considering my period based on the time zone, as in zones separated by four hundred years.

If I were in 1598, my period was a little over two months late. I would be rounding toward the end of my first trimester, which would explain the curious tenderness in my breasts and my sudden antipathy toward orange juice.

If I were pregnant now, in 2018, it would be an impossibility, no male part passing through my force field in a long while. Also, my period wasn't due for a few days. So theoretically, here, pregnancy was not even a question.

But the most quantumly physical question of all time—could I have traveled in time to another place, spent months there, gotten pregnant, and returned to my time where no real time had passed but pregnant all the same, despite the fact my period wasn't even late?

Chew on that, Einstein.

The real point was, where had my body been?

And for God's sake, could I have really time traveled at all? Despite the material I'd uncovered on Google, it was possible I'd either experienced total amnesia or was suffering from delusions. The world thought William Shakespeare had written well into his eighties, but maybe I'd made up all the earlier facts I'd believed to be true. The former truths I had once held dear could simply be my brain tripping on its own wires.

Or, according to those who believed in the many-worlds interpretation of quantum mechanics, I could simply be in a parallel universe. Problem solved, right?

"How are you doing in there?" a flight attendant said, knocking on the thin door. "Is there anything I can help you with?"

"I really doubt it," I said, pulling up my bright white underwear.

At Heathrow, I scanned the stores for something remotely drugstore-ish, but the international terminal was crowded, and I kept banging my shins with my wheelie. So I decided to forgo searching for a pregnancy test and focus on getting out of customs, security, and onto the Tube first. I bumbled onto the Piccadilly line, jostled and bumped until I managed to get a seat at the Green Park stop. At Holburn, I got off, and then took the 242 bus from Holburn to Bank. An hour and ten minutes after landing at Heathrow, I was back in my old stomping grounds, Cornhill Street, the same road Hugh had taken when carting Daisy and me to Cheapside. To my left, Poultry Street. But nothing was the same. There were banks built in the seventeenth and eighteenth centuries circling the roads. In the distance, skyscrapers. CCTVs at every intersection along with traffic lights. Zebra crossings (with warnings to look left and then right), cars, bikes, pedestrians, tour buses. Building cranes in the distance, the roar of planes overhead, the black huff of diesel gas. But the sky was the same. The wide blue sky with white clouds towering up and into a storm. This was the same sky William Shakespeare and I looked up into that first day in Bishopsgate. A true London sky, no matter what century.

On my way off the bus, I decided to ask the driver where I might find a drugstore. As I headed down the aisle, the accent and lilt of the passengers' voices almost made me say, "Dear sir, do you know of a likely apothecary?"

I started to laugh but swallowed it down, jetlag and insanity filling me like a swarm of bees. So I simply asked the driver where I could find a drugstore.

"Up there." He pointed. "Old Broad Street."

I thanked him and got off the bus, pulling my wheelie behind me. Old Broad indeed.

Since the drugstore was very close to my hotel (I had splurged on a five-star for two nights. If I needed more time, I was doomed to the Travel Lodge at sixty-one pounds sterling a night). I checked in, gave the bellboy my wheelie, and headed back out. I'd taken the redeye out of San Francisco and arrived at Heathrow at two in the afternoon, though it felt like two in the morning to me. What with my obsessing about my period and my general all-around unstable mental health, not to mention the two large men pressing me almost flat to the window, I hadn't slept a wink. The most I could expect from myself now was to get some supplies at the drugstore, hole up in my room until tomorrow morning, and then head out on my expedition.

Once I stood in front of the feminine products, I realized, alas, I'd overestimated myself. The last time I'd bought a pregnancy test had been in the United States and back in the first passionate weeks with Phillip. I'd thought we'd been very careful, but then my period did not show up on the twenty-sixth for its regularly scheduled program. No, it strung me along until the thirty-first, but by then, I'd bought three tests, all with the same, simple instructions: pee on the stick and wait for the red or blue lines.

These in London, though, were much more detailed. There was an "EASY" test with a "Colour Change Tip." Another one was perfect for obsessives like me with a "Double-Check and Date," which would tell me exactly how far along I was (which would certainly help with my time-travel conundrum. The science involved wouldn't care where my body had been). Finally, there was a digital test with a "weeks indicator" that promised to be as accurate as an ultrasound.

After reading the boxes repeatedly, I finally settled on the "Double-Check and Date," because if I didn't, I'd find myself back here buying another test if I only bought one. At this point, everything was suspect. As I walked back to the checkout, I grabbed a few things, including some apple juice, nuts, and dried fruit, trying to be healthy as well as keep myself out of the mini-bar. I wasn't sure if I was being healthy for myself or for the supposed baby. But as I paid my purchases, I realized this baby and I had been exposed to pathogens from centuries before and lived through them. Survived. And then some.

Before I took the test, I needed to be practical. I unpacked, hooked up my laptop to the internet, and checked my emails. A couple of screamers from my mother and Kate (*Where the hell are you?*—my mother. *Have you lost your mind?*—Kate). A terse note from Susan Franklin requesting an in-person meeting upon my return. A calm text assessment of my classes from Dan. The students listened, took notes, and loved the opening sequence of *Hamlet*.

Dear Jessica—

I brought in the Mel Gibson film version. We listened to the ghost's speech to Hamlet. The discussion was very rich, to say the least. I'll bring the film in for the "To be or not to be" soliloquy, too. Should help. Hope you are having a good time—or getting done what you need to. Sherry Maita's students had a lot of questions at rehearsal, so hurry back. I'm about tapped out.

Maybe one day, you'll tell me what's going on.

Best, Dan

I wrote back, thanking him for everything, and closed my laptop. The whole long trip on my skin and in my hair, I took a shower, made a cup of herbal tea, and then, wearing my cushy white robe, sat down on the bed and read the test box. Opening it at the bottom end, I pulled out the multifolded instructions and read them carefully, twice, double-checking already. Then, when I was sure I'd pass the exam on pregnancy test processes, I went into the bathroom with both tests clutched to my chest and closed the door.

Here's the way it is now with digital pregnancy tests. No equivocation. A plus or a minus, the symbol clear, the pattern unambiguous. The words "Not Pregnant" or "Pregnant." The numbers 1-2, 2-3, or 3+ to indicate how many weeks one is along the way.

I was "Pregnant." Twice. Both with big pluses. And the number? 3+. I was England now, and I'd been in England for well over three months, at least my female reproductive organs had been. Sitting in full on amazement on my king-sized hotel bed, I contemplated the truth: I was well into my first trimester and pregnant with William Shakespeare's baby.

Chapter Twenty – Back to Church for All Good Sinners

Even though I wanted to stay awake all night and obsess about my predicament, my body took over, the long flight and subsequent, stunning revelation pulling me into a deep, twelve-hour sleep. When I awoke, I ordered up some tea and toast and took a hot shower, using the spa shampoo, conditioner, and soap liberally. When I was done—ready for my adventure in jeans, running shoes, and large bulky sweater—I ate my toast and studied St. Helen's church online. I laughed out loud when I saw the images. Tiny little St. Helen's dwarfed by the Gherkin's pickle spaceship form rising behind it. But St. Helen's had been in that spot since the time of Constantine, the first century CE, named supposedly in honor of his dead mother, Helena. It would be there long after the Gherkin was imploded and rebuilt in some other century.

I clicked onto the first page of the church's images, all with neighboring glassy buildings dominating the squat little church. But last time I'd seen St. Helen's, it seemed enormous, solid, the exact place to hide Will's poems. All I could do was hope recent renovations hadn't touched the little hiding spot. But after searching for "Shakespeare poems found at St. Helen's" or "mysterious erotic poems discovered," I'd come up with nothing.

Brushing my hair and putting it in a ponytail, I packed my purse, popping in my fabric shopping bag, map, flashlight, and the screwdriver I'd bought at the drugstore as an afterthought. The air was crisp and slightly breezy. For the moment, not a cloud in the sky. I took in a breath, amazed at how much cleaner and fouler it was, light on dung and heavy on diesel. I was assaulted by light and noise and scrabbled in my purse for my sunglasses. Once arranged, I strode east toward Bishopsgate Street, toward what was once the parish of Bishopsgate. Now it was not a parish, but a ward of the City of London. London proper. Not outside the wall but inside England's version of Wall Street.

My purse banging against my hip, I ran toward a busy roundabout swirling with cars and buses. What if I could make a left and right and miraculously find Will at home, suddenly unmarried, writing at his desk, his quill feather swaying with every word.

"You'll never believe it," I'd say as I pushed into the room, setting down my packages of soap, ink, paper, and pasties.

"That's impossible." He would finish his exquisite sentence and put down his quill. "You are here in my world. I cannot help but believe it all."

Then I'd sit on his lap, put my hands on his face, and say, "We're going to have a baby."

He'd kiss me full on the lips and say, "Sweetling, only you can carry this fair creature. But I will be here, by your side."

Later, Daisy would bring up the tray with two mugs of beer, and we'd toast, though I'd have to explain the effect of alcohol on a developing fetus.

My breath coming in heaving punches, I stopped running, the sweater's wool rough and itchy on my cheeks. A couple of pedestrians gave me quick, furtive looks, probably worried they needed to call an ambulance, but they tucked back into their isolated, heroic storming of the morning, music pumping out of their earbuds.

None of that imagined scene with Will could happen. That world was gone. Nothing around me right now reminded me of where I'd been only days before. Will's London was lost, save for a tiny church almost stomped to death by the enormous buildings around it.

Finally, I blew my nose and took in a couple of deep breaths. Smoothing my hair, I strode on, down to Great St. Helen's Street and toward the little church.

First, I passed a few young male banker-types, their suit jackets slung on benches, their blue shirts open at the collars, ties loosened. Most jabbered into their cell phones. As I walked past, I stared at their shiny leather shoes, thinking about my perfectly worn-in pair back at Will's, wishing I could have brought them and about ten other things home with me. But of course, I'd brought home more than shoes. For a moment, I stopped again, remembering Mistress Meade's words:

"All I will say is to bring it back with you."

No shoes. No kirtle. But a baby brought home through time.

I walked on and turned into a dead-end street. Under a tree losing its leaves in reddish-gold autumn gusts, stood a crowd, milling in a loose circle around a woman who held up a pole from which fluttered a tiny red flag. Her short blond curls whipped around her small round reddish face.

"The church," she said, in a slightly posh voice I hadn't heard in a while, "is a true survivor. Not only did it withstand, mind you, the Great Fire of 1666 but many wars and changes of rule. As we go through the edifice, I will point out the various monuments. While small perhaps, St. Helen's has one of the largest collections of such in Greater London. Now, please follow me. Stay in strict accordance with the rules inside, the most important of which is 'Do not touch!' This way please."

A woman next to me smiled and said something in what I thought was Bulgarian. Clearly, Ms. Posh Tour Guide didn't seem to mind no one understood her. But I followed along, moving into the main door, pouring into the church with the tour. The Bulgarian woman stayed next to me. Maybe she had something to dig up here, too.

"Once a priory of Benedictine nuns," the tour guide droned on. In front of me, I saw evidence of her words—the former nun's choir. Slowly, I circled the circle of tourists, and then as the guide moved them along to the tune of "two parallel naves," I slipped toward the chancel as I'd done before.

Keeping myself hidden behind a column, I made sure the guide or any church staff wasn't paying attention to my stealthy moves. For a terrifying moment, Mr. Beadle strode toward me at a brisk pace. But it was only a father with a crying child, clearly in dread need of a toilet.

The coast clear, I moved forward, searching for the small stairwell that would lead me down to the room with the loose stone. But the stairs weren't there, dismantled during some renovation or another. I paced back and forth, half expecting to find it the next time I marched by, but no staircase appeared.

"Are you looking for the memorial to Sir John Crosby?"

Startled, I looked up into the wide blue eyes of a very earnest man. His name tag read "Douglas Outwich."

"Is it nearby?" I sputtered.

"Quite. Right under the arch." He had sort of an English *duh!* in his tone, and I glanced to my right. Indeed. And there were my old friends, Sir John Crosby and his wife Agnes on top of their tombs, Sir John resting his feet on a griffin. At his wife's feet, one headless dog, the other intact. I'd always thought they both seemed very peaceful in a dead stiff marble way. Will once told me that in old John's own lifetime, he'd risen from an apprentice to a knight.

"Thanks," I said to Douglas. "Um, can I ask? Is there a downstairs? I thought that's what my mom said." I motioned generally to the tour that was blobbing its way through the church.

"Oh, quite. But it's not open to viewing." Then Doug motioned vaguely toward the Lady Chapel.

I nodded. "Thank you," I said, admiring John and Agnes. Doug slipped away into the crowd. Glancing behind me, I saw the stairwell was barricaded with a blue velvet rope. My eye on Doug, I slipped into the Lady Chapel and then under the cord, into the stairwell, and down the steps. I fished around for my flashlight, turning it on and running the light over the stone walls. When I made it to the passageway, I sensed I was in the right area. But I couldn't be sure as this way hadn't existed the last time. Also, I'd been alone in the church, Mr. Beadle, a late arrival. Now the United Nations was upstairs learning about the memorials to Sir William Pickering, Sir Andrew Judd, and Sir Thomas Gresham; the arches and naves and altars.

Quiet as the rats in Will's rooms had never been, I moved along the wall, using my flashlight and feeling the stones with my hands. I tried one room, but the door was locked, and then I came to another, slipping inside and trying not to move as someone clomped down the passageway.

The footsteps fading, I focused the beam of my travel flashlight on the floor. But I couldn't see much. The room was crammed full, an apparent storage facility. Posters for St. Helen's galas, extra folding tables, stacks of tablecloths, and boxes of books and papers banged up against every wall. Going to the right-hand corner, I put the flashlight in my mouth and pushed a table away from the wall, the legs giving a terrible squeak. Pausing, I waited for security guards to come rushing in. But nothing. Using less force and more skill, I slid the table away from the corner, squeezed into the space I'd made, and lay flat on my stomach once again. How much easier to do this in pants. I reached out to the loose stone, but it seemed more firmly wedged into place. I yanked and pulled, sweltering in my big sweater as I rustled with the rock. I picked a little at the grout with the screwdriver, and then pulled and yanked the stone some more.

It was no good, wedged tight as it was. I wouldn't be able to get the poems. But how could I leave them in there? How could I possibly go home without his work? Could I leave an anonymous tip?

"I know it sounds crazy. But there's a whole folder of erotic poems by Shakespeare under your chancel altar? How do I know? For God's sake, man, I put them there in 1598."

Here I was, pregnant, flat on the floor, grit in my mouth, spiders probably crawling up my socks and onto my shins. Ridiculous. I breathed in dust and the cool chill coming up off the stone pavers.

In anger, I jabbed at the grout again, clicks and stabs echoing in the room. I put down the screwdriver and grabbed the stone again, but this time, I dug with my fingernails, pulling hard, and then. Yes? Yes! The stone popped out and clanked to the floor. Without wasting another second, I reached my whole arm into the space, felt with my fingertips the leather folder I'd put in there last week or four hundred and seventeen years ago. Slowly, I pulled it out and pressed the curl of it against my side, breathing hard. I scuttled like a crab out of the spot I'd opened between the table and the wall and then stood up. Without my flashlight on, I put down the folder, took off my purse, and then my sweater, The I took out the fabric shopping bag and slung it around my body. Carefully unfurling—gently, gently—the folder, I put it in the bag against my body, next to my stomach, and put on my big bulky wool sweater. Just as I was strapping on my purse, a light flashed on my face, so bright all I could do was shut my eyes.

"I quite had the feeling you wanted to come down here," Douglas Outwich said. Or, at least from the sound of his voice, I thought it was Douglas.

"Yeah, I'm sorry," I said, lifting my arms in a *you-got-me* posture. "Listen, I'm in this treasure hunt thing. I was supposed to find..." I mimicked looking in my purse for the list and then giving up. I recited as if from memory, "A stone from a 'Grade 1 listed church.'"

I pointed under the table. "There is one there, but, well, I have to say I feel guilty. I can't take it."

Douglas shone his light under the table, right on the one I'd moments ago wrested from its mortared place. "That would have made a delightful treasure. But I have to ask to look in your purse. Rules, you know."

I nodded my head and pulled my purse off my shoulder. Even in the dark, I noticed the bulge of my stomach. So as I handed over my purse, I made the gesture I'd seen so often with friends, colleagues, and Kate—the cupped palm over the rounded belly. "I don't know what I was doing signing up for this. I'm expecting, you know."

Horror rode across Douglas' face. He quickly shone the light into my purse, and then at the wall. "For goodness sake, there is electricity in here," he muttered.

I laughed. Of course. I'd almost forgotten about electricity, especially here.

He flicked on the switch, and I bent my body into a deeper, more pronounced pregnancy, my hand passing gently over my poetic stomach. Douglas opened my purse a bit wider.

"You can dump it out," I said. "Really. Just my wallet. Some prenatal vitamins."

Douglas closed my purse and handed it back to me. "I hardly think such a game is good for you at this particular moment."

Clutching my purse, I nodded, smiling. "You are so right. I'm giving up. Now."

He stared at me and softened. "I say, I'm quite ashamed to admit I know where there is a loose stone. Hold on one minute."

Douglas shot out of the room. As I waited, I closed my eyes, relief beating through every vein. Or beating into Will's folder. I could hardly wait to see his poems again. In that way, we could be together. Then I flushed at the thought, remembering what those poems did to me the first time I read them.

"Are you quite alright?" Douglas asked. He was back in the room, his hand palm up, a dark stone in the center.

"I need some fresh air," I said, rubbing my stomach again.

Invigorated and renewed, Douglas handed me the stone, led me up the stairs, and pointed me to the main door.

"I hope you win the treasure hunt," he said.

"Thank you so much," I said, holding up the stone. "I think I just did."

Chapter Twenty-One – The Shakespeare Switcheroo

My head up, I sailed out of the church, past the reassembled tour group, the Bulgarian woman waving to me. I waved back and headed toward the hotel, but I took another route, past the Superdrug, down Gresham Street toward a little park I'd visited once after a tour of St. Paul's Cathedral, the one built after the fire. To my left, the great white dome loomed. The shopping bag still under my sweater, I clomped on, my head a whirl of adrenaline and gratitude. The miracle of the folder still being in the same spot for four hundred years hadn't hit me, and as the sky was blue and billowing with clouds, the air fine and brisk, a walk was the answer. I needed to dispel the quake that threatened to take over my whole body.

Gresham Street dropped me into the circle of Postman's Park, and I let myself in through the gate, wandering the path, rounding the fountain, and walking over to The Memorial to Heroic Self Sacrifice. I'd walked this wall before, as painful and amazing a tragic viewing as any at The Mall in DC, but with more narrative.

For example:

Alice Ayres, Daughter of a Bricklayer's Labourer Who By Intrepid Conduct Saved 3 Children From a Burning House in Union Street Borough At The Cost of Her Own Young Life, April 24, 1885.

Frederick Alfred Croft, Inspector, Aged 31, Saved a Lunatic Woman from Suicide at Woolwich Arsenal Station But was Himself Run Over by the Train. January 11, 1878.

Harry Sisley of Kilburn, Aged 10, Drowned In Attempting To Save His Brother After He Himself Had Just Been Rescued, May 24, 1878.

I walked past the other plaques, finally pressing my forehead against the cool tile of John Cranmer's memorial. He'd been 23 and saved the life of a stranger and foreigner but drowned himself.

So sad. So wonderful. Will was dead now, but he'd lived until he was 88, written plays and sonnets I would have the joy to read for the first time. He'd had another child, who was now dead, too, but Will's next child was alive inside of me. I was without Will, back in my own time, but with his words. Somehow, I'd tumbled back into my life with things I'd almost given up on. Not since Phillip had I allowed myself to imagine having a child. The good news, I had a job, benefits, and paid maternity leave. After some explanation, my sister and Shelby would be ecstatic to help out. Finally, I could take care of myself in a way I could never have before.

I kissed my fingers, pressed them against John Cranmer's tile, pushed away from the wall, and walked toward an empty bench facing the memorial. Sun glinted on the roof of the memorial. The winds had settled, the sky still, no chance of rain or a sudden storm. There was no tree limb over this bench, no chance of one of the few pigeons aloft to drop a ripe present on me. No children were running around, no threat of splat of mud or chance of a wayward thrown ball. Lush fern fronds fanned wide over the lawns, dark green and majestic, urging for *hush*. The fallen leaves clumped in still piles. No dogs. In fact, aside from a couple of tourists at the memorial reading the plaques—an older white-haired woman and her middle-aged daughter—the park was all mine.

I took off my purse, sweater, and the shopping bag, sitting down with it tucked safely on my lap. It was a soft Trader Joe's bag, the type heaped in the back of my car. The ancient folder was the most unlikely object for it, as it was usually filled with crackers, coffee, and tubs of salsa, hummus, and spreadable cheeses.

Taking in a deep breath of Postman Park air, I opened the bag and pulled out the curled folder. Four hundred and twenty years ago, I'd rolled it up and shoved it into a hole in a church. Slowly flattening the folder, my heart fluttered, my throat dried, and, finally, my eyes did, too. I was ready to read. But when I opened the cover, I gasped, closing the folder again and looking at the leather cover. This was the same folder I'd grabbed from Will's desk. I'd seen it countless times, those many nights I'd read his poems, squirming to their fleshy juiciness. I opened the folder again. A letter from Will to me.

My Dear Jess—

If you are reading this letter, we broke the damned curse, most like with our reworking of Merchant. *What I know from my timeline is that sometime during the last act of* Richard, *you disappeared. I pray that you awoke in your life with electricity and cars and all the amazing contraptions of which you told me much. To be reading this letter, you must have discerned the changes in my life once you left. You assured me I was known to your world, so my hope was that you would be quick to find the newer works and decide to travel to London to retrieve the folder that is this moment safe in your hands.*

I hardly know where to begin. Decades have passed since I last set eyes on you and the sunshine of your face. I took all your health commandments to heart and removed to Stratford. Anne and I built on our friendship, surrounded by our daughters, living well in the way that we could. We even had yet another child, a son, Charles, who works with me in my profession. He helps me much with my industry, which most certainly it became, even in this lifetime. It has been a good and productive life, though I look back on those London years, those with Lord Pembroke, and those months with you as if perceiving a dream. Madness. Lunacy. Rapture. Amazement. Joy. Rage. The words on the page. The love in my heart and body whole. A cat! (Pirate lived a long and mousey life in the barn at Stratford). And you. All of it enough to take me forward into the good life of which I regret not one day. I know my family well. I will die here with them, too. As I write these words, I am six-and-seventy. Anne lives still, relaxing in her chair with her great-grandchildren in her lap. And my dear heart, you shall be satisfied to know I still have all my own teeth.

Tilting my head back, I laughed, face in the sun, tasting the minty vinegar rinse, his words making me swirl my tongue around my teeth. If my reproductive organs had been in Elizabethan England, so had my teeth. I made a mental note to schedule a dental appointment, among others.

Now as I write, I imagine you rescuing the poems from the tidy spot in the church. When I first visited, it was an easy reach. But, oh, what a bending it will be for an old man, hunched over to rip the stone from its moorings. Knowing there would be fewer and fewer trips to town, I made my decision to trade you poem for poem—

Poem for poem? I stopped reading the letter and moved into the poems, opening a page to read... to read an old standard, one I'd read many times, Sonnet 23:

"As an unperfect actor on the stage,
Who with his fear is put besides his part,
Or some fierce thing replete with too much rage,
Whose strength's abundance weakens his own heart;
So I, for fear of trust, forget to say
The perfect ceremony of love's rite,
And in mine own love's strength seem to decay,
O'ercharg'd with burden of mine own love's might.
O let my books be then the eloquence
And dumb presagers of my speaking breast,
Who plead for love and look for recompense
More than that tongue that more hath more express'd.
O, learn to read what silent love hath writ:
To hear with eyes belongs to love's fine wit."

I flipped page to page, poem to poem. These weren't the erotic poems about Lord Pembroke. Not at all. These were the poems the world used to know before my time travel but didn't upon my return. My mouth open, my eyes blinking into the sunlight, and the green of the park, my whole body sang at their return. Here were the poems that began it all, a call to Lord Pembroke to marry. They would not be lost to the world, at least for the world of the future. But the erotic poems? What did he do to them?

I know you loved the "sexy" poems, as you called them. In many ways, so do I. They are now by my side as I sit by the fire.

Let me be plain about how I crafted this scheme. In your feverish rants, you told me of your worries that I would destroy the poems. I divined you meant those of the more specific and particular nature. During our first days together, you told me St. Helen's survived the horrible world wars and fiendish fires. But with the strain between us after your illness and then with the flurry of rewriting, I forgot. Until the afternoon of your disappearance. Then I noticed the folder was missing.

Once I had managed to quell my grief and sadness over your swift departure, I conferred with Daisy and Hugh, and then with Mr. Beadle, who did see you running from the church that last night. Then, my dear love, commenced weeks of churchly visits. With luck and grace, I found the stone at the moment I was most despairing. I hastened home with the poems and commenced collecting the other sonnets from private and public sources. In the folder, I also placed those I wrote for you, my Dark Lady.

I stared at the words. Dark Lady. I was the Dark Lady? Or was this a jest, a jibe, as Will would have put it? Was he making fun through the centuries?

With my new son and my new life at home in Stratford, I wanted not my sonnets in a collection published without my say. While I take back not one feeling I wrote for Lord Pembroke, they are feelings not ready for my world. But your world is a world prepared. As I wrote into my life, I made well and certain to give my audience the views in the poems. The love of all. The need and gnawing, the hope and glory. The pride, shame, upset, and revelation. So not all was lost by my own clever plan.

Anne is napping, not another soul home. I will finish this letter to you, burn the remaining poems I searched for so long ago, and then on the morrow travel

to London with Charles and return the folder to the hiding spot. Mr. Beadle is
these many years dead, and I am an old man. My attempt may be folly, but if
you are reading, I have been successful.

Oh, time. Oh, how I can still see you. I imagine you, dear Jess, sitting
somewhere reading my words. Look up—

So I did. But instead of the world Will imagined I was viewing, I saw
everything transfigured, 1598 roaring past. Carts and coaches. People bustling
past on their way to market. Mud and pigs and cows. The sky opening to
downpour and then sudden sunlight. Clouds and arcing blue and golden sunset.

What a world you must see, so changed from when you last were here.
Many centuries. What a gift, my love. The time with you was a miracle, the
strangeness of the spheres opening a crack we both fell into.

Wondrous strange.

My dear Jess, I hope your life will be long and good, as mine has been. You
freed me from an enslavement of my own making, and you helped me find my
way to this vast comfort, free of the grief that had threatened to pull me under.

The folder in your hands is truly yours to use or to not. My life has been
my life. My choices informed by your good counsel. I wish you love and more
and all, now and anon.

And a final thought, my love. Know you I penned not Pericles. *Do but look*
for it, and you will note its glorious absence.

W

Gripping the pages and laughing, I looked up into the green of the park. The
past was wrapped up in this letter, the future unwritten, a promise in the poems
under my hands. But more than anything, was Will's trust. That I would do the

right thing with his true heart. More than anything anyone had ever said to me, his words gave me courage. Gave me hope. All that had happened to me in the past—my father, my mother, Phillip—was simply what had happened. I didn't have to press it to me like a nosegay. I didn't have to not do what I wanted because of what I did then. The point was, what I did with those experiences, and what I did with Will's trust, would craft the future. Here, at this moment (please forgive my Zen cliché), was only *now*.

A cab blared by, pigeons flapping up into the trees. Done with their slow read of the entire memorial, the mother and daughter walked past me on their way to the next tourist stop, both smiling. I smiled back, feeling that upturn on my lips all the way to my heart.

I opened the folder to the last page and found a sonnet I'd not yet read, not in 1598, and not in my life before I traveled back in time and changed the space-time continuum forever. I started reading and, by the middle, saw the message. Laughing, I read on, thinking of Will in the bath, his hair wet and curling down his back. Will approving the strange cleaning of his chambers, the restuffing of his bed, the refreshing of rushes. Will gagging up vinegar and mint. Will begrudgingly filling the water dish for Pirate (not to mention consenting to the windowsill kitty litter box).

The final lines of the sonnet read:

"This brand she quenched in a cool well by,
Which from Love's fire took heat perpetual,
Growing a bath and a healthful remedy
For men diseas'd, but I, my mistress thrall,
Came there for cure, and this by that I prove:
Love's fire heats water, water cools not love."

Not water. Not time. I slowly started to work back, flipping to the next poem, but I stopped, having not seen this one, either. It was to a woman, but not the Dark Lady with her black wire head of hair, the poorly described (but loved) woman from Sonnet 130, the poem Will once wrote but in another timeline:

"My mistress' eyes are nothing like the sun;

Coral is far more red than her lips' red;

If snow be white, why then her breasts are dun;

If hairs be wires, black wires grow on her head."

No, this new dark lady had long dark hair and blue eyes, her skin fair. Apparently, she taught him a thing or two about love. And cats. She spoke her mind, even though their minds were often in opposition. The last image of them sitting together on a chair, together, writing, the light fading.

"And yet, this candlelight glows her hair to flame

Without her, I am nothing, no matter what her name."

Sitting on his lap, my arms around his shoulders, the candle gasping. Our last night together. Our rewriting of *Merchant*.

I flipped through one poem and then another, amazed, distracted, astounded. This woman was different. This woman was me. And finally, was this last, his true goodbye:

"Methought at first that heaven played a jest

That tousled head beside me when I woke

Those plaints and moans did not befit a guest

And naught of sense didst come of what you spoke.

"What is't this, what means that, how com'th I here?"

A plague thy queries were from dawn to dusk

And aught of me it seemed that thou couldst bear

(Though true it is thy beauty woke my lust).

Then such a world thou introduced to me

Thy wisdom, thy goodwill wrought your Will good

And good grew great with boundless love for thee

But now a hollow space where once you stood.

Time make me more or thou four hundred less

Return to me my lovely, loving Jess!"

"Oh my," I said aloud to Will, almost able to breathe in the steam from the hissing water. I sighed, sat back, amazed.

I read the poem again and again, putting it down to look at the world around me.

At that moment, someone sat down next to me, and I wiped away a tear and tucked the poems close. Sniffing, I turned away a bit, hoping the person would get the message and move on.

"You got the package, I see," the person, a woman, said.

I looked at her, and saw a well put-together woman in sleek wool pants and matching sweater. Her graying hair was cut in a fashionable and shiny bob, and her teeth were very white and straight. I knew her right away.

"Mistress Meade!" I said, sitting back, blinking.

"You can call me Jessica," she said.

"What?"

"That's my name," she said. "At least here."

My breath and heart stilled. She smiled. "You didn't think you were the only one to stay?"

"But Will said—"

She held up a tanned hand, nails trim and neat, perfect for peeling potatoes for soup. "I misspoke. Stayed in the time. Maybe not with Will. He wasn't ready until you showed up."

So many questions rushed through my head. How did she come and go? Why didn't she tell me then what she was saying now? How could I go back? Should I go back?

As if sensing the thoughts clacking in my brain like pool balls, she reached over and patted my hand. "You were the right one to help him. You were the exact Jessica that was needed."

"But how can I go back?" I asked. "I have so much to tell him."

Mistress Jessica Meade leaned over, looking at me, her beautiful, clear face in front of me. "You are needed here more. Take what you have and give him life yet."

And in that sentence, I heard 1598, Will, and all that he was in her voice.

I nodded, swallowing down a lump of sadness. She stood, hooked her bag on her shoulder, and smiled.

"You know what to do now," she said.

But did I? Really? I wiped my eyes with a sleeve and looked up to ask her how she could possibly know I could do anything of import in this time line, but she was gone. Wind blew the leaves. A bus blasted by the park. I was alone again.

"Thank you," I called out to Mistress Mead; to everything and everyone, those alive and those dead. Those who saved people and died trying. Those who tried and failed, as so many of us did, time and time again. But the attempts. The struggle of it all.

The experience was here in my hands and inside my heart. Just as Mistress Meade had said back in 1598, I'd brought it back. The poems themselves and the little person I carried. Now it was time to go home and figure out how the story ended.

Wishing I had a beer and the company of Will and his fine fellows, I toasted with an imaginary mug, to the good and the bad, the very ordinary and extraordinary that led me here, both times.

Chapter Twenty-Two – Home Again with a Story

Upon arriving home from England and after a good night's sleep, I called Kate to arrange a pickup time for Horatio and then headed down to my bank to open a safety deposit box. A large one. Once the bank manager settled me in my private cubicle, I took Will's leather folder and his poems out of my bag and stared at them. Slowly, I flicked through the fragile pages, noting his half-moon handprints in the margins. The splotches, the scratching out of words. His revisions sometimes right there on the page, his wording, his changes, his decisions.

I ran my finger across his lines, seeing his hand as he worked, imagining his intent, candlelit gaze on his work. Sitting back, I closed my eyes. I would have to let these memories fade, or I'd never be able to live in the real true world of my own life. I breathed in and out, calming myself. But then with a great clattering of keys, a teller clacked into the steel vault, talking with a patron. Gently, I placed the folder in the box. I had a lot of work to do before I could begin to dip into Will's precious work. My life wasn't exactly ready for a historic literary reveal. My career was on shaky ground, my sister thought I needed a life coach, and I'd hidden for so long, I'd almost turned into a mole. I had friends and apologies to make as I dug myself out of some pretty bad habits. And somehow, I'd have to craft a fantabulous tale to explain how I, an ordinary Shakespearean scholar, came upon this raft of precious—not to mention authentic—words. Maybe a wardrobe or a trunk sent by mistake to the New World and passed down through the Randall generations to end up, by chance, in my grandmother's amazingly dry and mold-free basement, just waiting for me to reveal the treasures inside.

The good news was I had time to figure it out.

More importantly, there was the issue of getting ready for another big reveal, the baby.

But first things first.

Before I left home, I'd found the English department directory and tossed it in my bag. Now, in front of the bank, I pressed the address to my phone and followed the GPS directions downtown to a tree-lined street of charming bungalows, most covered with vines, the leaves just beginning to turn a brilliant yellow. Wind swept a few brown sycamore leaves across the wide streets, parents pushed children in strollers, followed by parades of older children on bicycles. Sad to say, I'd never ventured to this part of town. Mostly, I'd not ventured most places in town other than stores, school, and the dog park.

His yard was neat, well-maintained, surrounded by a swear-to-God white picket fence. Before I'd even closed the gate behind me, Dan opened the large front door and walked out onto the porch. Holding a steaming mug of coffee, he wore a pair of jeans and a gray t-shirt. He wasn't wearing his slip-sliding glasses, so he squinted a little.

"Jess?" he said.

"Yep," I said, my heart melting at the way he said my name. Just like Will did.

"What's up? A play emergency? Or did Sherry finally decide to stage *Merchant 2.0*? Make our lives easier."

Merchant 2.0. The second version. Our version, Will's and mine.

Dan shifted, gave a slight shrug. "Sherry doesn't do things the easy way."

I wanted to lie and tell him yes, the play was the thing. Horrible, the first version. Or maybe I could make up a plumbing disaster in the lobby. Or maybe Amber had taken her Jessica and gone AWOL. Or no. I wanted to say, "Thank you for taking my classes. Here's a fruit basket." Or really, I wanted to run. Far away from everything. Telling my family about my feelings or experiences had never gone over well. It had been a disaster with Phillip. My father had never stuck around to listen to anything. But Lady Mary Sidney had shown me something all my living had not. Sometimes you can tell someone the whole truth and survive.

And Master William Shakespeare had shown me that sometimes, people already believe in magic before you do.

"Do you have a minute?" I asked as I walked up the stairs. I noticed a cat curled up on a teak bench, its green eyes suspicious marbles.

"Sure." Dan opened the door, his blue gaze on me.

"I have a story to tell you," I said. "You'll probably think I'm crazy."

Dan raised an eyebrow, smiled, and then pushed his glasses back on his nose. "And?"

"I might actually need longer than a minute."

"Sounds good," he said, letting me into his comfortable house. Maybe a bit paper-strewn, novels and textbooks scattered here and there, but light and bright and warm. Colored pillows on the sofa, floor. *The New York Times* open on the dining room table. The smell of coffee in the air.

"It's pretty juicy," I said. "But I don't know the ending."

"Who does?" Dan said. "Have a seat. Stay awhile."

Instead of our regular post, today at *The Shakespeare Blog*, contributing editor A. Kendall Singh has the rare good fortune to interview Jessica Randall Gordon, the Director of Shakespeare Studies and Performance at California Mid-State University. Her discovery, publication, and subsequent book about *Shakespeare's Lost Sonnets* took the literary world by the heart and won't let it go. Years in the writing, her book presents sonnets that continue to inform and inspire Shakespeare scholars and students, writers, actors, directors, and general lovers of literature. Her book now in its 25th printing, Professor Randall Gordon is writing a novel set in Elizabethan England.

A. Kendall Singh: Welcome, Professor Gordon.

Jessica Randall Gordon: Jessica, please. And thank you for inviting me.

AKS: Are you kidding? I never imagined you'd have the time for this given your research, writing, teaching, and family.

JRG: The fact is, I'm so excited about this book. I still can't get over the breadth and beauty of the poems.

AKS: So for the three people on the planet who don't know how you came to find the poems, could you fill them in?

JRG: It's hard to believe, but I love this story. My mother's family has been in this country since it began. In fact, should I ever have the desire, I could be a card-carrying member of The Daughters of the American Revolution. But suffice it to say, a lot of "stuff" has come down through the generations. When I was clearing out my grandmother's house, I came across a small cabinet. Who knows what family member brought it or how it came to her. But there it had been for as long as she lived there, almost 60 years. I was in charge of the excavation, and the cabinet ended up with me. One night, I opened it up. Like magic, 178 new sonnets. So familiar in tone and form and structure, they had to be Shakespeare's. So I first confided the whole story to a friend and fellow colleague—

AKS: Now your husband.

JRG: You might say Shakespeare brought us together. So I filled him in on everything. Told him the entire story. Eventually, we went over the find, poem by poem. We both taught and still teach at the same university, so we knew who to call. The poems went through rigorous testing. Archeological, actually. The paper, the ink. Then the handwriting. The diction and syntax. It all checked out. When compared with the extant 250 poems, we can see writer's habits and preoccupations that run throughout the body of his work.

AKS: Well, people are teaching the poems all over the world now.

JRG: Better be real then!

AKS: And from what I've learned, you and your family aren't taking any remuneration for the book.

JRG: The first people I contacted after my discovery were the folks at The Shakespeare Family Foundation. After a frank discussion, we reached an amicable agreement. All proceeds are going to our foundation that gives grants to schools and programs that work with children to further creativity. So far, we have funded over one thousand projects. We also wanted to build up our own English department, and now we put on a world-renowned Shakespeare festival at Mid-State, funding plays, lectures, and readings.

AKS: In a couple of the poems, the love Shakespeare detailed caused quite a stir. Given the laws against homosexuality in Shakespeare's time—

JRG: Pretty harsh penalties. Hanging. Drawing. Quartering. Horrible, ghastly practices. Something never to be seen. Or even thought of. And all this for love that is no crime at all.

AKS: Right. So do you think he sent these poems out to the New World to get rid of them?

JRG: Who knows? This might have been just a shipping mishap. And not all the poems were penned for a male lover. It's hard to know what he was doing with them. The poems might have been going to a certain person. An editor or a publisher. The trail goes cold after the shipping label. But it's true that his expressions of love to the "Fair Youth" would have been transgressive for the time.

AKS: There are a couple in the book that one might need to read alone in the privacy of home.

JRG: (laughs) I agree. I needed a fan as I was reading them the first time.

AKS: Their discovery adds such a richness to LGBTQ+ writing. A history. A record of human feeling.

JRG: Absolutely.

AKS: How have the poems shifted your own studies? For instance, your published dissertation focused only on the early plays. Now you are writing more and more about the later work.

JRG: True. There was something very accessible about the earlier work, especially up to 1616. Reading the new sonnets gave new meaning to his later plays.

AKS: What are your favorite plays?

JRG: That's as hard a question as asking which child is my favorite?

AKS: Indulge us (laughs).

JRG: Okay, my stock answer has always been *Hamlet, King Lear*, and *Twelfth Night*. But I'm enamored with his last play, *The Face of Heaven*.

AKS: A comedy!

JRG: A love story. The main character Archibald—a pirate—finds his true love through time and space. A love found on the continuum.

AKS: Along with the later plays, you say the poems have changed your studies. How have they changed your teaching and research?

JRG: These new poems have the capacity to change lives in a long-lasting way. College students are grappling with all the confusion and love and hope and despair that Shakespeare writes about. Now more than ever we can say this writer knew more about the human condition than any other. These poems give me the opportunity to present Shakespeare fully, a man in love, a man with yearnings, a man who can turn away from one relationship to another. How can my students not relate?

AKS: You've written extensively about the differences between the two versions of *The Merchant of Venice*.

JRG: This play has always been a conundrum. In terms of the original version, it was at once of its time and beyond, but it morphed in the centuries after Shakespeare's death into something thematically not intended. Shylock was based on a stock medieval character, and in the 1598 version, Shakespeare almost forecast the way the play would age badly.

Later, he managed to revise and provide us with a play that grapples deeply with bias, stereotype, and racism. And forgiveness. What is interesting is to read them side-by-side to note his shifts of thought and theme. Many of his subsequent works build on the revision he did with this play.

AKS: On a more personal note, you named your first child William. Given your lifelong study, I would assume this is an homage.

JRG: Of course.

AKS: And I've heard tell your son Will, as you call him, bears a striking resemblance to the Bard.

JRG: Ridiculous. That's just people's imagination! He's a 12-year-old boy with long dark hair and big brown eyes. Right now, who else will people think he looks like?

AKS: (laughs) But your daughters? No resemblance to any famous literary characters?

JRG: My oldest is named Daisy, but she's not a bit like Daisy Buchannan from *The Great Gatsby*. And my baby Mary—which Mary should we work with? Too many to count! But she's a very good baby.

AKS: How has the rest of your family taken to your discovery and subsequent project?

JRG: My husband and sister have always supported me, despite the fact the work has kept me from being a fully-functioning member of the family. Things have settled down now. And because the poems and the book have been so well-received, even my mother has come around.

AKS: Finally, you are writing a novel now, set during Shakespeare's life. Can you give us a few hints about it?

JRG: Let's just say it's not literary per se. Genre with literary elements. And the fun part is the story involves time travel and love.

AKS: Comedy or a tragedy?

JRG: There are a couple of weddings at the end, so let's call it comedy. But I think it's my most important work.

AKS: I can't wait to read it. And thank you so much for spending some time with us. I look forward to reading your novel.

JRG: Thank you.

Author's Note

I am not by study or training a Shakespeare scholar. While I've taught his plays all my teaching career and taken my fair share of classes, read his work multiple times (my first *Romeo and Juliet* and *Othello* in high school, thank you Mr. Black, my real and true English teacher). But when this story called, I did my best. I read as much history and analysis as I could. I reread the plays and the sonnets. The members of my writing group are very well-versed in Shakespeare, and they went over this manuscript with a fine-toothed comb. Thanks to Gail Offen-Brown, Julie Roemer, Judy Myers, Marcia Goodman, Joan Kresich, and Maureen O'Leary for constant reminders of all things Renaissance and Jacobean. Thank you to Maureen O'Leary for her "sexy sonnet" when I asked her to write me one. Only she could have done such a great job. Deep thanks to Darien Gee, Kris Whorton, Warren Read, and Kent Meyers for their clear-eyed reads. Julie Roemer and Judy Myers read in group and separately, and deserve medals. Marcia Goodman would have been so happy to see this in print. She was my friend and colleague who lived and breathed Shakespeare, and one of my most treasured objects is a notebook that detailed her day-to-day teaching in her Shakespeare class.

For some specifics, I went to London with my mother Carole Barksdale and attended plays at The Globe. While there, I walked as much as I could, tracing the places where Jessica and Will traveled during this tale. If ever you make it to London town, go to Postman's Park and read the tiles.

And there are real people here in this story. William Shakespeare himself (more below on this). Lady Mary Wroth neé Sidney, William Herbert, 3rd Earl of Pembroke, Richard Burbage, John Heminges, Harry Condell. I've used them in my story, though I've tried to base their actions on historical record. Probably, I've been unfair to Lord Pembroke, but his various love affairs and perhaps sad life led me to my portrayal. Maybe he decamped to Wilton, found a great guy, and lived happily-ever-after.

But please, don't rely on me to give you the truth. This is truly a story. Because there are historical inaccuracies here. Anachronisms. This is not a textbook. (Though I provide some resources below). Furthermore, Shakespeare's life is a mystery. We have very few facts about him. Some people firmly believe the man from Stratford did not pen any of the plays or poems. One theory I read declared that the playwright Christopher Marlowe faked his own death, only to later reemerge and use hapless William Shakespeare as his "shield" as he continued to pen plays until his real death. I make a slight mention of this in the novel. But the theories about who the real Shakespeare are varied, multifaceted, and rife. I'm pretty much a believer that in a man's world such as Elizabethan England, a successful man needed no shield. And Queen Elizabeth—should she have written these plays—would have proudly had them produced. But that's just my theory.

Also, because this is a work of fiction and Shakespeare is a character in my story, I made stuff up about him and his life, too. I left stuff out. I've bent and twisted things a bit in terms of chronology so the story worked better. Kris Whorton and Darien Gee were my story proofers and busters, guiding me ever onward as I wrote. However, it is my belief that if you willingly suspend your disbelief and travel back in time with Jessica, you will feel you are, indeed, in William Shakespeare's world, circa 1598.

Reading List

The text below is an English major's Bible. My copy is the 1974 version. My older son used it as a booster seat back before we could afford a real one. I wrote this novel with the plays and sonnets in front of me the entire time, flip, flip, flipping away.

Evans, G. Blakemore, Ed. *The Riverside Shakespeare*. Boston: Houghton
    Mifflin, 1974.

These books were really helpful with the day-to-day details of living in London circa 1598. They are all much dog-eared:

Mortimer, Ian. *The Time Traveler's Guide to Elizabethan England*. New
    York: Penguin, 2012. Print.
Picard, Liza. *Elizabeth's London*. New York: St. Martin's Griffin, 2003.
Secara, Maggie. *A Compendium of Common Knowledge 1558-1603.*
    Elizabethan Commonplaces for Writers, Actors, and Re-enactors. Los
    Angeles: Popinjay Press, 1990-2008. Print.

I was reading this next book on my Kindle, and I knew something was up when it told me I had 20 hours left in the book and I'd been reading a very long time. But in terms of the plays and their interpretations, I would truly recommend it. In paperback, it's 1008 pages. But I found all her writing well-done, insightful, and funny. She has a great voice and brings the reader right into the plays.

Garber, Marjorie. *Shakespeare after All*. New York: Anchor, 2005. ebook.

I'm much in debt to Old House's *A Map of Tudor London 1520* and *Braun and Hogenberg's Map of Elizabethan London 1572*. Hard to know how to get a cart around otherwise. In that same vein, aside from Google Earth, this book helped me best to get a clear perspective:

Whitfield, Peter. London: *A Life in Maps*. London: The British Library, 2006. Print.

In terms of William Shakespeare's life, I'm indebted to:

Greenblatt, Stephen. *Will in the World: How Shakespeare Became Shakespeare*. New York: Norton, 2005. Print.

But let's also give great good thanks to the internet. I have two screens. One was open to my manuscript, the other on an aerial view of St. Paul's Cathedral or on Lady Mary Wroth's Wikipedia page. I read about the effects of the plague, typhus, and dysentery. The sites on clothing and hygiene and language were constantly helpful. The internet. Click, click, click. There you have it. That's true magic.

Made in the USA
Coppell, TX
09 August 2021